DEDICATION

This book is dedicated to my wonderful daughter Amanda.

The one who deserves to be loved.

If you believe in a world of magic, then come with me into a time that is long gone or never was.

All you have to bring is you imagination, and the willingness to dream.

Let us travel back to the year 1223 and visit Mackenzie's Inn near the small village of Dalmally in Argyll & Bute.

Visit lochs, rivers, mountains and the realm of the Seelie Fae, as we accompany four friends on their quest.

.

CONTENTS

1 BAD NEWS

Amanda felt a shiver run down her spine. So she quickly pulled the featherbed right up to her nose, buried her head deep into the soft pillow, and wondered if it was time to get up. It was market day, which meant lots of early guests, news and a visit from her best friend, Ursula. She opened her eyes and glanced around her room. Her windows were covered with ice flowers that sparkled in the morning sun, and the remaining embers from last night's fire filled her room with a soft golden glow.

"Amanda, mo lennan get up. Remember its market day today, the first travellers should be here soon, we have to get the fires going!"

"Oh no Granny, please let me sleep a little longer. The sun is only just coming up."

"No Amanda, we have to get the hall warmed up and prepare the food. Out of bed lazy head."

Amanda sat up and felt goosebumps creeping up her legs. *It's no use I better dress, and make my way to the kitchen. At least it should be warmed up by now.* With that thought, she slid out of bed, dressed, and washed her face, the water was ice cold, but it did the job she was awake now and ran down the steps, taking two at the time.

"Take it easy you could fall, and I might not be able to catch you, you are so big now," chuckled her father William who stood at the bottom of the staircase

Aye, but you manage to carry a cask of ale all by yourself, don't you? Amanda thought as she skipped the last two steps and leapt into his arms.

"See you can, I knew it," she whispered in his ear, ruffling his blonde locks and giving him a smacking kiss on his cheek.

"Well I say, you are in a good mood! Is there something that I should know about?"

"Aye da, don't you smell it? Granny is making pancakes, and I am sure they are for me," she said with a grin.

"Am I right, Granny?" called Amanda letting go of her father dashing into the kitchen.

This was Amanda's favourite place, especially during the winter month, it was always warm and filled with goodies. Smoked ham, bacon and sausages hung from the ceiling, and the shelves along the walls were stacked with jars of honey, jams, and jellies. Granny was busy sweeping ashes and wood chips away from the hearth. She only noticed Amanda as she lifted her head to brush back some long silver strands of hair that had come undone from her bun.

"Well good morning sleepy head. Your breakfast is almost ready," her grandmother said smiling. "But before you sit down to eat, go and start the fire in the hall for me please," she added handing her a clay pot filled with glowing peat from the kitchen fire.

The tab room was dark and cold, as Amanda rushed to the fireplace, placed the glowing peat on the flagstone, and covered it with straw, twigs and some small branches. The fire flared up with a roar and soon its flames and began to dance between the logs sending sparks up into the chimney like wild bees. Warmth and light spread far out across the room.

Amanda lit a few candles and placed them on the wooden tables before she stepped outside. The sun had reached the top of the hills by now and made the freshly fallen snow glisten like diamonds. She made her way through the knee-deep snow keeping close to the wall, to avoid the ice-cold wind, opened the shutters and rushed back inside.

"Granny I am done, are the pancakes ready yet?"

"Aye my bonny lass, they are on the table near the hearth, go sit down, I'll bring you a cup of tea and some blueberry jam," replied granny, while filling a cup with steaming herb tea.

Granny loved to cook and eat, which showed on her hips, but she had a good sense of humour about it. The people from the surrounding villages as well as travelling merchants and tradesmen came to enjoy her cooking and would never miss her special stew on market days.

"There you are, sweetheart, enjoy, but don't linger, I believe I hear a carriage," said Granny as she went into the hall.

Amanda sat down on a stool near the fire, warmed her hands, and lifted her skirt to dry the seam. She was in no hurry; *it is much too early for guests* she thought. Took a large spoonful of blueberry jam, picked up her tea and savoured her breakfast before entering the hall to help her grandmother.

So Granny was right. There is a carriage, Amanda thought when she saw four men sitting at the fireplace.

"Oh there you are Amanda," her grandmother said when she saw her entering the hall.

"Go on get some hot broth and bannocks for these poor men, they are frozen to the bone! And set these cloaks near the fire to dry," she said, handing her the wet cloaks and closing the door behind her.

"*What's the rush..., and why is she closing the door?* Amanda wondered as she placed the cloaks over a rack near the fire. She could not resist returning to the door to open it just a crack, listening to the conversation.

"Oh, dear Amanda the kippers are burning," shouted her father as he stepped through the back door, with a stack of firewood in his arms!

"What is going on? Why did mother leave the

kitchen with food on the fire? And why for goodness sake is the door closed?" he mumbled angrily as he dropped the wood and rushed to the hearth to pull the pan from the fire.

"I don't know da, Granny wanted it that way," Amanda shrugged her shoulders and reached for the handle to open the door when her grandmother stepped in.

"Oh William, I am glad that you are back, could you please help me to get some food ready for our guests?" Granny's voice was shaky and she looked pale and very nervous.

"Of course," William responded before adding with hesitation," why is the door closed?"

"Never mind that, I will tell you later," said Granny, tightening her apron as she began to chop some onions.

Amanda placed four bowls on the table and picked up a scoop to get the broth for the men when Granny called over to her.

"Never mind lass, I'll handle that. Go and fetch me a bucket of water."

Startled Amanda, rested the scoop back on the table, picked up the bucket and stepped out into the garden.

Clearly Granny wants me out of the kitchen so she could talk to da without me listening in. What's the big secret, and what could these four men have to do with it?

Ups! She tried to keep her balance as she walked, the ground underneath her was frozen solid and slippery under the freshly fallen snow. Her hope to return quickly, to pick up some of the news that Granny was about to share with her father was squashed. She had no other choice than to walk very slowly to avoid falling and the heavy bucket she was trying to balance didn't make it any easier.

It took her a long time to get back to the house. When she finally reached it and knocked the snow off her shoes, she noticed that she was alone. The door to the hall was still closed. She set the bucket down very carefully so as, not to make any noise, before she tiptoed to the door, opening it slightly to overhear the ongoing conversation.

"Ar ye telling me, that the Stranger returned?"

"Aye William, he was seen at the market last Saturday."

"Have any girls disappeared?" Her father's voice sounded hoarse and very concerned.

"Aye, Grace and Dallis, we are all very worried. We thought we better come to warn ya' before anything happened."

Amanda didn't recognise the voice and couldn't see anyone from where she stood.

What stranger, and how could Grace and Dallis just disappear? She wondered as she opened the door a bit more to get a glimpse of the men sitting at the fire.

"This is bad news. We hoped he had stopped coming. No one had caught sight of him in Ardteale for a long time," Granny said with quiet intensity making eye contact with each of the visitors.

"Oh no Maighread, he was always around, and every time he appeared one or two girls would go missing. It's terrible ten are gone so far."

The man that spoke sounded familiar, but Amanda couldn't place his voice.

"William we must get to the market and warn the other villagers. Quick get our cloaks. We don't have time." The man that had spoken got up. As he turned, Amanda saw him, clearly, it was Harris, the peddler from the neighbouring village. She would always recognise him by his height and his richly decorated wide rimmed green hat. *I have to get away from the door. Da is going to enter the kitchen any moment to fetch the cloaks,* she thought.

She barely made it to the other end of the kitchen, when her father stepped in.

"Amanda, come lass, help me with the cloaks. Our guests are ready to leave," he said, picked up the cloaks and handed two of them to her.

"Sure, Da but why are they leaving so soon? Their cloaks are still wet!" Amanda asked, hoping to coax some information out of him. He left back into the hall without answering. Amanda followed him quickly, eager to see the men that came to warn the villagers.

"Oh guid mornin me bonnie lass, how are you?" Harris addressed her with a big smile. "It's been such a long time since last I saw you, I believe it was last spring when you bought some pretty ribbons from me."

"Aye, right you are! Did you bring some with you today? I would love to take a look!" Amanda replied, hoping he would stay a little longer to answer some of the questions swirling through her head.

"I am afraid not my dear, I am not here to sell anything today. But I shall be back soon, and then I will show you the beautiful laces I got in Brussels." With these words, Harris swung the cloak over his shoulders and walked out, followed by the other three men

As soon as they had gone, Amanda swung around to face her family.

"What was that all about, and what stranger did they talk about? Please do not try to tell me that it is not my business."

"Amanda, calm down, we'll explain everything in time," her father responded in a low voice clearly disturbed by the news.

"It is time now! Dallis and Grace are my friends, so it is my business to know!"

She was not about to give in and looked her father straight in the eye. Seeing that he wouldn't budge, she left the hall, ran up the stairs and straight into her room, slamming the door shut behind her.

Her head was pounding from the hundreds of questions that were going through her mind.

In time, it is time now, how long do they want to wait before telling me? Could I be in danger, and who is this stranger? What does he want from Dallis and Grace? Where are they? She felt angry and frightened, so she lay down on her bed, closed her eyes and fell into a restless sleep.

It was already past midday when she woke to the sound of excited voices coming from the great hall.

Oh dear, I slept all mornin! Grandmother will need my help in the kitchen. She thought, splashing cold water on her face before she ran downstairs.

The hall was filled with people returning from the market by now. As Amanda walked through the crowd, she noticed the farmer John, sitting slumped on a bench near the door. His broad shoulders and flaming red hair stood out in the crowd. Amanda hurried over to greet him and find out if his daughter Ursula was with him today.

"Guid dai Farmer John, hou ar ye? And where is Ursula, I don't see her anywhere did she not accompany you to the market today?"

"Oh, guid dai Amanda. No Ursula had to stay back I am afraid the weather being bad as it is, I did not want her to leave the house. But don't fret, you will see her as soon as the snow stops," replied John in a soft voice. Something about his voice didn't seem very convincing.

"I don't mind the snow; may I come along when you leave? I need to speak to her, it is important," she urged, hoping he would agree.

"I do not think it is wise, and surely your Da wouldn't want you away from home now," John said looking over to the kitchen door, where her father had just entered the hall.

"Amanda, there you are," he exclaimed when he saw her. You had us worried. Now go and help Granny in the kitchen, would you?"

Amanda and Granny had lots to do till late in the

evening. Only after all the dishes were washed, and the kitchen cleaned was, Amanda able to join her father in the Great hall where she found him sitting by the fire. Next to him sat a woman, with hair as white as snow dressed in a colourful robe.

Amanda recognised the woman right away it was Adelaide, the weaver who lived near the edge of the forest. Amanda loved her dearly and visited whenever she could to help her spin the wool from her sheep and watch her weave the most amazing cloth. She especially cherished their walks through the forest collecting barks, flowers, and berries to make beautiful dyes. It was rumoured throughout the villages, that her cloth was able to protect the wearer against dark magic and spirits. Amanda loved these stories of magic but did not honestly believe them.

"It is nice to see you, Adelaide," she greeted her. "I was planning to visit you tomorrow and bring you a cake Granny made for you."

"Oh my bonnie lass, you can bring it along when we are leaving. Your Da asked me to keep you at my home until it is safe for you to return," replied Adelaide.

"Da, why didn't you tell me? Why do you want me to leave, and why would I not be safe at home?" Amanda asked surprised.

"You will be all right, my sons and I will look in on you regularly, do not be afraid!" Amanda spun around and saw Bhaltair, the miller. She had not noticed him before but was glad to see him.

"I would like that Bhaltair, but why all these secrets? And why do I have to leave?" her voice sounded frightened.

"The village elders agreed that all lassies your age should be taken in by childless people, to keep them safe from the stranger. He seems to be responsible for the disappearance of more than ten so far. We cannot prove it, but every time he is seen one or two will vanish," Bhaltair responded.

Amanda looked at him in disbelief. She felt that her knees were about to buckle, so she leaned against the wall and shook her head. Her father rushed over to her.

"Amanda I want you safe, and Adelaide offered to take you in. You were always happy to go to her, so we thought it best you stay at her home. Let's go and get the bag Granny packed for you, Bhaltair is taking you to Adelaide's home," said William, put his arm around Amanda's shoulder and walked her to the kitchen. She did not know what to think. Her heart pounded like a drum in her chest, and she began to cry.

"Granny, I don't want to go, no one would see me if I stay in my room," Amanda pleaded.

Granny stood near the back door holding a heavy travelling bag and was visibly shaken.

"It is hard for all of us, mo lennan, but we have no choice. You are not safe here at the inn," said Granny in a quivering voice. "It is time to go, the carriage is behind the house, Adelaide and Bhaltair are waiting."

Amanda climbed on to the carriage, waving to her Grandmother just before Bhaltair cracked the whip. The two brown horses fell into a trot, pulling the carriage away from the small inn that was Amanda's home.

2 ADELAIDE'S COTTAGE

It was a cold starry night. Flurries of snow danced in the moonlight, and the frozen ground cracked under the wheels as they passed. The wobbling of the carriage and the fresh night air had made Amanda drowsy. She fought hard to stay awake by looking at Adelaide and Bhaltair, trying to read their expressions. That's when she noticed that Bhaltair's eyes were scanning the surrounding trees.

"What is it Bhaltair? Do you see something"?

"No no, don't worry, I was just looking for Adelaide's house. We should be close by now."

"Aye, it's just around the next bend Bhaltair" Adelaide answered. "Soon we'll all sit by the fire enjoying mulled wine. It's not often that I have visitors, so I am glad of the chance to sit and chat with you for a while."

"I can hardly wait," he said with a smile. "I think we all could do with a hot drink by now, I just hope that I will be able to let go of the reins! My fingers are so cold I can barely move them."

"Goodness, why don't you wear your mittens!"

"I forgot them at your house when I dropped the lads. But never mind, it's not so bad, and in any case, we've almost arrived. Giddy up fellas!" shouted Bhaltair, to the horses.

Adelaide's cottage stood peacefully in the distance, its thatched roof and stained glass windows drawing them in from the cold.

Amanda pushed back her hood and grabbed her bag as the carriage rattled over the small bridge leading to Adelaide's cottage.

Just as the carriage stopped in front of the threshold, the door opened to Bhaltair's two sons, Hugh and Glen, who came running out shouting over to

Amanda.

"Hiya lassie, mighty fine to see ya again! It's been such a long time since you came to the woods!"

"That's not true, it has been only a month or two, I can't help it that you weren't around," Amanda teased.

"Never mind let me give you a hand with that bag! Glen, you'd better pick her up, so she doesn't have to walk through the snow and wet her boots."

"Aye right Hugh just as soon as you get out of my way," his brother responded. "Come on Amanda, jump on my back, I'll carry you."

"Are you sure, I am pretty heavy you know."

"Oh come on, you are light as a feather compared to the sacks of flour I lug around all day."

"If you insist," she replied with a grin as she and jumped onto Glen's back.

He truly had no problem carrying her, the work at the mill made him very strong. He carried her to the cottage, stooped through the doorway and safely sat her down near the fireplace.

"Thank you, Glen thought I'll admit the comparison with the sack of flour was not all that flattering," she laughed as she kissed him on the forehead.

"Aye, my dear brother is a real charmer, and he even gets a kiss. What about me! I carried your heavy bag all the way to your bedroom!"

"Oh come here, Hugh," said Amanda with a big smile, hugging and kissing him just the same.

"Goodness lads, that's enough hugging and kissing for one night! Let's sit by the fire and enjoy Adelaide's famous mulled wine before we have to go," said Bhaltair as he ushered the three of them to the fireplace.

The wine was delicious, and Adelaide had even found some gingerbread, nuts and dried fruits to go with it. The group enjoyed each other's company very much sharing not only the food but also many great stories till late into the night. Many hours later as the fire began to die down, Bhaltair spoke up. “Oh goodness me, lads, it’s very late. Your mother must be worried stiff. Let’s get on shall we? Hurry, along now.” with that he bid goodbye to Adelaide and Amanda and pushed his sons through the door, just leaving them enough time to pick up their cloaks and give a quick wave.

After the men had left, Adelaide turned to Amanda.

“That was a long day, my dear, I am tired, and I am sure so are you. Leave everything as it is and let’s go to bed.”

“Aye Adelaide, you go ahead, I’ll check the fire and close the shutters. Guid nuit!”

“Guid nuit, Amanda and sweet dreams,” Adelaide said as she made her way to her bedchamber.

As Amanda stepped outside to close the storm shutters, she was captivated by the bright night sky. The moon looked like a silver disk on black velvet, surrounded by a sea of diamonds. She was so mesmerised by the sight that she didn’t notice, how the wind was picking up and began to blow the snow from the treetops towards her. Just before the whirl of snow reached her, she felt a shiver. She looked around, barely avoiding being engulfed in a vail of the icy crystals. *Goodness, that was close*, she thought, pulled her shawl up over her head, and closed the last shutter.

On her way back to the door, she turned around one more time to take a last look. At that moment she noticed the shadow of a man in a whirling snow cloud.

After a moment of hesitation, she spoke up, taking a deep breath to steady herself for what might come.

“Who are you? What do you want?” she called over to the edge of the forest. She stood perfectly still as if she was frozen to the ground and listened intently for a reply. But there was only the hauling of the wind. The snow cloud and the shadow had disappeared.

I must have been dreaming, she concluded. *No wonder after all the excitement of today. Adelaide can give me some answers tomorrow. She is always well informed, and wise. She is not blinded by fear or rumours,* she thought, as she locked the door and made her way to her bedroom.

3 THE TRUTH

The sun stood high in the sky when Amanda was awoken the next day by the busy click-clack of Adelaide's loom. Adelaide had covered her straw mattress with soft sheepskins, and she felt so comfortable she could have stayed in her bed all day.

It is so nice not have to rush out of bed. Amanda thought, stretching her arms over her head as she let her eyes wander through the sunlit room. The reflection of the stained glass windows looked like coloured lights floating in the air. Amanda would have loved to look at it all day. But she wanted answers to her many questions, so she got up, readied herself and went straight to Adelaide's workroom.

"Guid mornin Adelaide, hou ar ye?"

"I'm fine. I hope I did not wake you, but I have to finish this plaid today. I trust you had a guid nicht," said Adelaide.

"Aye, I always do when I am here. The sheepskins are so soft, it feels like sleeping on a cloud," she replied with a smile. "But tell me, who is this plaid for? It must be a big woman judging by its size."

"Well, she is not that big, she just wants it to wrap around comfortably, but enough of that, it is high time to get food in you. I baked some scones and laid the table in front of the fire in the sitting room for us, we can talk there. I am sure you have many questions."

"Aye I do, and I hope you will tell me the truth. Please don't keep anything from me, I want to know if I might be in danger."

"Of course Amanda, I promise. But let's have some breakfast first, I am starving."

They went into the sitting room, sat down in front

of the fireplace, and enjoyed their scones with honey and a cup of tea.

Amanda had always loved the relaxed and peaceful atmosphere at Adelaide's cottage. It was so much calmer than the inn. No noise from rowdy guests, no rushing around preparing the meals and making beds. But it was time to find out what was going on, so she broke the morning silence.

"Adelaide, tell me. Who is this stranger everyone is talking about? Where is he coming from, and why do the people from Dallmally, and Ardteale believe, that he is responsible for the disappearance of the lassies?"

"Oh dear, one question at the time," said Adelaide. There is so much I have to tell you and it, might disturb and even frighten you. But I promise it is the truth," she looked at Amanda before continuing.

"Almost seventeen years ago your mother came to me, to order a baby blanket. She brought her own wool, which was so soft and fine, unlike anything I had ever seen."

"You knew my mother? Amanda asked in disbelieve. What was she like? Da never told me anything about her and Granny only cries when I ask."

"Aye Amanda I know her."

"What do you mean, you know her? She is dead. She died the day I was born."

Adelaide took a deep breath before replying.

"That's what you have been told. But it is not so."

Amanda stopped chewing the scone that was in her cheeks.

"No, no, that can't be true, Da would have told me. Why should he lie, about something like that?"

"Amanda, William is not your da. He swore an oath, to look after you, to keep you safe and to never tell anyone," whispered Adelaide, she rested her hand on Amanda's knee and continued.

"My dear, your real da is Gregor, the son of

Jonathan, the fisherman. The villagers believe that he drowned in a storm almost twenty years ago."

Amanda's head began to spin as she tried to take in everything she was hearing.

"So Jonathan is my grand da?" she finally asked.

"Aye Amanda, but he doesn't know that no one knows. They all believe William had gotten married while studying law in Edinburgh and that his wife had died in childbirth." Adelaide got up and went to her bedroom, leaving Amanda by the fire. Moments later, she returned carrying a small basket.

"This is the basket William found you in, under the old oak tree, near the lake."

"What do you mean he found me?" Are you saying that my real parents just left me in the woods?" whispered Amanda. She got up and paced back and forth in front of the door as if she was about to run out any second.

"Amanda please, mo lennan, calm down. It's not like that. You will understand when I tell you what happened." Adelaide urged, getting up to put her arm around Amanda's shoulders and leading her back to the fireplace.

"Sit down, I'll make us a cup of tea before I continue. Some lavender with honey will help you calm down," she said softly kissed her on the cheek and walked out.

Amanda found herself sitting alone, staring at the flames as they danced in the fireplace. She felt more confused than she had her entire life like her whole world had just crumbled in ten minutes. The man she loved and believed to be her da was, in fact a stranger, who found her in the woods. Her own parents had abandoned her.

Has there ever been any truth in my life? Whom can I trust? Is Adelaide telling me the truth, or is this just another deception? The thoughts raced through her mind, each one faster than the last. She took a deep breath to steady herself for what might be revealed today. Moments later Adelaide came back into the room, carrying a tray of tea and cake.

"Be careful, my dear, it is very hot," she said as she handed Amanda a cup. "I also brought you a few slices of Maighread's cake, to calm your mind. Are you sure you want me to tell the rest? Or do you want us to take a break before we continue?"

"I am fine, please don't stop! I need to know everything about my parents," Amanda urged moving her chair closer. Adelaide looked at her with a look that Amanda couldn't quite place and continued.

"Very well. It all began twenty years ago. Our fishermen had been returning with empty nets for months. It was terrible, many lives were threatened. That's when Gregor decided to row out every morning, long before the sun was up, trying to catch anything he could returning late at night.

One day the weather was so bad, that none of the fishermen dared to go out in fear of a storm. So they pulled their boats out of the water and secured their nets. Only Gregor braved the weather. But he never made it back. His boat washed up on the shore two days later, laden with fish. And ever since that day, the boat is filled with fish every morning. Jonathan blames the Seelie Fae for Gregor's disappearance. He is certain that the fish is restitution for the loss of his son."

"Seelie Fae, Adelaide this makes no sense, these are old wives tales," Amanda replied in disbelieve when she had finished.

"Amanda he is right, even if you have never seen any, elves exist and so do many other magical beings. Do you want to hear the truth, or do you want to continue to live in ignorance?" asked Adelaide, running her hand through her long white hair.

"Of course. I want the truth, Adelaide. But what you are telling me is so hard to believe."

"It may be hard for you to believe Amanda, but every word is true. So let me continue and please open your mind. There is so much in our world that you don't know," she said looking at Amanda solemnly.

"Remember how I told you, that your mother came to me to order a baby blanket?"

"Aye Adelaide, I do, and please forgive me for doubting you, you never lied to me, and I know that. But this is all just so confusing," said Amanda and hid her face in her hands.

"I understand Amanda, and I know that it must feel as if the world has turned upside down, but the time for the truth has come. Your mother expected you to be born around the summer solstice. She came to me asking me to spin the wool, weave the blanket for you and dye it with rose hips and Elderberries. She then handed me a feather from her golden eagle and told me, that she would receive any message I write using this feather the moment I write it. So naturally, I wrote her a message as soon as I had finished your blanket, and to my amazement, she arrived the same day to pick it up.

She offered to pay me with a beautiful jewel, but I told her no, and that I felt honoured by her trust. She smiled telling me, that any of cloth woven on my loom, will be protected, from now on, against dark magic and evil spirits, because of the magic left by the wool I used to make your blanket. Before she left, she revealed to me how she met your da and how much they look forward to the birth of their daughter they are going to name Amanda, which means, *the one who deserves to be loved.*"

"So how did she meet my da?"

"Gregor's boat had capsized in the storm, and he was drowning. When he had no more strength to fight the waves, he sunk to the bottom of the loch. At that moment, your mother came, pulled him to safety and brought him to her Island. She healed all his injuries and nursed him until he had regained his strength. When the time came for

Gregor to return to his father, she told him, that she had watched over him for many years and that she wished he would stay. He too had strong feelings for her and didn't want to leave, but he could not stay, because of his elderly father, who was no longer able to fish and would surely starve without him. So, with a heavy heart, he said goodbye, and held her one last time, before he pushed his boat away from the shore and started to row. He didn't turn around because it was too painful, so he stared at the floating islands of bonnets and water lilies, and that's when he saw her, gliding effortlessly through the crystal clear water next to his boat.

Before he could make sense of it, she surfaced right next to him and told him that she was Murigen, the Goddess of the loch. She promised him that his father will be cared for as long as he lives if he would marry her and live with her in her kingdom. He accepted immediately, and they got married on the night of Beltane. Since then your father has gone out fishing every morning, and the Ashrays pushed the boat filled with the finest fish up to our beach before sunrise," Adelaide continue.

"But if they wanted me so much and if they loved each other so strongly, why did they leave me all alone in the forest?" Amanda urged grabbing Adelaide's shoulders.
"That I don't know, mo ghràdh. All I know is that something terrible must have happened on the island so that the golden eagle had to bring you to safety under the old oak tree. You were wrapped in the plaid with another eagle feather and a message to the one who would find you, asking to keep you safe, raise you as their own, and never to tell anyone how they found you. Thank heavens it was William, who saw the eagle and followed him to the oak tree. He took you home and told everyone that he had gotten married in Edinburgh and that his wife died giving birth to their daughter. The moment I heard about it, I went to offer them my help, but when William showed me the basket with the blanket and the feather, I knew who you really were. Ever since that day, I have kept this secret and made sure that you have been safe. I decided

to keep the basket with the blanket and the feather here at my home until you were old enough to know the truth, or in case you needed its protection. I am afraid the time has come," with these words, Adelaide handed Amanda the ruby red blanket and the eagle feather.

4 IMBOLC

Two days had gone by since Amanda had learned the truth about her parents, and that magic was not only real but a part of her. The thought that her parents might be in danger kept her up all night and even erased her fear of the stranger. She was the first to wake up that morning. Adelaide had worked on the loom till late at night and was still sleeping soundly.

Adelaide will be surprised when she gets up. I just hope she likes my baking. Amanda thought as she took the shortbread and bannocks out of the oven, placing them in a large basket covered with a cloth. *Okay then, that's done I better go and check the fire in the sitting room again, and fix our breakfast. It will not be long until Adelaide gets up and then we will be busy as bees. There is still so much to do for tomorrow's celebration* she thought as she began to set the table in front of the hearth

"Dear me, guid mornin Amanda, when did you get up?" Adelaide exclaimed in surprise as she entered the kitchen. Her greeting gave Amanda such a fright that she almost dropped the jug of milk she was carrying.

"Goodness, you frightened me. I just thought what else I could do before you get up."

"Well lass, I am up and ready to continue with the preparations for our Imbolc celebration. Sorry to have startled you." Adelaide said and cracked up laughing.

"Aye right, you go ahead keep laughing, I'll just wait till the next mouse comes running through the kitchen, let's see who will be laughing then!" giggled Amanda and gave her a wink.

"Fair enough, but let's have a quick bite before we start. We have to finish cleaning the house, wash the linens and start with the decorations."

"I took my sheets off this morning and they are already

soaking. I'll go and get yours now while you fix breakfast."

"Alright, but don't be long!"

Adelaide and Amanda went straight back to work after they had finished their breakfast. There was so much to do. Imbolc was the first big celebration of the year, welcoming spring and the rebirth of nature. So they began with the shores to prepare for the event, first cleaning the house making sure that all their clothes and linen were washed, and tidying up the garden. When it came time to clean the windows, Amanda was a bit uncertain.

"What shall I use to wash the windows?"

"Just put a little vinegar in the water, and take a soft cloth, that will be fine."

"Are you sure? Wouldn't the colours come off Adelaide?"

"No silly lass, they are not made of glass, the panes are made of finely sliced precious stones, quartz, amethyst, amber, beryl, and aquamarine. They are a gift from the Drows. They dispel black magic, and protect the people within from any kind of negative attack on body, heart, mind, and spirit."

"Who are the Drows? And where do they live?"

"They are mountain elves and live in caves in the highlands. They are very gifted crafters and blacksmiths. Their metal work is said to have magicalpowers."

"Really," asked Amanda intrigued. How did you meet them, and why have they given you such a precious gift."

"Well, I met them many years ago when I came to this house. Three of them were chained to a blacksmith forge down by the brook and forced to work for the laird who use to own this land. I freed them, destroyed the forge, and thereby broke the spell that bound them to this land," Adelaide explained. "They were so grateful, that they returned a month later with their brothers, built my windows and exchanged all of hinges and locks on this cottage. Thanks to them no one with ill intent can open or break the windows and doors nor can they enter the cottage."

"What a fantastic gift, no wonder that I feel so at ease

when I am in your home. Have you ever seen them again since that time?" Amanda asked. She was hungry for every scrap of information she could get about this newfound magical world.

"No Amanda, but I know that they come around now and then," Adelaide responded with a smile. "Oh dear, talking about coming around, let's make sure we have enough food for tomorrow. We will have at least seven guests!"

"Well, I baked a basket each of scones, shortbread, and bannocks this morning. The Bonnach bride and the apple fruschie should be about ready now," she responded leaving Adelaide in the pantry to look through the shelves, for some blackberry jam, dried fruits, and nuts.

It's time for winter to end, Adelaide thought while putting the third jar of blackberry jam in her basket. Our stocks are getting low, and we could really do with some neeps and carrots.

"Adelaide! I hear a carriage, are you expecting anyone?" Amanda called, hurrying to the door taking a look at the approaching guests. To her big surprise, it was farmer John and Ursula. She was so happy to see them that she picked up her skirt and ran as fast as she could to the bridge to meet them.

"Oh, I am so happy to see you, Ursula. I have so much to tell you."

"That's nice, but what about me, am I invisible?" asked John as he stopped the carriage for Ursula to get off. The two girls hugged and ran into the cottage.

"It is farmer John, and he brought Ursula! I am so happy Adelaide! We are going up to my bedroom, we'll not be long I promise," shouted Amanda, pulling Ursula up the stairs and into her bedroom. Just as they were about to get comfortable on Amanda's bed, the door opened, and Adelaide stepped in.

"I am very sorry lassies, but I need your help. But don't fret, you can talk all night, Ursula is staying with us for a while."

"Really, Adelaide? That's fantastic, I am so happy! You

go ahead, we are coming. Ursula just needs to change."

"Alright, but don't be long! I'll go and help John unload the carriage in the meantime. See you in the kitchen," Adelaide responded and went back downstairs where she nearly ran into John as he walked through the door holding a basket filled to the brim with eggs.

"Gee Adelaide we almost had a calamity here!"

"I say, that would have been a lot of scrambled eggs," she responded bent over in laughter. Hearing the commotion, the girls poked their heads out of their room.

"What's so funny, what did we miss?" Amanda shouted over the bannister.

"Well, lassies we almost had scrambled eggs right here on the threshold," John answered them, joining Adelaide in laughter as he rested the basket with the eggs on a shelf.

"Ursula. Come, lass, help me with the milk, and Amanda, bring in the cheese, please. I'll carry the butter and the vegetables," he continued after he caught his breath. Picked up a large basket and walked back into the pantry.

"Oh dear, John, I don't know how to thank you," Adelaide said, seeing the goods in his arms. "We were almost out of neeps and carrots and had absolutely no onions left, now I can prepare a nice stew for tomorrow."

"Aye, you most certainly can, look what I got," he replied and picked up the back leg from a wild boar.

"This fellow made a mistake to come into my barn trying to steal the food from my hogs. Well, now he is a roast. I can't wait to taste your stew tomorrow, but I have to hurry back home before my wife puts me out. See you tomorrow morning Adelaide!"

"Goodbye John. Give my love to Anette!"

After all the food was securely stored in the pantry, the three women tightened their aprons and went back to work. It was already afternoon when they decided to take a break and sit down in front of the fire to enjoy a cup of tea and some shortbread.

"Well lassies, I think we are about done," Adelaide said

with a satisfied sigh. “The stew is on the fire, and the linens are washed. The only thing left to do is the prettying up of the cottage. Ursula, did you bring the straw I asked you for?”

“Aye Adelaide, I put it to soak in the barrel outside. It should be nice and soft by now.”

“Fine, then you two can weave Brigid’s cross, and pick some heather when you are done. I look after the stew and finish up the kitchen,” she instructed them.

“Alright, but isn’t it better if we go for the heather now? We’ll head out now to make sure we’re back by nightfall,” Amanda and Ursula said in one voice. They picked up their shawls and baskets and ran out of the house.

Amanda and Ursula were happy to be alone and finally have the chance to talk about all the things that have happened, since last they saw about a month ago. They discussed the disappearance of Grace and Dallis, and Amanda’s rushed departure from the inn, but soon ran out of time. The sun was already low in the sky, and the light began to fade.

“We will talk tonight,” shouted Amanda panting as she hastened up the knoll, trying to catch up with Ursula.

“Oh Amanda look, isn’t this magical!” exclaimed Ursula grabbing Amanda’s hand to pull her up. The rays of the setting sun made the heather glow like a purple sea and the evening mists floated above it like a silvery vail.”

“Aye it is magnificent, Ursula, but let’s get the heather now. We have to make it back before dark.”

They did not waste another moment and hurried back to the cottage as soon as their baskets were filled. The sky had already begun to darken, and the full moon was slowly rising spreading his silver light, over the fields and the forest when the cottage finally came into sight.

“Oh, good we are almost there. I am so hungry, my tummy is growling like an angry bear,” giggled Ursula as they rounded the corner and stepped on to the small bridge leading over the brook to Adelaide’s cottage.

“Stop and be still!” whispered Amanda all of a sudden,

grabbing Ursula's hand and pulling her down.

"What is it, what did you see?"

"Don't you see the shadow near the barn? I swear it's the same one I saw the night I arrived."

Amanda and Ursula stooped low and continued walking cautiously across the bridge, and up to the barn.

"Do you think that it is a good idea to look for him? I think we should go and tell Adelaide, she would know what to do!"

"Oh don't be such a coward Ursula."

"I am not a coward!" Ursula protested. But what do I do if he attacks, hit him with the heather?" she chuckled as she lifted the basket, spun around and swung it as if she was going to knock out an invisible assailant. All of a sudden a hooded man stepped out of the dark and spoke in a calm voice.

"Guid evenin, lassies. You should not be out so late. It is not safe for you to roam through the woods at this hour."

The girls felt as if their limbs had turned to stone. Their hearts and minds screamed for flight, but they could not move or even breathe until Amanda finally gathered some strength and spoke. "Who are you, why are you following us? And why do you sneak around the cottage at night?"

"My name is Ralston. You do not have to fear me, Amanda," he answered in a voice as soft as velvet. "Lady Murigen asked me to guard you and keep you safe. I am sorry if I startled you and your friend, but I think it is best when you return to the cottage now. We can talk tomorrow at sunrise. I will be waiting for you in the barn," he whispered and faded into the darkness of the night.

"Goodness, where is he gone? I didn't see him move, he just vanished."

"Well then, let's not wait for him to reappear," Amanda replied. She picked up her skirt, grabbed Ursula's hand and began to run.

"Ursula you have to promise that you are not going to say a word to Adelaide about this," insisted Amanda before she opened the door.

Ursula looked at her friend in hesitation for a moment, then agreed.

"Alright, I promise," the girls pushed the door and entered.

"Adelaide, we are back, and hungry as a pack of wolfs. What's for supper?" Amanda called out, as they entered the cottage.

"Oh I am so glad that you are home, you had me worried," Adelaide said drying her hands on her apron and taking their baskets.

"The heather is very pretty. Thank you. We will put it up with Brigid's cross, tomorrow after breakfast. But it's time now for some food. The pottage is ready, and I even have some stewed blackberries with cream for you."

"That sounds yummy! We just go and freshen up a bit," called Amanda as she and Ursula ran up the stairs. We will be back in a flash!"

The supper was scrumptious and very filling. The girls felt quite tired after they had finished their bowl of blackberries and cream.

"Adelaide that was a great supper. Thank you so much," sighed Ursula and rubbed her tummy.

"I am stuffed too, I could fall asleep, right here and now," chuckled Amanda as she stretched and got up. "Do you want us to do anything else Adelaide, or can we go up now?"

"Of course you can go up my dears. You worked so hard all day. I'll take care of the kitchen. See you tomorrow, have a guid nuit."

Amanda and Ursula ran up the stairs as fast as they could. It was finally time talk things over and share the latest news.

5 RALSTON

Amanda and Ursula didn't sleep a wink that night. All the exciting news and the prospect of finally getting some answers had made them restless.

"In the name of the wee man Amanda, come back to bed. You can see the rising sun from right here, the window is facing directly east," sighed Ursula as Amanda got out of bed for the fifth time.

"I think he is already in the barn, we should get down there now. Come on, get out of bed, let's get dressed," Amanda urged.

"What gives you that idea? You can't even see the barn from here."

"I don't need to see the barn to know it. I have a strong feeling that he is here."

"Yeah, right," grumbled Ursula rolled her eyes, as she got out of bed and dressed quickly.

"Oh come on a snail moves faster than you."

"Can I at least wash my face and ran the brush through my hair?"

"Aye do that if you must, but then let's go. Watch your step we don't want to wake Adelaide," whispered Amanda. She opened the door very slowly to stop it from creaking, as she had done many times before, she knew just how far she could open it. They squeezed through the narrow opening, tip-toed downstairs, and stepped out.

"Oh dear, it is freezing, why did you agree to meet this early?" Ursula complained as they stepped out into the cold. "I bet not even the chickens are up at this hour."

"Och stop fussing Ursula, the barn is just there. Walk a little faster if you feel cold."

After a few steps through the freshly fallen snow, they

had reached the barn. Amanda attempted to open the large door. “Ursula, can you give me a hand please to open the door. The snow is blocking it."

"Sure, just step aside and let me handle this, sweetie,” replied Ursula as she leaned against the barn door and gave a strong push. “There you go. Let’s get in there then and meet your protector, shall we? I bet he is not even there."

"Are you talking about me, lass? I am right here."

"Och must you always do that!” snapped Ursula. “Can't you just walk up to people like a normal man?"

"Sorry lass, that I can't do. I am not what you call a normal man."

"Aye right, so then what are you?"

"I am a Pict," replied Ralston with a big smile and bowed to Ursula.

Choosing her words very carefully so as not to offend him, Amanda asked. "You are a Pict? I have never heard of a Pict before, are you an elf?"

"Sort of. My ancestors were elves. I am part mortal. But let’s not waste time talking about me,” Ralston said as he took off his cloak and gave her a smile that would melt the largest glacier.

Amanda and Ursula were startled by the looks of him. He was a very handsome young man, with long hair as black as a raven’s feather. His eyes were dark brown and mystifying.

Amanda was spellbound and unable to move or take her eyes off him, which reminded her of the night when she saw him for the first time in a whirl of snow. Just when she had found her voice again and was about to ask, if she truly was in danger, he spun around and disappeared like a flash of lightning.

"Wow, did you see that? He is as fast as a shooting star!" Amanda exclaimed in wonder.

"I was more impressed by his armour and his weapons."

"Don't be silly, Ursula."

"I am not being silly, I am dead serious. He looks as if he has emptied the Laird's armoury. But I bet the only thing you saw, were his eyes," said Ursula with a frown.

"He carries a dirk in each boot, a sword, a bow, and enough arrows to wipe out our entire village."

Amanda blushed and nodded. "You are right, but you have to agree that he is truly fascinating. And yes the only thing I saw were his eyes," she added with a grin.

"Who is fascinating?" asked Ralston, who had just returned.

"Goodness you nearly made me faint! I wished you could stop doing that," sighed Amanda and let herself drop on to a heap of straw.

"What is the matter, what did you see?" Ursula asked as she looked around nervously."

"No need to worry, it was Adelaide who had gone to the well to fetch some water."

"Oh dear, she is up let's hope she thinks that we are still in our beds fast asleep. Ralston, let's not waste time please, tell me if I am in danger. Where you met my mother, and why she did not come with you?"

Ralston leaned against the barn wall and began his story. "Alright! Two years ago the golden eagle Ioroth brought me a message from your mother Lady Murigen, in which she asked me to watch over you and keep you safe. She wrote that Lord Dougal is searching for you. So yes, Amanda, you are in danger. He is the one who has taken your friends and is holding them captive in his caves. She further wrote that she is bound to her Island kingdom by a curse and that we can only communicate with her through Ioroth or her Ashray warriors," Ralston explained.

"I'll tell you more tonight, but for now, you better return to the cottage before Adelaide notices that you left.

Meet me in her workshop around midnight," he concluded. With that, he wrapped the cloak around him and pulled the hood deep into his face before he disappeared.

Amanda and Ursula were relieved when they made it back into the cottage and their bedroom unnoticed.

“Well, that was interesting,” said Ursula, as she kicked off her boots and lay down on her bed.

“We still don't know much, but I hope that he will clear it all up tonight. I am not going to let him get away this time before he has answered all of my questions."

"Alright Amanda, but this time you'll have to go without me. I can't make it one more night without sleep. I am truly sorry."

"No problem, you can stay and sleep. I am not leaving the cottage, but now is not the time to get comfortable,” said Amanda. “It is very late, we have to go down before Adelaide starts to get worried."

"Right, but first you have to brush the straw off your skirt, or Adelaide may think that you busted the mattress," giggled Ursula and pulled bits of straw out of Amanda's auburn hair.

"Guid mornin’ lassies! I thought you two would stay in bed all day. Come on, and grab a scone, there is no time to sit down for breakfast. You can eat while you are setting the table. I’ll go and set up the kitchen, Harris should be here soon, and I am certain that the others will not be far behind."

Amanda and Ursula picked up the scones Adelaide had laid out for them and began to set the table in the sitting room, taking a bite now and then. In no time the table was beautifully decorated with heather and covered with baskets filled with all sorts of cakes, pies, scones, loaves of bread, and a large cheese.

"Well done you two, we are almost set. All that’s missing are the bowls and tankards go, and get them quick,

I think I hear Harris's drum!" said Adelaide as she lifted her skirt and rushed out the door.

"Adelaide is right, do you hear the drum, Ursula?"

"Aye, but who are the pipers? Don't you hear the pipes?"

"Now I do! Come on, we get the tankards later!" called Amanda, took Ursula's hands and pulled her out of the cottage.

The sound grew louder, and moments later they saw three beautifully decorated carriages coming around the bend and over the small bridge. Bhaltair, Hugh, and Glen were playing the pipes and Harris accompanied them on his drum.

"I wish you all a blessed Imbolc! Welcome to my humble home," Adelaide greeted the guests warmly. "I am so happy that you are here so early."

"Blessed Imbolc Adelaide! We had to come early. John didn't want to wait any longer, he wanted to try your stew since last night. He has been talking of nothing else!" Annett said laughing and ruffled John's hair.

Amanda and Ursula stood in the doorway holding hands, listening to the music.

"Oie lassies, stop holding hands and get over here to help us unload!" called Bhaltair. "And you lads, stop the racket and get the ale in the kitchen. I am thirsty!"

"Aye Da, that is a pure dead brilliant idea, let's get to it, Glen!"

"Sure thing Hugh. Lassies step away from the door, the ale is about to roll in!"

"When you are done with that lads come for the wine!"

"No, bother Harris we will get to it right away."

All of a sudden the serenity in the cottage was replaced by excitement and happy bustle. Everybody was rushing back and forth in order to get things in place for the celebration that was about to start. Hugh and Glen rolled the heavy casks of ale and wine into the pantry, where

Harris and Bhaltair propped them up on short stools and knocked in the tabs. Adelaide and Annett carried the cauldron with the stew to the heart, lifted it up and placed it on the cast iron hook over the fire, while Ursula added more wood.

I wonder how Da and Granny are today. The inn will surely be packed with people from the villages by now. How will they handle all the work without me? Amanda thought as a deep sadness started to fill her heart and tears began to blur her vision. She had to get away from all the excitement and commotion around the cottage. She needed time alone to make sense of all that has happened. She pulled her shawl tied around her shoulders and walked to the edge of the forest where she sat down on a tree stump near an old rowan tree.

"Why are you so sad, Amanda? You are surrounded by people who truly love you and care for you."

She turned around slowly to see who had spoken, though she was pretty sure that it was Ralston. And there he was, right behind her, reaching out his hands to pull her up. She was surprised at how relieved she was to see him.

"Everything is going to be alright," he reassured her. We will find a way to lift the curse that binds your mother and free your friends."

"I hope so Ralston. But what will happen to Granny and my da, I mean, Maighread and William, they are all alone now. The work at the inn is too much for the two of them."

"Don't fret they are not alone. I asked a group of Brownies the night you left to move in and to stay as long as they are needed."

"Oh thank you, Ralston!" she exclaimed, her eyes filling with tears of joy. "Please forgive me, but I am struggling to make sense of what has happened. Not even a month ago, I thought elves and fairies only existed in tales, and now, here you are. You have to tell me all you know about Lord Dougal, my parents and why he is looking for me. But right now, I think it is best to return to the cottage before I am missed. See you tonight," she said and walked back to the cottage, hoping that nobody had noticed her absence.

"Come and have some stew Amanda, it's delicious!" Glen called to her as she saw her appear. "Adelaide is a master when it comes to seasoning. Do you think she would be willing to share her secret ingredients? Say where were you?"

"Oh, I just went to check on the animals," Amanda lied, "I would love some stew, I am starving. All I had so far was a dry scone for breakfast."

"Well, that's no good, let's go and have some ale and stew then." giggled Glen. He placed his arm around Amanda's shoulders and gently led her back to the cottage, where the celebration was now in full swing. Bhaltair played the pipes and Harris was beating the drum like there was no tomorrow. Everybody danced and sang praises for Brigid and the return of spring.

"Amanda, Ursula, come along lassies, we are going to light the bonfire!" called Hugh, and Glen, from the field behind the cottage.

"Aye, we will be right there!" the girls replied. "We'll just fetch some ale, don't start without us!"

"Right then, but don't take long, the sun is already setting!" called Hugh and added more logs to the already towering stack of wood.

Amanda and Ursula rushed to the kitchen and pushed the door open almost knocking over Annett.

"Look out lassies!" cried Annette as she struggled to regain her balance and keep the Bonnach bride from falling.

"Sorry Annett, we were in such a hurry to fetch some ale and get back the bonfire that we did not see you,"

"No harm was done, I am heading there myself. Everyone else is already there so don't linger."

Amanda and Ursula hurriedly filled some jugs and rushed over to the bonfire.

"Put the jugs down lassies and join the circle! Blessed be everyone," John announced as he lowered his torch and lit the fire.

The celebration lasted well into the night and ended with the burning of last year's Bridges cross. It was close to midnight when the house finally fell silent. Adelaide and Ursula were fast asleep when Amanda quietly walked down the steps to meet Ralston in Adelaide's workshop.

She placed her steps very cautiously to avoid the creaking floorboards and not stumble into anything in the darkness. She knew that Adelaide was a very light sleeper and would wake at the faintest sound. She was relieved when she finally made to the workshop, took a deep breath and closed the door. Only now did she notice how cold it was. Her hands and feet felt like ice. She hurried straight to the fireplace and ran her hands over the mantle in search for the flint when she heard a rustling noise near the window behind her.

"Ralston is that you?" whispered Amanda. She tried to adjust her eyes to the darkness of the room, as she listened anxiously, but the only thing she could hear was the faint gurgling of the brook.

I am hearing ghosts now, this is getting ridiculous. I have to get it together, she thought and continued to search for the flint. She was very relieved when she finally found it. She kneeled down and tried to strike the flint, but her hands were so cold and numb that she dropped it twice. She began to rub her hands together until the feeling in her fingers returned, and she was able to create some sparks to light the tinder. It did not take long before the fire was blazing and its warmth and brightness helped her to regain her courage and clear away the fear she had felt, but it did not stop her mind from racing.

I wonder where Ralston is, it has to be long past midnight. I hope nothing happened to him. He is the only connection to my parents. What if the mysterious Lord Dougal has caught him too? I can't just sit here by the fire and do nothing. I have to go and look for him, what if he needs my help? Amanda thought. She got up and walked to the door leading to the garden when she heard the rustling sound again and felt a cold breeze on the back of her neck.

"Where you think you're going?" asked Ralston as he climbed in through the window.

"Well, as a matter of fact, looking for you! I thought something happened to you since it is long past midnight," said Amanda and put her hands on her hips.

"Please forgive me, I didn't mean to worry you. But I had to make certain that we were alone and your presence here remains unknown."

"Aye right, I forgive you. Just don't do it again!"

"Aye, I'll try my utmost best, Amanda."

"Oh, and one more thing," she added. "When you next approach me or enter a room, knock! My heart always skips a beat when you just suddenly appear out of thin air like that."

"I promise," he replied with a smile. "But it may not always be possible."

"Fair enough," she consented. "I am feeling very cold, let's sit by the fire while we talk."

"I can see that you are shivering and your lips are blue. Why don't you use your plaid to keep warm?" Ralston picked up the plaid and placed it around her shoulders.

"It is not mine, Adelaide made it for some noblewoman," Amanda responded absentmindedly "But wait come to think of it... why hasn't she picked it up yet? Adelaide was in such a hurry to finish it that she worked on it throughout the night."

"I am sure there will be no harm done if you wear it for one night. It will keep you warm and comfortable while we talk."

The pair settled down by the fire and warmed their hands. They sat in silence for a moment before Amanda spoke up.

"Ralston, tell me about my parents, Lord Dougal and what you are planning to lift the curse."

He turned to face her, his eyes filled with warmth and mystery.

"Your mother, Lady Murigen, is the Goddess of the loch and the Island Kingdom" he began. "She is very loving, beautiful, and just."

"What about my father? Do you know anything about him?"

"I have never met him, but your mother told me that he is very courageous. It seems to me that you have inherited this trait from him along with your beautiful auburn hair and your gentle hazel eyes."

"Now I understand, I have always wondered why my hair was not blond like William's. But let's not talk about looks," she pushed forward, not wanting to get distracted. "It is far more important to talk about what has happened and what we can do to lift the curse."

"I am afraid I can't tell you that, I don't know what happened on the island. We will have to try to find out from your mother."

"How can we do that? You told me yourself that she is bound to the island and that there is no way to directly communicate with her."

"There is one way. We should be able to talk to her during the night of the next full moon. We'll take Gregor's boat out to the middle of the lake, and call her name. She may be able to bring us close enough to the island to talk to us."

"Why not tomorrow night! Why do we have to wait so long?" Amanda urged, full of impatience.

"We need the protection of Arianrhod, the Goddess of the Moon and Stars. Her silver light will guide us and make us invisible to all malevolent entities. For now, let's plan how we get you out of the cottage unnoticed."

"Now that is no problem at all," Amanda said. "Ursula sleeps like a stone, and I know my way around the cottage in the dark. No one is going to know that I am gone as long as I return before sunrise."

"You will be back long before then, trust me," he said with confidence. But there is one more thing. You must tell no one about our plan, not even your best friends or Adelaide. Do you promise?"

"I don't understand why not…" she began to protest. But the look of seriousness in Ralston's eyes made her stop. "Alright, yes, I promise."

"Good Amanda, I will hold you to your promise, but I think it is high time for you to get some sleep. I will be around if you need me, even if you don't see me. Guid nuit Amanda," he whispered as he squeezed her hand and disappeared into the night.

The room suddenly feels so much colder, Amanda thought. She pulled the plaid tighter around her shoulder and looked around. *Well, no wonder the window is wide open, why can't he use the door like any normal human being? Oh right he is not a normal human being, he is half elf,* thought Amanda and chuckled silently.

She got up to close the window and returned to the fire, where she remained for many more hours to think about her conversation with Ralston and the upcoming journey.

Why am I not allowed to share this information with my friends? I would feel much safer if they could come along. After all, they say that there is safety in numbers…, not that I don't feel safe when I am with Ralston, I most certainly do. It feels as if I have known him all my life, and that we belong together. I miss him and long for his return the moment he leaves, which is truly strange keeping in mind that we only met yesterday. She interrupted her daydreams as she looked outside. *Anyhow, it is time to go to bed, the sun will be up soon and so will Adelaide. How would I explain being in her workshop at this early hour?* With this thought, Amanda got up and rushed back into her bedroom.

6 THE PLAN

Ursula was still fast asleep and snoring loudly when Amanda finally climbed into her bed.

I desperately need a few hours of sleep, she thought. She closed her eyes and tried to free her mind from the thoughts buzzing through her head when she suddenly felt a strange sensation. She opened her eyes, sat up and saw that the new morning was already downing. Its bright cold light shone through the window and painted a rainbow on the floor, which grew and steadily moved closer with the rising of the sun. Amanda was mesmerised, finding herself in a cocoon of brilliant light. She felt as if she was floating in a sea of warmth, and serenity, all her anxiety, and questions gave way to tranquillity. She closed her eyes and fell into a deep dreamless sleep.

The sun stood high in the sky when she woke up, feeling refreshed and full of energy as if she had slept for days. She stretched like a cat in the sun, jumped out of bed, and walked to the window to pour water into the small basin and wash her face. The cold water felt wonderfully refreshing and soothing on her burning eyes. *These long nights and all the secrets have to stop,* she decided. *There is no reason to continue the whispering like this and hiding of the truth. It is time to share what I have learned with Ursula, Glen, Hugh, and Adelaide.* She dressed and made her way to the kitchen, determined to tell Adelaide and Ursula all about last night's talk with Ralston. She was very surprised and a bit worried when she found the kitchen empty and silent.

"Adelaide, Ursula where are you?" she called, walking out into the garden.

"Oh, good afternoon, Amanda. We thought you might sleep through the rest of winter like your little friends the squirrels. Come on over," called Adelaide from the workshop window.

"Will do, just let me have some breakfast, I am starving."

"Well better make it lunch," giggled Adelaide. "There is a bit of stew left from yesterday, and fresh bread is in the oven."

"Thanks, Adelaide."

Amanda helped herself to a bowl of stew and a large chunk of the freshly baked bread before she sat down on the bench near the hearth. *Hugh is right, Adelaide is a master when it comes to seasoning, I wonder where she finds all these spices,* Amanda thought while enjoying the savoury taste of the stew.

"Are you done yet, Amanda? Hurry up, we could really do with your help!"

"I will be right there Adelaide, just fetching some water," she replied trying to buy some time as she walked up to the well looking for Ralston. *He has to be here somewhere, he said that he would always stay close. But where is he?* She thought, scanning the surrounding intensely. Seeing nothing, she went back inside.

"What would you like me to do, Adelaide?" asked Amanda, as she entered the workshop.

"Add some logs to the fire, it is getting kind of nippy in here which is strange, considering that the fire burned all through the night, don't you think?"

"I supposed so," Amanda replied. "But what makes you think that the fire burned throughout the night?"

"Well, there were some embers left this morning," Adelaide replied. "Though none of us remembers lighting it yesterday, isn't that strange?"

Amanda nervously cleared her throat.

"Aye very strange indeed," she looked away, trying to change the subject. "What else can I do to help?"

"Get me some spools of the brown and green yarn so that I can finish before the light goes. They are on the shelf next to Ursula."

Amanda placed one more log into the fire before she went to the shelves near the window where Ursula sat at the spinning wheel.

"I need to talk to you," mouthed Amanda as she picked up a basket full of spools. Ursula looked up and nodded with a broad smile on her face.

"What's so funny?" whispered Amanda, narrowing her eyes.

"I tell you later when we are alone."

"What are you weaving Adelaide? Is it another plaid?" Amanda asked as she placed the basket near the loom.

"Aye mo lennan it is, I have one more to do when I am done with this one."

"Goodness that is a big order! Who are they for?" Amanda exclaimed as she admired the cloth. "Why did they choose such dark colours? They look almost like the forest floor."

"Well, that's the whole idea! They are meant to blend in with the colours of the forest."

"So they are for a group of hunters!" Amanda exclaimed.

"Precisely," Adelaide responded with a mile.

The women worked for the whole afternoon, stopping only as the sun began to set and the light in the workshop was fading.

"Come on lassies, it's time for a cupa, we got a good bit done today," Adelaide said. "If we keep on working like this, we should be finished by Sunday."

"I'll say! My back is killing me!" Ursula complained. "How do you manage to do this every day?"

"Well, I don't weave every day. I spend a lot of time in my garden, and in the forest collecting roots, plants, and berries," Adelaide replied. "You'll see when you come along, we'll take a walk as soon as the snow has melted."

"But surely that time I will be home helping mum

and da in the field," Ursula affirmed.

"Hmm, actually you will not be able to do that, at least not this year." Adelaide said softly. "At least not this year."

"What do you mean, I will not be able to do that? Da is coming to pick me up in three days," she said louder this time.

"I am sorry lass, but he wouldn't be. He asked me to keep you here together with Amanda until it is safe for the two of you to return," Adelaide said, looking at the girls with a look of concern. "Please don't get upset. Let's have some supper and sit by the fire."

Amanda saw the frustration in Ursula's face. *I can imagine what is going through her mind, I was right there when her father told her that he would be back before Sunday to take her home,* she thought as they made their way to the sitting room. *I am sure that she was happy to spend some time with us, but she most certainly didn't plan to spend weeks or month away from home.*

"My sweets, help yourselves to some food while I pour the wine," Adelaide said gently. "I am sure we all could do with a drink right now."

"Thank you, but I am not hungry," Ursula responded with her arms crossed.

"Come on Ursula, you have to eat something, it will make you feel better," Amanda tried to calm her. "It's not Adelaide's fault that you have to hide out here with me, it is because of me and for that, I am truly sorry. Ralston told us that Lord Dougal is searching for me and that the only thing he knows about me is my age. This must be why he has abducted all the girls in the village. And now we are the only ones left."

Ursula looked to her friend weakly.

"But I didn't think for a moment that he would be looking for me."

"So you met the elf, did you?" Adelaide spoke from

behind them, overhearing the conversation. "And what did he tell you exactly?" her voice sounded angry.

"He told me things about my parents that you didn't know," Amanda replied. "He believes that there is a way to contact my mother and to find out what happened the day she had to send me away. And he knows how we could lift the curse binding her to the island."

"What curse?" Adelaide stopped, clearly confused. "I don't know about any curse, all I know is that Lady Murigen never responded to any of the messages I wrote."

"Well, you can ask the elf when he chooses to show his face next. I know that he is close by and can hear us," Amanda said, looking around the room for something she couldn't see.

"He is most likely upset because I broke the promise not to tell you anything."

"So how do you plan to contact Lady Murigen? And what will you do to lift this curse?" Adelaide asked, caught between anger and intrigue.

"We plan to row out to the middle of the loch during the next full moon. Ralston believes that my mother has the power to bring us close enough to the island to talk to us."

"Maybe she can," Adelaide said softly. "But you can't go alone you need protection."

"Ralston knows that. That's why he has chosen the night of the full moon so we will be protected by Arianrhod. And I am certain that Hugh and Glen will come with us. I'll send them a message tomorrow morning and ask them to meet me here."

"What about me," Ursula spoke up. "Do you think that I am useless?"

"Of course not!" Amanda turned to her friend. "I never doubted for a moment that you will come with me."

"You're damn right I will."

"So how are you planning to get the message to the lads?" Adelaide asked. "You can't very well send Ralston."

"That's no bother, I know a way that has never failed. You'll see, I have done it for many years, but kept it my little secret," Amanda said. "Say speaking of secrets - who are you weaving these plaids for? Nobody came to the cottage. How did you get the order?"

Adelaide looked at Amanda, impressed for a moment by her cleverness.

"You are right. There is no order they are for you and Ursula. They will keep you safe whenever you leave the cottage. The third one is for me, in case Lord Dougal tries to get you through me. He is desperate and would not hesitate for a moment to do whatever he feels necessary to get hold of you. These plaids will make you invisible. They keep you warm, dry, and safe from dark magic."

Amanda looked at Adelaide, moved by her kindness.

"Adelaide how can we ever thank you for all that you have done for us?" she asked.

"My bonnie lass, there is no need. Protecting you is the most important thing I can do."

Amanda felt the words give her a strength she did not recognise. She looked at Adelaide with admiration.

"Adelaide, do you think that there is enough yarn left to make two more?"

"Of course. I should have just enough. But I will need your help, so let's not talk any longer, we have to get up very early to get it done. Up to bed lassies, have a guid nuit and sweet dreams!"

"Guid nuit," Amanda replied and pushed Ursula up the stairs.

Once they were back in the bedroom, the girls exchanged stories from the day.

"What was the grin all about this afternoon?" Amanda asked. "You said you would tell me once we are alone. "Well, we are alone now so spit it out."

Ursula laughed.

"It was nothing. I just loved how you played the

innocent when Adelaide mentioned last night's fire. She knew all along that you lit it during the night. She also knew that you met Ralston of course, but she wanted to hear it from you."

"Oh dear, she must be very disappointed in me," Amanda said with dismay. "Only I did not want to worry her. I'll explain everything to her in the morning. But for now, let's go to bed," she sighed."

"Yes, you need your beauty sleep, I don't want you in a grumpy mood tomorrow." giggled Ursula and closed her eyes.

Amanda smiled and blew out the candles as Ursula curled up in her bed. She couldn't help walking up to the window to look one last time into the dark, hoping to catch a glimpse of Ralston. But all she could see was the night sky and the black silhouettes of the forest.

7 THE MESSAGE

Amanda and Ursula got up and made their way down to the kitchen long before sunrise. They were surprised to find all fires lit and a breakfast with freshly baked scones and steaming hot milk waiting for them on the table near the hearth.

"My goodness, Adelaide must be up for hours," Amanda exclaimed. "I thought she was so tired last night that she would sleep a little longer today."

"Really Amanda did you not hear the click-clack of the loom last night? Maybe she did not sleep at all."

"I didn't hear a thing. I slept like a stone.
But where is she?"

"She must be in the workshop," Ursula answered. I think I hear the taping of the spinning wheel, hang on, I go and take a look," she turned to open the door to the workshop, but it did not move. *What's wrong, why is it stuck? It was fine last night, that's strange,* she thought puzzled. She leaned against it with all her weight, but the door did not budge.

"Amanda, can you give me a hand? The door is jammed, I can't seem to open it."

Joining her both of the girls pushed with all their might until the door swung open with a bang. They stumbled into the workshop, surprised to see all candles lit, and the spinning wheel turning, but no sign of Adelaide.

"Oh, wow this is spooky. Pinch me, Amanda, I must be dreaming."

"You are not, I see it too."

"Seeing what?" they heard Adelaide's voice calling from the kitchen. "What is going on?"

"How on earth did you do that?" Amanda said startled "We just heard you in the workshop. The spinning wheel is still moving and you are in the kitchen," she hesitated a minute before asking. "Are you an elf too?"

"No Amanda I am not," Adelaide replied. "Come back and sit with me you two, I'll explain everything over breakfast."

The women made their way back to the kitchen, sitting around the hearth.

"Years ago a family of Brownies came to my cottage asking for shelter," Adelaide began. "They had been living and working in the kitchen of Kilchurn Castle, but could no longer bear the cruelty of the Laird. I offered them my barn, and since that day they cared for my animals and helped me in the workshop."

"Oh, please, can I see them, Adelaide! Ralston told me that a group of Brownies moved in with William and Maighread to help them run the inn. I would love to speak to them," Amanda pleaded.

"I am sorry my dear, but that will not be possible. They are extremely shy and do not trust mortals. Maybe they will show themselves to you after they got used to you being around."

"It's not the Brownies that interest me we have some of them helping us when it is time for the harvest," Ursula interrupted. "The story about the Laird, I want to know. Da told me that he is a very wicked man."

"He is not, he is a good friend of my da. I mean William," Amanda said. "He made him the justice of the peace for Ardteale, Auchtermally and Edendoich."

"Well that may be so, but Ursula's da is right, he is a very sly and dishonest man. He tried to take the cottage and all the land from me after his father had bequeathed it to me shortly before he died. If it had not been for William's help, he would have succeeded. But apparently, he did not want to risk their friendship, so he gave in. But enough of that, it is time to start working, let's go lassies." Adelaide stopped the girls got up and walked into the workshop.

"You go ahead, I will join you soon," Amanda said. "I just have to get the message on the way to Glen and Hugh."

"How are you going to do that? Sending a pigeon with a letter?" Ursula asked.

"No, I send it by water. The brook is my messenger. Tell Adelaide that we will be with her just now, and meet me under the bridge," Amanda said. "Hurry!"

She ran up to her bedroom, pulled a wax-coated piece of red cloth from her travelling bag and hurried down to the brook.

"Ursula where are you?" Amanda whispered and looked under the small bridge for her friend.

"I am right here. What are you planning to do with that old thing?"

"That is my message, I throw it into the brook, and the current will carry it right up to the mill, where it will get caught in the wheel and stop it," Amanda explained. "Don't worry Glen and Hugh know the procedure. Come up here as soon as they freed the wheel. You will see."

"That will not work said Ursula full of doubt. "The cloth is going to sink to the bottom as soon as it is wet!"

"Yes it will, I have done it hundreds of times, I coated the cloth with wax so it cannot sink," Amanda retorted. She went to the edge of the water and let go of the cloth, which floated on the water like a leaf.

"Believe me now? Let's go back to Adelaide the lads will be here soon."

"That is pure dead brilliant Amanda," Ursula laughed taking Amanda's hand and pulling her up on to the bridge. "Let's go, Adelaide is waiting. We have a lot to do if we want to finish the plaids in time for the next full moon."

8 GETTING READY

"Amanda, did you get your message on the way?" Adelaide asked.

"Aye, it should not take long, the brook is flowing fast today. The snow on Ben Croachan must be melting."

"Alright, let's get to work lassies. Ursula, can you please comb the fleece and Amanda I need you to do some spinning so that we will have enough yarn to get the plaids done in time for the next full moon."

"Aye, Adelaide. But please, tell us a bit more about the Drows and the magic of your windows while we work, I have never seen anything like them before," pleaded Ursula as she picked up a basket with the fleece.

"Alright then," Adelaide conceded with a smile. She sat down at her loom and started to throw the shuttle, telling the girls stories as they worked. The harmonious and hushed tapping sounds from Amanda's spinning wheel, and the click-clack of the loom created a dreamlike atmosphere that seemed to carry Amanda and Ursula away into the mythical world of the Drows.

The hours passed by like clouds in the wind, and it was already afternoon when the workshop door opened.

"Guid efternuin, lassies!"

The sound of Hugh's voice echoed through the workshop as he stepped over the threshold.

"We tried knocking, but I guess you didn't hear us over all that click-clack. Anyhow here we are. So what's the reason for the red flag you sent?"

"I am so happy that you are here," Amanda said, stopping the wheel to greet her friends. "We have so much to talk about!"

"I am so sorry for causing you this much trouble," she added.

"We tried to get here earlier but the brook is running strong today, so we decided to get as much grinding done as possible. That is until some cursed piece of red cloth got caught in the wheel," Glen explained. It was a real task to get it out of the gears this time."

"Well then, let's call it a day!" Adelaide said. "Nice to have you here lads. To be honest, I did not believe that Amanda's message would work, but I was proven wrong. I reckon it's time for some good food, wine and talks so let's pick up the candles and move over to the sitting room."

"Brilliant idea, we are starving! What's for dinner Adelaide?"

"Bread, cheese and ham lads. The stew is done, but there is some broth in the cauldron if you'd like something hot. Amanda and Ursula, you lassies, get some wine and ale for us. And you lads take care of the fire while I get the food." It was not long till they all sat comfortably in front of the fire and enjoyed the food and drinks. In the calm, Amanda and Adelaide could finally share all the long-held secrets with the men. Hugh and Glen were stunned by all that was revealed. They looked at Amanda as if they were seeing her for the first time.

"This is incredible. Of course, we've always believed in magic ourselves," Glen exclaimed. "After all, we have a load of Brownies helping us at the mill. But we have never met an elf before. Are you sure this Ralston is truly an elf?" he asked raising his eyebrows.

"I am half mortal," to be more precise." Ralston appeared as if out of nowhere.

"Ralston, you did it again!" Amanda exclaimed. "You promised me that you would make yourselves known whenever you enter a room!"

"And you promised not to tell your friends about me and our plan," Ralston responded. "So we are even."

"Dear me, don't argue it is better this way," Adelaide jumped in. "There has to be an end to all the secrets at least among us. I am delighted to see you again, Ralston, it has being a very long time."

"I was always around Adelaide but could not show myself to you, I am glad that all this hiding is finally over."

"How long have you known each other?" Amanda asked confused.

"From the day Adelaide came to this cottage and freed the Drows."

"That can't be!" she exclaimed. "That was at least thirty years ago, you were not even born then."

"Do you remember me telling you that I am part elf?" Ralston explained to her. "Well, we do not age like you mortals do."

Amanda was thunderstruck by this revelation and looked bewildered at Adelaide and Ralston.

"Never mind your age," interjected Hugh. "All we should be talking about is what you are planning, since we only have ten days left till full moon."

"How long would we be gone? And do we need to arm ourselves?" asked Glen, walking over to Ralston and embracing him like a good old friend.

"We should be back before sunrise," Ralston replied. "And no you don't have to arm yourselves, all you need is warm clothes and good control of your senses, so that strange sounds or visions wouldn't fool you."

"We can do that no problem. We spent many nights hunting in Eredine Forest since we were small," Hugh said. "The real problem is finding warm clothes for the lassies."

"I think that they should dress like us. I'll get them proper buckskin truis and lambskin boots," added Glen.

"I like that," Amanda agreed. "And Adelaide is making thick woollen plaids for all of us that look like the forest floor and will make us almost invisible."

"Good, but keep in mind that it will still be dangerous," Ralston said. "We have to be vigilant and keep what we are about to do secret. I'll go and talk to my brother about our plans and ask him to be our guardian for that night. Take good care, my friends," he said and vanished.

"Goodness that is truly magical, I wish that I could do that."

"Aye, right, and leave me with all the work, I can just see that happening my dear brother," chuckled Hugh and slapped Glen on the shoulder.

"Come on lads, settle down. I think it is time to find a place for you to sleep," Adelaide said. "I gather that you are going to spend the night with us."

"Aye, it's Saturday so da would not need us tomorrow. We'll sleep in the barn, don't worry yourself," Glen replied stood up and winked at his brother to follow him.

"Oh well, yes, guid nuit," grumbled Hugh as he stood up and followed his brother.

"The lads are right. I think we should go to bed as well," Adelaide said. "The night is short, and we have to get up early if we want to finish the plaids in time. Guit nuit lassies see you tomorrow and Amanda, promise me not to come down if you hear the loom tonight. You'll frighten the Brownies, and we need their help now more than ever before," she looked sternly at Amanda and left.

"I can't sleep now. I am too excited! I think we should make a cup of tea and bring it up with us," Ursula said after Adelaide had disappeared.

"Good idea, what do you think about lavender tea with a big scoop of honey?" Amanda replied with a smile.

"That sounds like my kinda cup of tea, and we can surely do with something hot when we go up."

"Why is that?"

"Well because we forgot to restock the fire in our bedroom. I am sure that it has burned out long ago."

"Oh no, don't tell me that, I was so looking forward to our cosy little room! It will take half the night before it gets warmed up," Amanda groaned. "Let's take some of the glowing peat with us, so it won't take that long for the fire to start," she handed Ursula a bucket with peat, picked up her cup and a candle as she left the kitchen.

"Don't forget your tea, you will need it," she added.

"Oh no, I wouldn't. Let's go and face our icy chamber, brrr…," chuckled Ursula and gave a shiver. The house was dark and quiet except for the creaking of the staircase. The girls had made up their minds to spend the night in a freezing bedroom but were startled when they opened the door and found the fire blazing.

"But who lit the fire! We were downstairs for the whole day?" Amanda exclaimed in surprise.

"I am sure the Brownies did it, they are a very helpful bunch."

"Oh yes. Speaking of the Brownies, how come that you never told me about them, Ursula?"

"Well, you have always been so adamant that magic beings do not exist, that I did not see the point in arguing with you."

"What makes you think that I would have argued with you?" Amanda protested.

"Let's just say that I had a strong feeling and anyway, it no longer matters because now you know that magic does exist."

The days passed quickly and tonight was the long-awaited night of the full moon and the start of a great adventure. Hugh and Glen had arrived before sunrise and were sitting in the kitchen enjoying a hearty breakfast while talking excitedly about the upcoming journey. Adelaide had not slept all night and was still busy trying to finish up the seams and edges of the last two plaids when she heard Amanda and Ursula coming down the steps and into the kitchen.

"Oh dear, what are you doing here this early in the morning? We are not leaving before dark, you must have smelled our breakfast all the way up to the mill, am I right?"

"Yup, I guess we did Amanda, but we left some for you lassies. After all, we are no scoundrels," replied Glen as he jumped up and embraced the two girls.

"Crivens Glen, don't frighten the lassies, you unkempt wild man!" called Hugh pushing his brother aside. "Guid mornin ladies, I hope you had a good rest. Your knights are ready to accompany you on your journey."

"Come on you noble knights try your plaids and leave the lassie alone so that they can grab a bite too," called Adelaide from the workshop.

"Aye fair lady Adelaide, as you command. We are at your service," giggled Glen, nudging his brother with his elbow and walked into the workshop.

"These plaids are huge Adelaide! Thank you, they will keep us warm even on the coldest nights."

"You are welcome, lads. Just make sure to fasten your belts correctly so that they don't slip."

"Come on lassie it's your time now to try on your gear for tonight, I made some heavy tunics for you to go with your truis."

"Oh that's terrific Adelaide, we're coming," shouted Ursula excitedly and came running into the workshop pulling Amanda behind her.

"You look even better as lads," teased Glen and walked around them to fully appraise their looks. "Hugh you have to see this, the lassies can truly pass as one of us that is after they hide their long locks of course."

"Oh yes, Adelaide, we have to braid our hair and find a way to cover it," Ursula urged.

"Don't you worry I already have a plan."

Glen and Hugh decided to walk up to the lake to check the path for the night and try out their new plaids, while the girls were busy in the workshop.

It had been snowing for days so that the old familiar path lay hidden under a thick layer of snow. Hugh and Glen had no choice, but to search for a new way down to the lake which could easily be followed at night. They tied strips of cloth onto lower branches and laid twigs on the ground wherever the path changed its direction. It was freezing even though the sun was sending her rays through the treetops making the glazed branches and ferns sparkle in her golden light. Glen and Hugh struggled on through this crystal forest until they finally saw the azure blue of the frozen lake through an archway of snow-covered willows.

"I am so glad we got here without any frostbites. We would not have made it if it wasn't for Adelaide's plaids. There are simply no words that can express how grateful I am," said Hugh in a hushed voice. His eyebrows were encrusted with ice, and his lips cracked, but he felt quite warm under his thick plaid.

"You're right, these plaids are magical, but never the less, we have to go back, have something to eat, meet with Ralston and discuss our next steps, so let's go."

As they made their way back, Hugh and Glen re-checked all their marks and made sure the strips of cloth were tied correctly. Exhausted but satisfied they walked into the cottage in the late afternoon, took off their plaids, and slumped down in front of the fireplace in the sitting room.

"Goodness lads I am so relieved that you are back, you were gone for such a long time."

"Well Adelaide, our old path was buried under a deep layer of frozen snow and blocked by many branches that had broken under the heavy weight of the snow, so that we had to find and mark a new one."

"Oh dear lads, why didn't you leave your boots outside! Get up and go into the kitchen and have something to eat while I take care of that mess. Amanda, sweetie, bring some rags and woollen socks for the lads so that they can dry and warm their feet."

"Sorry, Adelaide, we forgot, all we wanted to do is to rest and warm our feet, they feel like lumps of ice."

"I can well imagine, I'll place your boots near the fire so that they will be dry by tonight, and when you are ready to go, we will make sure that they are properly stuffed with the fresh straw that should keep your feet warm."

"Thank you, Adelaide, you always know what to do."

"Enough with the compliments! Now go eat and rest you need your strength later, Ralston will be here before sunset to make sure that you are ready for your quest."

"Somethings smells good lassies, I hope it is ready. We are famished!" Glen said went straight to the hearth and picked up a ladle. He was just about to help himself when Ursula took the ladle from him and slapped his hand.

"Just what do you think you are doing? Go and sit down, I'll bring you a bowl in a moment. Have some bread in the meantime."

Glen smiled at Ursula and threw her a kiss before he sat down next to Hugh who sat slumped over the table, his head resting on his folded arms.

"What's so funny? Come on, if you have something to say, say it," hissed Ursula and curled her lips.

"I was just admiring your colourful new hairdo," responded Glen, bending over laughing as he looked at Ursula.

"You can laugh all you want, it is warm and comfortable," said Ursula, throwing her head back as she left the kitchen.

"What is the racket all about?" asked Hugh, lifting his head from the table and rubbing his eyes.

"Well, you would have noticed if you weren't sleeping all the time. The lassies have braided their hair with strands of green and brown yarn," Glen laughed. "It looks as if they were wearing a big woollen cap."

"Well, that's a good way to keep warm! You are just jealous because your hair is not long enough to do it."

"Yeah right, let's have some food. It smells like pottage and knowing Adelaide's cooking it will have a good bit of meat in it," said Glen picking up his spoon. At that moment the back door swung open with a bang and Ralston bolted into the kitchen.

"What on earth were you thinking, didn't I tell you to keep what we are about to do a secret?" shouted Ralston furiously throwing off his cloak.

"What is your problem, we didn't tell anyone, not even our parents, so what are you on about?"

"You trampled through the forest and left a trail in the snow worse than a herd of wild boars! And to make things worse, you tied bloody strips of cloth to the trees. Even a blind man could follow your trail. You could have gotten us all killed," Ralston raged. He was breathing hard, trying to control his anger.

"We thought it would make it easier to follow the path," answered Glen in a trembling voice.

"Yes you did, for Lord Dougal and his Red Caps! We are lucky that a group of Dryads followed you and erased any sign of your presents, foolish mortals."

"Oh dear, please forgive them, Ralston, they meant well!" Adelaide said. "Do you think that Lord Dougal would be looking for the lassies here at Teatle Water?"

"He has his spies everywhere, especially around the loch, so we have to be extremely vigilant," said Ralston calming down as he embraced Adelaide. "Don't worry, we will be safe Ghilli Duh asked Laratbogh and Faerydae to remove all of our footprints. My brother Asanopirh and my sister Sorcha will be our wardens tonight."

"Good, that gives me peace of mind, now shake hands with the two lads to make peace please, they are still very young and can act foolish sometimes," whispered Adelaide looking deep into Ralston's eyes.

9 ERIDINE FOREST

"Dryads, what are they exactly Adelaide? Are they elves like Ralston?" Amanda, whispered pulling Adelaide closer.

"Not quite, Dryads are female fairies that live in the tree-tops of the forest. They have the most beautiful voices I have ever heard." Adelaide responded.

"Have you met any of them? What do they look like?"

"These fairies are as beautiful as their voices," she said. "Their clothes are made of feathers, ferns, and flowers, and their long hair glows like the morning sun."

"Oh, I would love to meet them, Adelaide. Do they show themselves to mortals?" Amanda responded dreamily.

"Seldom, but even if they don't, they will always help you if you ask politely, and may even share some of their secrets of divination with you. Laratbogh, which means the Gem Falcon and her sister Faerydae, the Dark Child are the only ones I have ever met. They are the guardians of Eredine Forest and live in the Willow Grove near the lake. I'll tell you more about them when you return, but now it is time to dress," said Adelaide. She took Amanda's hand and walked with her to the hearth where her friends were getting ready.

"What did you do to our boots, Adelaide? They look so different," the men said as she entered.

"I smeared them with hot wax and sealed the stitches so that they keep your feet dry. But remember to stuff them with a bit of straw before you put them on so they will keep warm as well."

"Aye right Adelaide, that is a brilliant idea thanks," said Glen and began to stuff his boots withstraw.

"Well, then my sweets it seems that you are all set, but

wait a moment before you go so I can say a prayer to Arianrhod asking for her protection." She closed her eyes and began to speak in a melodic voice.

"Fair Lady of the silver moon,
Watch over yer bairns tonight.
Send them your wisdom and
your shining light. Return
them safely to my side."

"Don't worry Adelaide I will make sure that they stay safe and return to you by morning," said Ralston, kissing her on the forehead before he stepped outside.

"Keep safe my bonnie bairns," called Adelaide from the kitchen as Amanda and her friends left the cottage.

The moon had not yet risen, so the woods were still shrouded in darkness which provided a perfect cover for the group of friends as they followed Ralston slipping and stumbling through the snow. The forest looked so different this way, it appeared almost to be alive. The frozen leaves on the forest floor cracked like crystals under their feet and bits of snow fell softly from the treetops.

Amanda felt uneasy as if eyes were on her back while they walked ever deeper into the forest. Shadows were dancing above them in the faint light of the rising moon, and there were strange sounds like whispers in the shrubs and trees. *Something or someone is following us* she thought.

"Hush, be still," whispered Ralston, and signalled them to hide under a large fir tree with unusually low branches.

"What's the matter Ralston, are we being followed?" mouthed Amanda.

"I am not sure, but you better take cover you should be safe under the tree," he replied. "Your plaids will hide you well. Wait here until the moon has fully risen and you can see the loch. Tell your friends to keep perfectly still until I come back."

"Aye, Ralston but how are we supposed to see the loch from here? We are not anywhere near it yet!"

"Trust me, Amanda, you will. But for now, join your friends and wait," he whispered before he disappeared into the dark forest.

The ground under the ancient tree felt like a soft carpet made from layers of pine needles and moss. Its low branches provided a perfect sheltered from the cold and prying eyes.

"This is a fantastic hideaway, I could stay here all night! How come that we have never noticed it before," murmured Hugh as he lay down and curled up in his plaid. "Hugh come on its no time to sleep you lazy head, we can't stay here all night," Ursula said nudging him in his side before she crawled over to sit with Glen and Amanda.

"What are you looking at, Amanda?"

"The rise of the moon, Glen don't you see its growing light on the snow? It will not be long before we can get back on our way," she replied.

"Aye, you are right," Glen replied parting the branches to get a better view.

Moments later, Ralston appeared. spoke in a hushed voice.

"Come on, the moon is up. We can now step onto the loch safely."

"We have to get to it first, don't we?" replied Amanda as she stepped out from under the tree, brushing some pine needles from her plaid before looking up. The loch lay inexplicably in front of her. How is this possible? She thought and took a deep breath while staring at the snow-covered loch that lay before her in the brilliant light of the moon.

"Its magic, pure magic," she whispered and stepped on to the ice.

"Be careful, don't be fooled by the snow, Amanda, it is just a thin layer. You will be fine as long as you do not lift your feet, just slide them over the ice and try to keep your balance! Let's go, Ursula, and you lads, close your mouths and follow us. We have no time to waste," Ralston said with a big smile and a twinkle in his eyes. This was undoubtedly his realm, and he was happy to be back.

Moments after the friends had left the shore, a gust of wind swept the powdery snow from the lakes icy surface towards the edge of the forest like a wall of icy mist. With the snow gone, the lake now looked like a mirror that reflected the night sky with a myriad of glittering stars and the bright full moon, giving the group of friends the feeling of being suspended and transported into another world.

"This is some truly powerful magic, Ralston," said Amanda in amazement.

"It's the magic of the Moon Goddess. We are now under her protection until we re-enter the forest."

"This is wonderful, and I am certainly very grateful, but how will it help me to find my mother?" Amanda asked. "All I can see is the sky and the loch, there is no sign of an island anywhere.

"All you have to do is call her, and she will show you the way."

"How?" asked Amanda, looking pleadingly at Ralston.

He nodded, looked at her with a gentle smile, then raised his arms to the sky and called out,

"Fair Lady Murigen hear our
plea. Open the sky and show us
the way. As we bring your daughter
to thee!"

The sky lit up in the most vibrant colours the moment he had spoken and lowered his hands.

"Is this the sign from my mother, Ralston?" implored Amanda anxiously. She turned around slowly, trying to comprehend what had just happened.

"Dear me, look at the beautiful northern light!" exclaimed Ursula in admiration.

"They are moving! Shall we follow them, Ralston?" Glen asked.

"Aye, the light is our guide to Lady Murigen."

The group of friends followed the band of light

gliding effortlessly across the ice until it suddenly stopped and descended onto the icy surface. Everyone held their breath and gazed at this beautiful apparition when they heard an ethereal chorus of elven voices reverberating from the cloud of light.

Amanda closed her eyes and felt how the voices lifted her up and carried her into a world illuminated with a brilliant light and filled the scent of thousands of flowers. As she floated through this otherworldly realm, she heard a soft voice calling her name. Somehow, she knew that it was the voice of her mother.

"Amanda mo ghràdh, I missed you so much that I thought my heart would break and now you are standing before me so beautiful and brave. My beloved daughter, it grieves me that I must ask you to accept tremendous challenges and face extreme danger to defeat Lord Dougal so that we can be reunited again. Lord Dougal has taken your father from my side and vowed to kill you if I did not relinquish my power and thereby accept the annihilation of my kingdom. I could not yield as it would have meant to sacrifice my folk and to lose you and your father forever."

"Lord Dougal is mortal but draws magic powers from a Sapphire he had stolen from my sister Cailleach, to break his power and vanquished him the Sapphire must be returned to the Blue Glacier of Ben Nevis. You will find Lord Dougal and the Sapphire in the mines of Wemyss where he keeps your father and the girls from your villages as slaves. If you accept this quest all the Elven clans, warriors, and white light spirits will fight on your side and protect you with all their might against anyone that means to harm you."

"Choose wisely my daughter, but whatever you decide Ralston will be your counsel and guardian throughout your life. But now you have to return to your friends and Adelaide the wise crone of the forest, as my sister Arianrhod has to make way for the rising sun. Farewell, mo ghràdh," Lady Murigen's voice softly disappeared, taking the beautiful sound and the Northern Light with her into the darkness of the night.

"Where has the light gone? And where are the beautiful voices?" Ursula asked looking crestfallen at Ralston after all was quiet again.

"Why have they just vanished Ralston? Weren't they meant to show us the way to the island and to Lady Murigen?" Glen asked.

"They have, everything is as it should be, let's return to Adelaide before the sun begins to rise."

"How do you mean everything is as it should be? Hugh shouted. "We did not hear a word from Amanda's mother, nor did we see the island!"

"Calm down Hugh I will explain everything as soon as we are back in the cottage."

10 THE ULTIMATUM

The way back to the cottage was arduous. No one had the energy to speak. Everyone seemed lost in their thoughts. The forest was black and lifeless as if every living thing was holding its breath. The friends felt relieved when the lights from Adelaide's cottage appeared in the distance.

"Oh dear, I am so glad to be back. All I want to do now is sleep for days," sighed Hugh quickening his steps.

"Wait, something is not right. Let me take a closer look," Ralston said lifting his arm to stop Hugh. "I know that you need rest, but believe, me it is not wise to let our guard down now," he whispered, pulled his hood deeper into his face and disappeared in an instant.

"What's the matter, Hugh? Where has Ralston gone?" Amanda asked looking around nervously.

"To the cottage. He said that something is not right and that he wanted to take a closer look before we approach."

Amanda felt her breath fasten, and a sense of danger rising in her chest. She crouched low to the ground, hid in the tall cotton grass, and crawled slowly towards the cottage. As she came closer, she noticed that the barn door was ajar and made a run for it.

"Are you perfectly mad, Amanda? You were supposed to wait until I told you that it is safe to step out in the open," Ralston hissed angrily pulling Amanda behind the well.

"No, I am perfectly sane, but we are talking about Adelaide here, and in case you didn't know, I love her and will not sit idly hidden behind bushes while she might be in danger. So what did you see?" replied Amanda defiantly as she shook off his grip."

Ralston looked at her in admiration for a moment

before conceding.

"Alright let's get into the barn, I will show you."

Ralston and Amanda stayed low to the ground and slipped into the barn hidden by the shadows of passing clouds.

"What is John doing here at this time? Something bad must have happened," whispered Amanda her eyes wide with terror.

"We'll find out, but we must wait while my brother makes sure that no one is lurking in the bushes before we walk up to the cottage."

"Your brother? I haven't seen anyone near the cottage where is he?"

"That's because my brother and sister are invisible to the ordinary human."

Amanda was about to protest and give Ralston a piece of her mind when she felt a presence behind her. She spun around and almost choked on her breath when she looked into a pair of green eyes.

"Forgive me, your majesty, I did not mean to startle you. I am here to escort you to the cottage where you and your companions will be safe."

Amanda was lost for words. She stood frozen staring at this luminous elven warrior waiting for Ralston to break this awkward silence.

"Amanda may I introduce you to my brother, Asanopirh. He and my sister Sorcha guarded us throughout the night and are about to leave, so let's not waste any more time, the sun is rising, and we need to get you safely into the cottage."

"Yes sure, thank you Asanopirh," stammered Amanda as she followed him and Ralston to the cottage.

"Oh, Amanda I am so happy that you are back unharmed. Sit down my bonnie lass and rest, you must be exhausted, cold and hungry," Adelaide greeted them with a heavy sigh as the group walked through the door. She pushed Amanda in a chair near the fire covered her with a thick quilt before she ran off to the kitchen to get her a cup of hot broth.

"Thank you, Adelaide, yes, I am freezing," replied Amanda with chattering teeth, pulling the quilt up to her shoulders and stretching her feet towards the fire.

"Amanda, my parents are here, you won't believe what's happened!" shouted Ursula

"I know, Ursula, Amanda answered. "I saw your father's carriage in the barn! Tell me what's happened!"

Ursula's father spoke up from the corner of the room. "The young Laird and his men came to our farm looking for you two," he said in a trembling voice. "They turned everything upside down, and when they could not find you, they took all of our livestock and threatened to burn down the farm if you don't show up at the castle before the next full moon. I tried to stop them telling them that you lassies had gone to visit family in Edinburg, but they did not believe me and told me to swallow my lies or I will end up like William and Maighread," He sobbed embracing Ursula and Anette.

"Why?" Shouted Amanda as she threw off the quilt and jumped up. "What does he have to do with anything and what did they mean when they said you would end up like William and Maighread?"

"We will know in a while Amanda, calm yourself," said Ralston, "Hugh and Glen are on their way to the inn to make a delivery and check on William and Maighread. No one suspects them. We were able to bring them back to the mill unseen. You all should go and rest, the cottage is impregnable and surrounded by white spirits no one can harm you while you are in here." he said in a soft voice before he took the bow from his shoulder and left the cottage.

"Ralston is right, you are safe here, go and rest I have set up bedsteads for you in my workshop. We all need to calm ourselves and gather strength for what might come," Adelaide agreed ushering John and his family into her workshop before she returned to look after Amanda.

As she entered the sitting room and walked over to the fireplace, she found Amanda all curled up in the armchair fast asleep. Adelaide picked up the quilt and started to tug it in around her when two brownies stepped out from behind the chair and spoke. “Do not worry mistress, we will look after her you go and sleep, we keep watch.”

Adelaide was exhausted. She had not slept for the last two days and nights, and the recent events began to wear her down. She sunk down on her cot and closed her eyes when she heard the gentle and familiar voice of the Goddess Momu speaking to her.

“Adelaide, me bonnie lass, everything is going to be alright, we are at your site do not despair. Sleep my love, we will take care.”

The cottage lay silent in the rising sun as the Goddesses Coventina and Momu appeared raised their hands and placed a shielding enchantment over the cottage, and all its inhabitants repelling any ill intent and dark magic.

*

At the mill, Glen and Hugh had just loaded two sacks of flour and an empty ale barrel onto the carriage and were ready to leave when they heard their mother calling from the barn.

“Wait you two, you have to take a sack of oats as well! I am certain that Maighread could do with some!”

“Oh Mum, we just brought her one last week,” quarrelled Hugh as he entered the barn.

“Look at me Hugh, and listen. If you are being asked to open the sack, do it from the end with the loop and leave the two last stitches intact. I tied a message to the other end before I filled the sack. Maighread will find it as soon as she pours the oats into the box.”

“That’s brilliant Mum! Don’t worry. I’ll be careful,” replied Hugh.

“Let’s go, Glen. Da wants us back before midday.”

"Aye right, hang on, here we go," said Glen as cracked the whip in the air.

"What do you think they have done to William and Maighread?" Hugh asked once they were on their way.

"Nothing, I reckon. After all, he is a close friend of the Laird. I believe they just wanted to intimidate John."

"Well, we are about to find out."

Hugh and Glen fell silent and paid close attention to their surroundings. As they drove up to the inn and saw about twenty horses tied to the nearby trees.

"Just as mum expected, the Laird sent his men to the inn to watch William so that he has no chance to warn the lassies."

"Aye right, but he thought wrong, didn't he?" chuckled Glen as he jumped off the carriage.

"Damn right he did, come on and let's announce ourselves," whispered Hugh with a big smile on his face and opened the door to the inn.

"Guid mornin William, where do you want your flour to go?" shouted Hugh. He walked straight up to the counter where William was busy pouring ale for some soldiers.

"Well, you are busy this morning, is the Laird holding a tournament? Good morning noble knights, gentlemen," called Glen bowing to the men at arms.

"Oh guid mornin lads, you can bring it straight into the pantry and then go to the kitchen. My mum is going to fix you something to eat," replied William.

"Hold it right there lads, two of my men have to inspect the sacks first," shouted one of the higher ranks. He waved two of the soldiers to follow Hugh and Glen.

"As you wish Sir," answered Hugh, leaving the inn followed by two armed men.

"Hang on gentlemen, that's a dusty business. I don't want the flour to make a mess of your beautiful uniforms," said Glen winked at his brother and let the sack hit the ground hard sending a cloud of flour up in the air.

"Oi, look out you eejit!" screamed one of the soldiers.

"I am sorry, but you can't say he didn't warn you," replied Hugh picking up the sack and bringing it into the pantry.

"We would be done much faster if you give us a hand. Look, why don't you take the sack of oats, it isn't that heavy," said Glen and handing the sack of oats to one of the soldiers.

"Open them up lads so that I can have a look."

"As you command my man, just look out, or you get powdered with flour," answered Hugh as he opened the stitching of the two sacks of flour, while the second soldier placed the sack of oats next to the door and sat down on it.

The armed soldier drew his sword and pushed into the flour a number of times, then nodded, satisfied and left the pantry followed by his comrade.

"Oh Glen, don't you ever do that again! I thought that I'd drop dead right on the spot."

"What? It worked, didn't it? They are too daft for their own good," laughed Glen and went into the kitchen.

"Where do you want the oats, Maighread," asked Glen and winked.

"Oh if you could be so kind and pour them into this box, me lad, that will make it so much easier for me," replied Maighread with a big smile and a nod.

"Aye will do, but then I afraid we have to go. Da wants us back before midday. I'll just have to go to William and fetch our ale." Glen said.

"No need, William already loaded it for you. Take good care, me lads, and give my love to your mum and da," said Maighread, as she waved goodbye and closed the door.

"Well, that was short and sweet. I wonder why she was in such a hurry to get rid of us." Glen said to his brother with raised eyebrows as they were left outside.

"Let's check the barrel as soon as we reach the forest

Glen. I have a funny feeling that she somehow hid a message for us."

"Aye, but we have to be careful, just in case we are being followed. It'd be best if you check Bessie's huff while I inspect the barrel."

"Pure dead brilliant," murmured Hugh as he re-tied the barrel and got back on his seat. "She must have dropped something in it, the cork is wrapped with something and feels kinda loos. Let's hurry home and find out."

"So how did it go, how is Maighread?" called Bhaltair as he saw his lads drive into theyard.

"Fine da, and mum was right! Maighread was waiting for the oats. Where do you want the ale to go, da?" called Glen tilting his head in the direction of the carriage.

"Ah, I think you better bring it in the cellar, so it keeps cool. And while you are at it, why don't you open it just a smidge, I am thirsty. Madge, my mo chridhe, bring us the tankards and have a drink with us."

"Aye, Bhaltair, I will be right there."

Moments later the men looked anxiously at Madge as she removed the strip of cloth from the cork and pulled it out.

"Maighread is a smart lady, look at that lads. She placed a message in a vile and tied it to the cork. No wonder that William was so quick in loadingit."

"What does it say, Mum? Come on. don't keep us hanging here." Hugh urged impatiently leaning over her shoulder.

Dear friends,

I hope that you all are safe and well when this message reaches you. William and I have been held captive at the inn since the young Laird had raided it last night. He is desperately trying to find Amanda and Ursula and threatened to throw us in the dungeons if the lassies don't turn themselves in before the next full moon.

Dear John,

I beg you to take Annette and seek shelter at Adelaide's home. The laird has given the order to burn down your farm and everything in it.

Bhaltair,

It seems that the laird is still unaware of your family's involvement, but I think that you would be wise to plan your escape in case the situation changes.

Adelaide,

My wise friend and mentor, please provide shelter for our friends and seek help from your elven guardians, I fear that we will not be able to survive this dark time without their protection.
Blessed be)0(

"Oh dear, this is far worse than I thought," Madge said. "We have to tell John and get his valuables out of his home before it is too late."

"But how are we going to do this without leading the Laird's men straight to Adelaide?" Bhaltair asked through concerned eyes.

"I am going to ask the Brownies for their help. After all, they also have a family at the farm that needs to be warned." Madge replied as she hurried out of the house and straight into the mill to warn her little helpers.

11 THE LAIRD'S SECRETE

Amanda was woken up by the rumble of thunder and the patter of rain against the window. She felt exhausted even though she knew she must have slept for hours. She rubbed her eyes and looked dreamily into the smouldering fire when her memory brought back the events from the morning. *Oh dear, I hope Hugh and Glen made it to William and Maighread, in that kind of weather, where is everyone?* She thought as she walked over to the kitchen, hoping that Adelaide or Ursula would be up.

"Oh, you are up! Did you have a good rest, Amanda?" Adelaide greeted her. "How do you feel?"

"Stiff, the chair is not as comfortable as my bed. But how are you? You look exhausted."

"I'll be fine, don't worry me lass. Come to sit with me and have something to eat."

"Where is everyone?" Amanda asked. "Did you hear anything from Hugh and Glen?"

"Not yet, and I do not expect any news before nightfall. Ursula, John, and Annette are still sleeping. We should not wake them till we've heard from the lads."

"You are right. They have gone through so much and need all the rest they can get."

"So, tell me about your journey. Did you see the Island and did you speak to your mother?" Adelaide's eyes shone with curiosity despite herself.

"We did not see the island, but we saw the most beautiful northern light."

"Are you telling Adelaide about last night, Amanda?" asked Ursula in a sleepy voice as she and her parents entered the kitchen.

"Yes, I was just about to do that."

"How did you all sleep? Are you feeling a bit better

now?" Adelaide asked.

"A bit, but we are anxious about what the Laird might do next," answered John sinking down on the bench near the hearth.

"Did you hear anything from the lads?" asked Annette.

"No, and I do not believe that we will before dark. But Amanda was just telling us about their journey last night. Come sit with us, Annette, and have some tea."

Come on Amanda, tell us what happened!" Ursula urged impatiently.

"Part of it I know, but I have no idea what happened when we were surrounded by the light and heard the beautiful voices."

"That is strange, did you not hear what my mother said? It was loud and clear."

"Nope, not a word. So come on let's hear it."

"It was like a dream." Amanda started, her eyes gazing out the window. "I was floating in bright white light and was bathed in the fragrance of thousands of flowers when I heard my mother voice."

"What did she tell you, Amanda?" asked John moving closer.

"She told me that Lord Dougal had taken my father and vowed to kill him and me if my mother would not relinquish her power and accept the destruction of her kingdom. She also told me that Lord Dougal is mortal and that he gets his magic powers from a Sapphire he had stolen from the Goddess Cailleach."

"Crivens, what can we do?" exclaimed John

"She told me that we could break his power and vanquish him by returning the Sapphire to the Blue Glacier of Ben Nevis."

"Perfect, but how do we get the Sapphire? He is not going to give it to us, and we don't even know where to find him."

"I do," Amanda said with determination in her voice. My mother told me that he hides in the caves of Wemyss and that he keeps my father and the girls from our villages in there as his slaves."

"Blood bas! So when do we leave?" Ursula jumped up.

"After you have learned how to fight," replied Ralston who had once again appeared without warning.

Amanda was about to say something concerning his disregard of their agreement but was too relieved to see him.

"After we've learned to fight?"

"Yes Ursula, fight. He is not going to just hand us the stone and give up his strive for the island kingdom. He commands an army of Red Caps and controls the men at arms from Laird Duane not to mention the Boobrie."

"Aye right and the five of us will triumph over them," remarked Amanda and shook her head.

"With what, may I ask?" Ursula asked, her voice thick with scepticism. We have no weapons unless you call a rake and a spade weapons."

"Not quite, but Glen is skilled with the staff and knows how to set fires. Hugh is a very good bowman, and as far as I know, you are a master with the slingshot."

"Ah, and what am I good at, throwing a tantrum?" asked Amanda and stemmed her fist in her hips.

"No my fair princess, you are going to use the sword. In fact, two of them. You have the swordsmanship in your blood. After all, you are the daughter of the Goddess Murigen."

"I don't know what is in my blood, but I never held a sword in my life," giggled Amanda, picked up the fire poker and spun around like a skilled swordsman.

"Damn Amanda, he is right! I don't want to see you with a sword in your hand," said Hugh who had just entered the cottage through the back door.

"Goodness lad, you are drenched. Hang on. I'll fetch you some dry clothes from John," exclaimed Annette and disappeared into the workshop.

"Did you swim? Why are you so wet?" teased Ursula

nudging his shoulder.

"Go and change, lad, I placed dry clothes on John's cot. And hurry! We want to hear about William and Maighread," Annette said pushing Hugh into the workshop before she went to the hearth to fill a bowl of hot pottage for him.

"That feels better, thanks for the clothes," said Hugh. He sat down right next to the hearth and enjoyed his food before he shared the news.

"Well, the Laird has gone mad. Why is he doing this? What has he to do with any of this?"

"Lord Dougal threatened him to take his little daughter Lucie if he does not deliver Amanda and Ursula before the next full moon," explained Ralston.

"He has a daughter?" asked everyone in one voice. They all looked around at each other in surprise.

"I didn't even know that he has a wife," John said in wonder. Did any of you know that?"

"It's the first time that I hear about it," said Adelaide

"When did he get married, and why did he keep it secret? Who is his wife?" Annette and Adelaide asked.

"As far as Nissa knows, he had bought his bride from the Mac Neil's of Barra," Ralston replied.

"They are bloody pirates! Their chief is not a Scotsman, Ruadhri is one of the last Vikings They are known for their raiding trips from their island stronghold of Kisimul. He was arrested for piracy of an English ship last year. Where is the lassie from, Ralston?" asked John in an angry voice.

"Nissa told me that she is a young lassie from France."

"Did you say France, Ralston?" asked Adelaide, staring at him in disbelieve.

"Yes, Nissa told me that her name is Anne and that she is the daughter of a Scottish nobleman in Touraine."

Adelaide went pale and had to hold on to her chair.

"What's the matter Adelaide, are you okay?" shouted Amanda jumping up to keep her from falling.

"I think Anne could be my niece," she replied in a

voice, barely over a whisper." I expected her five years ago but was told that the ship sunk near Edinburgh and that there were no survivors. Who is this Nissa and can I talk to her?

"Well, she is a Brownie that lives in the household of the midwife that delivered Lucie and still looks after her and her mother at Kilchurn Castle," Ralston said. "I will try to get her to talk to you."

"Please, I need to know if this lassie is my brother's daughter," Adelaide sighed wiping her eyes.

"Speaking of Brownies, Mum has asked ours to help your Brownies to remove all your valuables from the farm and bring them here to Adelaide, as far as we know the Laird's men have been given the order to burn the farm down before sunrise," said Hugh laying his hand on John's shoulder.

"Goodness, what will happen next? We have to stop those men!" cried Annette.

"Don't worry, we will build it back bigger and better than before. Let's just give the bairns all the help we can to vanquish this so-called Lord," said John defiantly, taking his sobbing wife in his arms.

"Well then, let's make some room for all the things the Brownies are about to bring," said Adelaide, took Annette by the hand lead her into thepantry.

"Now while ma is gone, Ralston, tell us more about the Redcaps and the Boobird," said Ursula.

"You mean the Boobrie," answered Ralston andcould not suppress a smile. "Well, the Boobrie is a giant savage bird which will devour anyone who dares to cross his path."

"If the bird is that big, how come that we have never seen it?" Hugh interjected. "You can consider yourself lucky. That beast lives near water so it could show up at the mill at any time. It can transform itself into a horse and canter across water and land."

"Good crivens, so what about the Red Caps? I have heard that they live in ruined castles and caves, but I don't know anything else about them," said, John.

"Well, they are even worse than that bloody bird," Hugh replied. "The villagers say that the Red Caps are murderous goblins that soak their caps in the blood of their victims and that no human, even if he is as strong as an ox, could overcome them."

"Oh come on Hugh, if they are goblins you just outrun them," replied Ursula

"Sorry, Ursula but there is no chance that a mortal can outrun a Red Cap. They are extremely fast, even with those heavy pike staffs they carry and the iron-tipped boots they wear."

"So if they are that strong and that fast, how are we supposed to fight them?" Amanda asked turning to Ralston.

"They turn to yellow ashes when they are struck with an elven blade or injured by one of our arrows. That is why I am going to take you all to the Seelie Court, where you will learn how to use our weapons," Ralston replied.

"Brilliant. But we have to make sure that our families are safe before we leave and find a way to communicate with them," interjected Hugh.

"It would be best if your parents use the night of the dark moon to move in with Adelaide. The cottage and the land around it is the gateway to the Seelie Court and therefore well protected.

"Oh, that is why you can always just appear out of nowhere! Good to know," said Amanda with a smirk.

"Yes, my dear princess and I have to return there now to prepare for your arrival and ask Cait Sith to be our messenger for the time of our absence. We'll leave the night of the new moon. Please only leave the cottage during the night while our warriors can protect you. I'll return for you as the moon is rising," said Ralston and disappeared.

12 THE SEELIE COURT

Amanda and her friends had waited in great anticipation for the night of the new moon and the journey to the realm of the Seelie Court. Now that the time had come the wait had become almost unbearable. They knew that the acceptance of strangers to the realm of the Seelie Court was extremely rare, especially if they were not of pure fey or elven blood. Permission for mortals to enter had been given to only a few over many centuries.

"Come on lads, it is time to go. Ralston is waiting for you at the bridge," said Adelaide with an uneasy smile.

"I wish that I could go with you. The realm of the fey is so beautiful."

"Aye Adelaide believe me, we all would love to have you by our side, but who would look after our parents while we are gone?" answered Glen, as he stormed out of the cottage.

"You'll have to forgive him, Adelaide. My brother is not very good at saying goodbye. Take care, and please watch over our parents. Da has a very short temper, and ma always worries too much."

"Crivens, are you talking about me lad? I am as calm and controlled as anyone, and your ma worries so much because she loves you," called Bhaltair from the kitchen.

"Never mind, I know your da my lad, just look after yourself. Go now, the others are already down by the brook," said Adelaide and pushed him out the door.

Hugh's knees felt as if they would buckle at any moment as he walked down the gentle slope to the bridge. *Get yourself together unless you want to tumble down into the brook in front of the lassies,* he thought.

"Well, well it's about time you made it down here, my

dear brother."

"Where are the lassies, Glen? I thought they left before me."

"Aye, they are waiting for us under the bridge, let's go."

"Why are we hiding down here? I thought that Ralston was taking us to the Seelie Court. Where is he?" Hugh asked suspiciously.

"I am right here, Hugh," Ralston said as he stepped out from the shadow of the bridge.

"Finally. Can we get on our way now? My boots are soaked, and I am freezing."

"Certainly Amanda, just follow me," said Ralston stepped into the brook and disappeared.

"What just happened, where is he gone?" asked Ursula, startled.

"Oh come on you guys just step into the brook and pass under the bridge," said Amanda stepped into the icy water took two steps and disappeared.

"Jinks, that's a great trick! Well, don't just stand there lads, come on, let's go." laughed Ursula. She grabbed their hands, took a deep breath, and stepped into the brook and under the bridge.

The three friends did not believe their eyes as they left the shadow of the bridge and found themselves standing in a crystal clear pond surrounded by islands of white and yellow water lilies and the brightest sunlight they had ever see.

"Come on, don't just stand there, we still have ways to go before we reach the great hall of the Seelie Court," said Ralston as he helped Ursula to climb out of the pond.

"My boots are dry! How is that possible?" exclaimed Ursula in surprise as she gazed at the staggering beauty of the landscape.

They wandered for hours through meadows of soft grass and wildflowers, petals from blooming trees and butterflies danced in the gentle breeze. No one spoke a word until they noticed a majestic forest in the distance.

“Is that the home of the Seelie Court, Ralston?” asked Amanda.

“Aye. The throne hall is in the centre of the forest and is guarded by Dryads and elven warriors. But don’t worry Asanopirh and Sorcha are going to escort us to the Queen.

“Who are Asanopirh and Sorcha?” asked Ursula

“They are my brother and sister, and the commanders of the royal guard.”

It did not take long until they found themselves standing at the edge of the forest and had to take the first step into the imperial grounds of the Seelie Court. They all felt that this was a great moment, by far greater than the step into the darkness they had taken earlier. This was the gateway to the ethereal world of the Queen of Lights. After a moment’s hesitation and with a pounding heart, Amanda stepped under the leafy canopies of the tree giants and felt a deep sensation of peace and happiness. She turned to her friends and waved them on before she continued her walk into the ancient forest.

“This is unbelievable. Pinch me, Glen, I must be dreaming,” whispered Ursula as she strolled through an ocean of bluebells.

“You are not, you are in the forest of Elfame. Welcome Ursula,” said Asanopirh bowed and walked on.

“Oh my goodness, was that Asanopirh?” Ursula asked Ralston.

“Yes, and to your left, you see my sister Sorcha. She does not speak your language and therefore never makes contact with mortals,” he replied.

“Glen, what are you looking at? Come on, we are going to lose the others.”

“I don’t know, I could have sworn that I just saw a beautiful young lassie behind that big oak tree. Actually, it looked as if she was part of the oak tree,” answered Glen in a dreamy voice staring at his brother in disbelieve.

“You saw the Dryad Faerydae, one of the guards of the forest. She and her sister Laratbogh were the ones that removed your tracks in Eredine Forest. Come on, hurry, we are not far from the throne hall now," Ralston pushed them along.

"Aye, but why did you not tell me that Dryads are beautiful fairies?"

"I thought it best if you find out yourself," laughed Ralston.

After this encounter, Glen paid close attention to his surroundings as he followed Ralston. His eyes scanned the trees, ferns, and patches of primroses and buttercups for any sign of the beautiful fairy.

As they walked on, the trees became even more magnificent and began to look like marble columns, their branches interlaced and forming a living canopy from which silken ribbons in the softest shades of lilac floated in the air.

The path had changed from the mossy forest floor to ivory coloured flagstones with embedded crystals that sparkled like diamonds in the glowing rays of the sun that filtered through leaves.

The friends were captivated by the beauty surrounding them and ambled on like in a trance until they found themselves standing in front of a luminous arbour and the Queen of Lights.

"Welcome to my court, Amanda, daughter of Murigen. I am honoured by your visit and hope that I can be of help to you to free your mother from the dark powers that bind her to the island."

"Dear Queen of Elfame, I thank you for allowing my friends and I to come before you, and for your generous offer to help my mother to regain her power and reunite my family."

"Dear Amanda, it is our tribute to your mother for all the wealth and security that she afforded us. I, therefore, pledge my incessant and unconditional support to you and your companions. My commanders Asanopirh and Sorcha will arm and prepare you for your quest and my warriors will fight on your side until the end.

"Go now and rest, you must be exhausted. My servants will tend to your every need," said the Queen of Lights and left.

"Perfect, let's go and eat, I am famished. I wonder what sumptuous treats they have for us."

"Oh Glen, how can you think of food in such a moment?" Amanda asked.

"What, I am starving! What's wrong with eating, aren't you hungry too?"

"I bet you all are. Keelin is going to escort you to your chambers. Eat and rest my friends."

"Thank you, Ralston, but when will we see you again?" Amanda asked.

"I'll come for you in the morning, and take you all to our armoury to get your amours fitted and receive your weapons. Sleep well," he said before walking away.

"Please follow me your meal is ready and fresh garments are laid out for you in your bedchambers," Keelin said in a soft voice, leading the friends into the castle. Their chambers were bright and airy and decorated with the most delicate carvings and gossamer veils.

"Oh look at this, isn't it just wonderful," said Ursula as she ran her fingers gently over the opalescent gossamer veils.

"Aye, it is. Look at all this food, roasted beef, chicken, lamb chops, bacon, tatties, peas, carrots, and gravy. I am in heaven!" shouted Glen pulling up his sleeve ready to dig into the food.

"Och, stop it, Glen you should at least wash your hands, you greedy scoundrel," Ursula scolded him.

"Why the harsh words Ursula? I am hungry, what's wrong with liking food, especially when it looks as good as this!"

"Glen is right, but let's freshen up a bit before we eat," said Amanda, pointing to a small waterfall and pond right outside. "We have all night, there is no need to hurry."

"We have our very own waterfall! Come on you guys, let's check it out," called Ursula as she hurried out into the garden. She kneeled down at the water's edge, and dipped her hands into the crystal clear water. "The water is warm, how wonderful is that?"

"Let's not worry about water when there is such sumptuous feast waiting for us," laughed Glen while he hurriedly washed his hands.

Hugh and Glen loaded their plates with meats, veggies, and tatties and then smothered it all with gravy like men who hadn't had a meal in days.

"Are you going to eat all that?" asked Amanda shaking her head in disbelieve.

"Aye, we are hungry! We did a lot of walking today, remember."

"Right and what did we do, fly? This is nasty, it's a good thing that we are alone! I would be so embarrassed if anyone would see you eating like that." Ursula said, her eyes squinted in disgust.

"Amanda, let's take some of the fruits and eat in the garden, I can't look at this."

"I am a step ahead of you, Ursula. Come on. I took the fruit basket the lads would not want any of this anyhow," Amanda replied and pulled Ursula into to the garden.

13 THE ARMOURY

Ursula, Hugh, and Glen had gone to bed, and the chambers finally lay silent. Amanda was grateful for the time alone and took a walk through the garden. The night air was warm and heavy with the scent of lilies. She enjoyed the feeling of the moist grass under her feet and the gentle touch of the breeze that played with her hair and her silken gown. As she dreamily walked closer to the glimmering fairy pond, she felt a strange pull. So she walked on until she was completely immersed in the deep blue water floating effortlessly on her back. She felt neither fear nor the need to breathe. It was as if she had become disembodied, and one with the water.

So it is true that the magic of my mother also lives in me, Amanda thought as she begun to glide calmly through the water when she suddenly heard a gentle ambient voice.

"Welcome, Amanda, to the realm of your mother, our divine Lady Murigen." Amanda spun around in surprise.

"Where are you? Please show yourself,"

"I am right here," answered the water spirit appearing in front of Amanda.

She was stunned by the beauty of the young fairy that stood like a crystalline statue in front of her.

"My name is Ariana, and I am here to bring you a gift from your mother, Lady Murigen. She sends you this pearl as a token of her love, and asks you to wear it at all times and to dip it into the water if you need help or protection," said the fairy. She carefully placed the necklace around Amanda's neck and disappeared. Amanda could not believe what just had happened. It seemed like a beautiful dream, but it was as real as the pearl on her neck. She did not feel the night slipping away until the rising sun began to replace the dark starry sky with her golden shine. Amanda realised that the time had come to leave the warmth and serenity of her mother's realm to return to her friends and left reluctantly. She felt her weight return with every step until she stood in the soft light of the new morning.

Hoping that her friends would still be asleep, Amanda rushed to her bedchamber, dressed and dried her hair as Ursula stepped in.

"Goodness, where have you been?" Ursula exclaimed. "I got scared when I saw your bed empty this morning."

"Oh Ursula calm down I got up early, to go for a walk in the garden. Let's go and have some breakfast before Ralston gets here," she replied, walking over to the table and join Hugh and Glen for breakfast.

"Guid mornin folks, I trust that you had a good rest and feel as fresh as a fish in the water," Ralston said. He smiled when he saw the pearl on Amanda's neck.

What does he mean, feeling like a fish in the water? Did he see me in the pond last night? Wondered Amanda trying to avoid his gaze.

"It is time to get on our way to the armoury. Bilobeal is waiting to fit your armours. I hope you did not eat too much for breakfast so that your armour can get a nice snug fit."

"What do you mean by fitting the armour? Hugh asked puzzled. Don't we just put it on?"

"The leather for your armour is softened in hot water and then wrapped around you. It shapes itself to your body as it dries."

"How can a leather armour protect us from blades and arrows," Amanda asked sceptically. Isn't it too soft to withstand such a force?"

"Bilobeal hardens it after it has reached its final shape. I am sure that he will be happy to explain it to you," responded Ralston as he led the group of friends out of the forest and into the mountains. It was a long, hard climb up the snow-covered slopes of Ben Lomond. The sun stood high in the sky as they reached the icy peak and squeezed through a crevice in the rocks into a cathedral-like cave. After their eyes had adjusted to the dim light of the cave, the friends walked on through a large cave system deep into the mountain until they reached a brightly light chamber.

As usual, Glen could not tame his curiosity and was the first to enter, heading straight for one of the silver armours hanging from the ceiling. A very strong Drow with long flaming red hair stepped into the light and approached them.

"Aye, you made it! I am glad to see you, Ralston. Are these bairns your brave warriors?"

"Aye Bilobeal, this is Amanda, the daughter of Lady Murigen, and these three are her friends."

"What's your name my bonnie lass," asked Bilobeal as he walked up to Ursula and bowed politely.

"My name is Ursula. It is a pleasure to meet you Sir Bilobeal."

"There is no need to be so formal, Ursula," he laughed. "But tell me what are the names of these two strong lads?"

"This is Glen, and this is his brother Hugh," replied Ursula, pushing them forward to greet Bilobeal.

"Aye right, let's get to work then, now that we've all been formally introduced. Your armours are nearly ready, all that is left to do is to fit and harden them. Once they are done, they will feel like your second skin and protect you from any blade or arrow. So let's get the armours wrapped around you while they are still soft so that they take their final shape on your body as they dry," explained Bilobeal as he pulled four soft pieces of leather from the steaming cauldron.

"Hold on, I am not going to have my skin burned off for some boggin leather armour!" shouted Hugh, taking a strong step back.

"It's not going to burn you, my brave young lad. It will be quiet cool by the time it touches your skin."

"Goodness Hugh, how embarrassing! Bilobeal, you can

start with me so that my brave friend can see how it is done," said Amanda, and stepped forward to be wrapped in the soft leather.

It did not take long before all of them stood wrapped in their leather armour and listened to Bilobeal's explanation of the hardening process.

"We are going to glaze your armours with pine resin and ground garnets, which will render them as hard as the stone itself. We will also add silver rivets for more resistance. Your arm and leg braces are made in the same way to protect and support you. Everything will be ready at the next full moon."

"Bilobeal, my armour is getting pretty tight is that normal?" asked Ursula fidgeting uncomfortably under the layer of leather.

"Aye right, my armour feels like a corset," added Amanda, as she tried to loosen the leather straps holding it together.

"Aye right, that is how it should be, it means that they are dry. Let me help you to take it off," Bilobeal replied.

"How come I don't hear anything from you lads," inquired Ralston with a broad grin.

"That is because we cannot breathe," whispered Glen.

"Well, let's get them off you too, so that my apprentices can now take them all to be glazed and hardened," said Bilobeal laughing as he placed the armours into a cart.

"Shall we go to our weapons arsenal now to arm your friends, Ralston?"

"By all means, Bilobeal. We have to make sure that they have the right size and weight, Amanda's wrists are very delicate, so she needs good braces. The same goes for Ursula."

"No, bother, Ralston. I thought of that and made special braces for the lassies. Follow me," he replied and led the group of friends into a large chamber crammed with racks of gleaming blades, lances, bows and other weapons. Hugh and Glen were speechless, staring in admiration at the sheer number of weapons on display and the magnificent craftsmanship of the Drows.

"Aye right, let's begin with Amanda. I made two short blade swords for you. Their grips are dragon claws, and the single edge blades are made from elven steel that can cut through even the heaviest armour. Your scabbard was crafted to go on to your back so that your hands remain free when you are not in combat. Your arm and leg braces have silver shields," said Bilobeal. He bowed deeply and laid the weapons at Amanda's feet before he turned and looked at the lads.

"Well, let's continue with our bowman. Which one of you is he?"

Hugh stepped closer in great anticipation.

"That would be me Bilobeal. At least that's what Ralston said," he answered.

"Aye right," said Bilobeal as he lifted a beautifully shaped longbow from a rack near the wall. "Your bow is made from the wood of an ancient white oak and strung with the hide from a stag. The arrows shafts are birch, fetched with falcon feathers and tipped with elven steel. We also made this special quiver for you that can hold up to thirty sixty arrows and a dagger," he said proudly displaying the weapon in his hands. Hugh was overwhelmed by this generous gift and bowed to Bilobeal before he took his splendidly crafted weapons.

"Now Glen, Ralston told me that you are the master of the staff. I made your staff very strong and reinforced its ends with elven silver rivets and black iron braces. I am a staff fighter myself and can assure you that a hit with your staff is deadly even for Red Caps."

"That leaves only you my bonnie lass," he continued with a smile as he walked over to Ursula. "Ursula your slingshot is made from elder wood and strung with dragon sinew. It is extremely powerful and has a brace attached to the handle which straps on to your wrist to strengthen and support it," he said, showing her how to strap the slingshot to her wrist.

"So now you are all armed for your quest. It was a pleasure to work for you, and I am looking forward to seeing you all again in combat," said Bilobeal extremely proud and pleased with himself.

Amanda picked up the scabbard with her swords and pondered how to strap it to her back.

"Let me help you, Amanda. It is hard in the beginning, but you will get the gist of it very soon," said Ralston as he helped her to strap the scabbard onto her back so that she was able to draw the blades for the very first time.

"You have to cross your arms over your head, grab the handles tightly and draw your swords upwards and in an arch with outstretched arms down to your side."

"Aye, I will give it a try," replied Amanda. She crossed her arms and pulled the blades without any effort from the Scabbard but shuddered when she heard the deadly hissing sound as she drew them.

"Perfect, I knew that you are a born swordfighter, just like your mother and all your ancestors. Tomorrow we will begin to strengthen your arms and wrists, and work on your balance, rhythm, and speed to prepare you for the battle," said Ralston with a smile before he turned to Glen and Hugh.

"And you lads, let's not get carried away and risk getting injured. You still need to learn how to handle your weapons."

The initial excitement over the newly gained status of a fully armed warrior wore quickly as the friends descended from the mountain.

"Ralston, please, let's rest for a moment I can't breathe," called Amanda as she sat down on a boulder.

"We can't, we need to keep going," answered Ralston, turning around to look at the red faces of Amanda and her friends.

"You have to adjust your breathing, or you will be

helpless and dead before the battle even begins. You have to learn to breathe into your belly. Try it as we continue to walk, and we will practice it tomorrow at the start of your training," Ralston said and walked on.

The friends were relieved when they arrived back at the palace and their chambers.

"Oh dear I never thought that it would be this tough," Glen sighed in exhaustion.

"Never mind Glen, we will get the hang of it. For now, let's just eat and go to bed I am dead tired," Amanda responded and placing her swords on her bed before she joined her friends at the table.

14 CAIT SITH

That night the friends felt restless and could not sleep. The importance and urgency of their quest had become all too real that day, and occupied their minds and conversations. Ursula, Hugh, and Glen were admiring each other's weapons and talking excitedly about the start of their training when Amanda interrupted.

"Guys, you should stop talking and go to bed, we have to be up early in the morning and will need our strength and concentration if we want to make it work," she said in a stern voice.

"What's wrong with you, Amanda, stop quarrelling. Where are you, anyhow?" Glen asked.

"I'm in the garden, trying to get some peace and quiet."

"Aye right, your highness, no need to ruffle your feathers. Let's go, guys, before Amanda loses her temper," said Glen closing the door to the garden.

At last silence. I did not want to be mean, but I need some time alone. I hope they understand, Amanda thought. As she sat down on the steps to the garden, rested her head on her knees, and listened to the calming sound of the wind. Suddenly a warm breath on her neck sent shudders down her spine. She jumped to her feet and spun around to see who was standing behind her but couldn't make out anything in the dark.

"Who is there? Show yourself," she whispered with a trembling voice, trying to sound brave.

"Amanda, you do not need to fear me. I am here to bring you a message from Adelaide."

"I do not have to fear you, why are you hiding in the shadows?" responded Amanda not entirely convinced.

"I am not what you would expect, so I think that it

would be best if you sit back down before I show myself."

"Aye right, I am sitting, so come out now. I don't frighten that easy."

"That's what Ralston told me. I am Cait Sith."

Amanda turned her head toward the sound. She could not believe her eyes when she saw a large black cat with a white spot on her chest standing right next to her.

"Please, forgive me for staring. Ralston never told me that you were a cat…, I expected a fairy or an Elf."

"I am a fairy, but I can only show myself as such nine times during my life, and I have only four times left. So tonight you see me as a cat."

"You are an unbelievably beautiful cat, Cait Sith. Tell me what the message is."

"Adelaide told me that she had spoken to a Brownie named Nissa and found out, that the young laird's wife is her long-lost niece, Anne. Nissa told Adelaide that the ship Anne sailed on from France was attacked by a Brilinn as they were approaching the harbour of Edinburgh. The crew was caught completely off guard, and could only offer little resistance as the mob of the Mac Neil's clan boarded the ship, stormed into the captain's quarters and demanded his surrender at gunpoint. All the women and children on board were sold into slavery as they made port in Oban. This is when the young Laird Duane Campbell bought Anne and forced her to be his wife. Anne, her daughter Lucy, and the Laird's mother, Julia, now live locked up in the castle."

"Crivens, we have to free them! Amanda exclaimed as soon as the cat had finished delivering her message. Especially since Lord Dougal has vowed to take Lucy if Ursula and I don't show up at the Castle by the next full moon. Cait Sith, please tell Adelaide that we will return within the next three days to free Anne, Lucy, and Julia. Forgive me, but I have to go now to wake my friends and devise a plan how to liberate them," Amanda said. She was about to run into the palace when Ralston stepped out in front of her.

"Slow down Amanda, let's talk first. There is a way to free them without putting anyone in danger."

"Oh yea, is there such a way?" said Amanda impatiently. "Go on let me hear it then."

"Yes Amanda, you don't have to do it alone. All you have to do is to ask the Goddess Momu for help. She will be able to bring Anne, Lucy, and Julia safely to Adelaide without anyone noticing."

"And how is she going to do this, may I ask?" she responded, her tone caught between sarcasm and hope.

"Momu is the Goddess of all wells and hillsides. She can take them to Adelaide unharmed. All we have to do is to convince the three of them that it is safe to climb into the castles well. Cait Sith, go and inform Adelaide. She will know what to do, and Amanda you come with me," said Ralston leading her to the fairy pond.

"Dip your pearl into the water to call Ariana. She will deliver your call for help to Momu," he instructed her calmly.

"How do you know about the pearl?"

"It's my job to know everything. And anyway it was foreseeable that Lady Murigen was going to send you one of her pearls and an Ashray to watch over you. But let's not talk any longer, call Ariana, time is of the essence."

"Aye right," Amanda responded. She took the pearl from her neck and dipped it into the water. "So what now?"

"Now we wait, Amanda. It will not be long before Ariana appears. Ashrays are faster than any current I know."

Ralston had only just finished his sentence when Ariana emerged.

"How can I be of service to you, Amanda?"

"Ariana, I need the help from the Goddess Momu to free three captives from Kilchurn Castle and bring them safely to Adelaide's house," Amanda explained. Before she had a chance to clarify it further, Ariana was gone. Amanda shuck her head and stared into the water in disbelief.

"Why did she leave? I didn't even tell her about Anne, Lucy, and Julia," whispered Amanda.

"There is no need, she would have overheard our conversation. She always stays close to you but will only show herself when you call her." Ralston explained.

"Don't worry Ariana, is going to deliver your message and Momu will get Anne, Lucy, and Julia to safety. But it is time now for you to rest. I will return for you at sunrise," said Ralston and left.

15THE TRAINING BEGINS

"Amanda wake up, it's late. Ralston will be here any minute."

"Oh dear, sorry Ursula but I went to bed late and didn't sleep well at all. Just after you went to sleep, Cait Sith came and brought me an important message from Adelaide. Can you wake Hugh and Glen? I'll tell you everything over breakfast."

"The lads have been up for ages! Just get yourself ready I'll go and tell them that you have news for us," said Ursula.

"Goodness Glen, take it easy on the food, you won't be able to start the training if you keep stuffing yourself like a pig," Ursula said as she walked into the hall.

"Oh come on Ursula, who knows when we are going get some food next," replied Glen picking up another meat pie.

"Give it up Ursula, you should know by now that he never listens to reason," said Hugh and shook his head.

"He will listen to the news I am about to share with you," said Amanda as she joined her friends. She sat down and began to recount last night's occurrences. After she had finished, Hugh spoke first.

"Oh wow, I would have loved to meet Cait Sith, I hope she will be back soon to let us know how the escape went."

"Aye, Cait Sith will be our messenger whenever we are away from home."

"Good morning folks!" Ralston's voice echoed from the garden. "I hope you are ready to go, Keelin is waiting for us in the meadow."

The friends left the palace and followed Ralston through a small grove of oak trees and into a sun-drenched grassy meadow, where Keelin was awaiting their arrival.

"Welcome, I hope you had a good rest so that we can start. "Keelin addressed them. "In the beginning, I will work with you as a group, and show you how to increase your strength and perseverance. Then I'll teach you to move with ease, graceful, and sleek, help you to improve your breathing and finally enable you to control your anger to remain mindful in combat," he explained.

"Laratbogh and Oren are going show you how to calm your mind, use all your senses, disguise yourself and stalk your enemies safely.

After you completed this basic training, you will learn how to use your weapons efficiently.

"Amanda," he continued. "Lord Ralston is going to teach you to fight with two swords and how to use a dagger.

Hugh, Lady Sorcha will help you to refine your skills to become a master bowman. Glen, Edana is going to teach you, to set and control fires, and I'll show you how to use a double bladed sword and help you to improve your techniques with the staff."

"Aislinn is going to train you in the use of a slingshot, Ursula, and share her secrets to heal injuries through the use of herbs. But enough of that, let's start with our basic training by practising deep and controlled breathing. I want you to focus as you inhale and hold your breath while balancing on these small rocks."

The group spent the next hours working on their balance under Keelin's gaze.

"Oh man, I can't take much more of this. My feet are hurting, and my head is spinning from all this funny breathing," Glen complaint.

"It's not the breathing that is troubling you, it is the food you had before the training. You have to get used to eating smaller amounts of food," Ralston said smiling.

"Well done, you guys. I think it's time now to work on

your strength and stamina, so let's climb some trees," shouted Keelin, disappearing in a giant oak.

"Aye, that's fine with me. I was climbing the wings of our mill before I could walk properly," shouted Glen. He grabbed one of the lower branches and followed Keelin up the tree like a squirrel.

"Well, that is easy for you to say, I don't have the strength to pull myself up and look at the size of these trees," sighed Amanda.

"Let's do it together. Come on, I help you up," giggled Hugh, forming a step with his hands for Amanda's foot and lifting her up.

"Take hold of the trunk and then step on to my shoulders so that you can reach the first branch."

Amanda wrapped one arm tight around the oak tree, swung the other over the nearest branch for balance, and lifted her feet off Hugh's shoulders and onto a large sturdy gnarl. She was truly grateful now for her new soft leather boots which allowed her to feel her way up the tree. Exhausted but proud of her achievement Amanda sat down as she reached the first fork of the tree, rested her back on the tree trunk, and took a deep breath to inhale the tree's fresh and spicy scent. A glorious feeling of strength and oneness with the trees around her filled her body as the green essence flooded her lungs. She felt content and let her eyes wander up to the canopy of lush green leaves and branches when she noticed a faint movement next to her.

"Stay calm Amanda and sit tight, I mean you no harm. My name is Laratbogh, I am one of the protectors of the forest."

"Oh Laratbogh I've heard about you and your sister Faerydae from Adelaide, where are you?"

"I am right by your side holding your hand. Promise me you won't let go," whispered Laratbogh. *Holding my hand?* Amanda thought. She looked bewildered at the large branch she had rested her hand on to steady herself when a beautiful woman with delicate features appeared from the wood. Her skin looked as if it was carved from softwood and her hair resembled the lush green foliage of the tree.

"Are you a part of this tree Laratbogh?" she asked.

"Yes and no. My sisters and I are a part of all trees, but we favour the oak as our home. We never travel far from it unless we carry one of its acorns with us to remain in contact with it at all times," Laratbogh explained.

"So that is how you were able to accompany us through Eredine Forest," Amanda said, slowly understanding. "But how come I did not see you? Your green hair should have given you away between the snowy trees."

"Our hair changes its colour as the seasons' change," she replied. "During the spring and summer months, our hair is lush and green, while during autumn it turns red and eventually brown or white in the winter."

"Well that explains it," said Amanda.

"I have to leave you now. I just came to assure you of our help and protection on your quest. My sisters and I will see you all tomorrow morning, goodbye Amanda," whispered Laratbogh and vanished.

Amanda remained in the tree for a little while before she joined her friends again. The group practiced swinging from branch to branch until the sun was setting and it was time to return to the ground.

"That was great, but how do we get down without breaking our necks," shouted Ursula looking lost.

"That is not as hard as you think. Whenever you need to jump or drop from great heights, look for a mossy or sandy landing spot. But never land straight-legged as the amount of impact would risk injuries to your knees and hips and therefore risk your life."

"Thanks, Keelin, we'll try our best. Come on Ursula, let's do it," said Amanda and let herself drop to the ground.

"That was fun, but don't look at my hands now!" Ursula said, looking at her hands in disgust. My fingers are swollen, and my nails are black from the tree sap."

"It's a good thing that you can't see your hair, Ursula. You look like a tree yourself with all the leaves and twigs in your locks," laughed Hugh and began to pull some of them from her fiery red hair.

"Hugh, Glen, come and join me for a moment I would like to show you something before we return to the palace," shouted Keelin from the edge of the woods.

"We'll see you later then," called Amanda and Ursula as they hurried out of the forest and straight into the fairy pond. They had just leaped into the clear warm water when Ariana suddenly surfaced next to Ursula.

"Oh dear, you startled me!" Ursula jumped. "You must be Ariana. I am Ursula."

"Aye I know who you are, you are Amanda's best friend," replied Ariana with a big smile and swam towards Amanda.

"Oh Ariana, I didn't expect you back so soon, do you have news from Adelaide?" Amanda asked as she climbed out of the water.

"No, I can't reach Adelaide's cottage the brock is too shallow. But I bring you a message from Lady Momu. She will help Anne, Lucy, and Julia to escape from Kilchurn Castle under the cover of the next dark moon so that no one will be able to see them leave."

"How she is going to do that without harming them?" Amanda asked, a concerned look crossing her face.

"Lady Momu is going to create a large air chamber around them once they are in the Castle's well, and I will move them through an underground river to Adelaide."

"Oh thank you, Ariana that eases my mind. I hope Cait Sith was able to contact Adelaide so that she can make the necessary preparations and get the message to Anne and Julia."

"You can ask Cait Sith, she is waiting for you in your bedchamber," replied Ariana

"Well, let's go then, Amanda! I want to meet her before the lads get here, hurry," called Ursula and rushed into Amanda's bedchamber.

"My goodness, is that Cait Sith Amanda? Let's not wake her who knows how she would react," mouthed Ursula as she saw the large black cat curled up on Amanda's bed.

"It's her, but you can relax she is not dangerous, at least not for us."

"Are you sure about that? I think I'd rather keep my distance. You go and wake her," whispered Ursula, hiding behind Amanda.

"No need to whisper, I heard you come in," murmured Cait Sith. She arched her back and stretched.

"Ariana told me that you have a message for me from Adelaide, Cait Sith," Amanda said.

"Yes, Adelaide is very excited and has begun to make preparations for the arrival of Anne, Julia, and wee little Lucie after she sent Nissa to talk to them. Nissa informed them about the plan and is going to stay at the castle to make sure that everything goes well."

"That is great news."

"Yes, but I also have bad news. The laird's men burned John's barn, stable and root cellar and placed a group of Red Caps in his house to make sure that he and his family can never return."

"Aye, that is bad news," Amanda said, a tear escaping from her eyes. "But at least we were warned and able to move all his belongings to Adelaide. But what about the mill, who is running it now since Bhaltair and Madge, left?"

"Nobody, I am afraid. The laird's men plundered their stocks, blocked the wheel, and removed the sails from its wings." Cait Sith said. "But you should not worry about any of that now, just concentrate on your training."

"Aye right, we will. But let's go now and join Hugh and Glen. They are eager to meet you," said Amanda and waved Cait Sith to follow.

"Help ma boab, that's a big cat!" exclaimed Hugh, taking a step back.

"Lads, this is Cait Sith. She came to bring us a message from Adelaide. Everything is lined up for the escape of Anne, Julia, and Lucie," Amanda exclaimed and could not suppress a smile.

"Thank you, Cait Sith. Please forgive our reaction, Amanda had told us about you but failed to mention your size," stammered Hugh and bowed.

"That is quite alright laddie. I am used to mortals staring when they see me, I would love to stay, but I am needed at the cottage to keep an eye on things for Lord Ralston. Take care," replied Cait Sith and gracefully pranced out of the palace.

"Dear me did you see the size of her paws? They are as big as a platter, and her green eyes gleam like fire." Hugh exclaimed in amazement.

"Aye, and she moves as silent as a ghost and her black fur blends in with the trees perfectly making her almost invisible," Glen remarked.

"Right my dear brother. She must be deadly when she prowls the forest at night."

"Come on you two, Cait Sith is our friend and protector," Amanda said. "The only ones that should fear her razor-sharp teeth and powerful legs are our enemies. I am sure that they will know the meaning of fear and terror whence they hear her roars."

"That's for sure, but let's not worry about that now," Ursula spoke. It's late, and I am sore from head to toe. Let's call it a day."

"Ursula is right we should go to bed. Tomorrow will be another demanding day," Amanda said. "Guit nuit, sleep tied."

"Guit nuit Amanda!"

16 LARATBOGH AND OREN

Exhausted and sore from the strenuous training, Amanda let herself collapse onto her soft bed. She closed her eyes and thought back to her encounter with Laratbogh high up in the majestic old oak tree. All of a sudden she heard the muffled sound of steps in the garden.

Who could that be in the middle of the night? Cait Sith is at the cottage and Ralston is surely sleeping by now, wondered Amanda. She got up and walked quietly to the door leading into the garden to take a closer look and was surprised to find it wide open.

Who opened the door? Ursula and the lads are in bed fast asleep...? She thought, went back to her room, put on her clothes, and picked up a candlestick on her way out as a weapon, just in case.

She felt foolish with the candlestick in her hand. *Who on earth could harm me here, with all these guards around?* She walked out into the garden and noticed fresh footprints in the grass leading into the woods. She followed them until she noticed the glow of a small campfire and saw Hugh, Glen, and Keelin sitting at the fire talking to another man.

"What are you guys doing out here in the middle of the night?" she called as she approached.

"Crivens, Amanda, I could ask you the same thing! Why are you out of bed at this late hour?" replied Glen. He stood up blocking Amanda's view.

"Well, I was following you! Who are you hiding there? I thought that we agreed to have no secrets," she said, crossing her arms, vexed.

"That's right, we most certainly don't, but Ghilli Duh is extremely shy and wanted to gather some courage before meeting you," Keelin explained bowing to Amanda.

"Am I so terrible that a grown man needs to gather the courage to meet me?"

"Well, to be frank, yes. After all, you are the daughter of a Goddess and cannot just be approached like a mortal," explained Keelin.

"Where are you, Ghilli Duh? Please step forward so that I can see you."

"As you wish Amanda, daughter of Lady Murigen," answered a voice, coming out of the shadows. As he stepped into the light of the fire, Amanda could see that Ghilli Duh was an extremely large fairy with long black, hair deeply tanned skin and gentle eyes. His clothing was made of leaves and moss, and he carried a heavy staff.

"I am honoured to meet you Amanda and humbly offer you my help and protection in your quest to free your mother."

"I am very pleased to meet you Ghilli Duh and thank you for your generosity. But I can't stay and talk to you tonight, as I am exhausted and need to rest. I am sure Keelin told you that we all are undergoing rigorous training to prepare us for our quest, so please forgive us for cutting our meeting short tonight. I hope that we will meet again soon," said Amanda. She bent her head and returned to the palace with Hugh and Glen.

The following day began entirely different with Laratbogh, Faerydae and their younger sister Oren taking them on a relaxed walk through the woods to identify and follow the tracks of all the creatures living in the realm of Elfame. They introduced the group to their little cousins the pixies and taught them how to walk through the woods without leaving the faintest mark, before approaching the more difficult lessons of disguise and stalking.

"When you stalk your enemies or plan an ambush, place a branch between your teeth to hide your face and wear the light, soft leather shoes that the elves gave you instead of your heavy boots so that your steps are soundless and leave little or no imprint," Oren explained and showing them how to cut a branch without leaving a trace on a tree or shrub.

"We've brought you some green suede jerkins made for you to wear over your armour. They will hide you just as effectively as your plaids but won't slow you down or hinder your movements," said Faerydae, turned and parted the branches of a hazel bush, revealing a Dryad child holding a large basket filled to the brim with wild berries.

"This is our youngest sister Hazel. She has been up since dawn to pick berries for you and fetch cool water from the spring, so let's unwind for a while," Oren said, kissing her little sister and sitting down on a large stone.

The friends were grateful for the break. They spread out their soft plaids and enjoyed the sumptuous treats and fresh water while basking in the afternoon sun and chatting with their gracious hosts.

"Now, let's listen to the gentle sounds of the forest. Hear the wind as he is playing with the leaves and branches of the trees, the hum of the bees, and dragonflies. Listen to the sound of birds flapping their wings and their beautiful songs. Pay attention to the thud of the deer's huff as it ambles through the woods without worry or fear," whispered Oren with closed eyes.

The friends followed her example and sat perfectly still, silent, and focused, listening to the beautiful songs of nature. Suddenly, they heard the trot of the deer quicken and turning into a gallop. The birds began to beat their wings in fright, and the sound of breaking branches echoed through the woods.

"What is happening, Oren?" shouted Ursula, scanning their surrounding nervously.

"Something is approaching, so the forest is sounding the alarm," replied Oren as she jumped to her feet.

"Did you do that to show us a reaction to danger, or is it real?" asked Amanda sounding tense. At that moment Cait Sith appeared out of the trees.

"It's real alright. Look at Cait Sith. No wonder that every creature is trying to get away. No offence Cait Sith, but I am sure you know your effect on your prey," Glen said.

"No offence taken, Glen. After all, I am a predator. But I am not here to hunt. I have an urgent message for you all."

"What's wrong? Is everything alright at the cottage?" asked Amanda looking alarmed.

"Nothing happened at the cottage, but we got word from Nissa that William and Maighread were taken to Kilchurn Castle last night."

"Why, what could they have possibly done to warrant an arrest?" Amanda asked.

"Nothing, but after the disappearance of John, Annette and now Bhaltair and his entire family, the Laird is suspicious of William and Maighread especially since they were the last ones to speak to them. He has sent his men out to search for you and your families. We can only pray that he doesn't make the connection to Adelaide."

"He can't possibly suspect Adelaide. We were so careful, and the cottage is supposed to be protected by powerful magic."

"Yes Amanda, they will all be safe as long as they remain at the cottage. The Goddesses Momu and Coventina placed another enchantment over the cottage and the land around it. No one with malicious intent can pass over the bridge or approach the cottage from the fields or the forest. So you bairns need not fear for them."

"We should go to the fairy pond and call all of our friends and allies to gather and assess the situation," said Faerydae with determination. She walked up to a large rowan tree and began to drum rhythmically on its trunk.

"What is she doing?" asked Ursula, looking wide-eyed

at Laratbogh.

"She is calling the Dryads, the Pixies and Ghilli Duh to assemble at the fairy pond. The tree is going to send her message through the root system of the entire forest," replied Laratbogh.

Glen, Hugh, and Ursula stood rooted on the spot. All colour had drained from their faces, and their eyes were wide in terror.

"Snap out of it," Amanda ordered. "Come on, we have to act. There is no time to hesitate. Let's get to the pond to make a plan of action." With that she ran into the forest.

17 THE GATHERING

Dark storm clouds soared through the blazing red sky like birds of prey while the sun melted in the meadow like iron ore in a black smith's forge.

It's a bad omen, Amanda thought as she ran panting and with a stabbing pain in her side through the thickets of the woods.

"Amanda, stop. There is no need for haste. Do not allow your feelings to blind you," said Ralston as he appeared right in front of her blocking her path.

"That is easy for you to say!" she replied angrily. "William and Maighread mean nothing to you, but they are everything to me. They are my family, and I will not abandon them."

"I would never ask that of you, but we have to be cautious and plan our actions well, so we do not place William and Maighread at risk. Please Amanda stop and breathe. We will find a way to free them. Let's talk it over with our friends, they are waiting at the fairy pond," said Ralston softly, taking her hand gently in his.

"Look at the sun, Ursula. It looks as if she has been drenched in blood. I am sure that this is a warning telling us that the time has come to fight."

"Oh Hugh, what's wrong with you? You used to like a red sunset! Why are you in such a dreadful mood?" asked Ursula, shaking her head and walking away.

"Since our homes and livelihoods have been destroyed and our families are forced to live in hiding," shouted Hugh behind her with an angry expression.

"Come on laddie, chase the dark clouds out of your mind," said Ghilli Duh, as he walked up to him. "You are not alone in this. We will all be at your side until we have defeated this evil."

"You are right," Hugh said, gaining courage with his words. "Let's join the others at the fairy pond to devise a plan of action."

"That's better, Hugh. Lift your head and face whatever comes your way. Speaking of what comes your way. I have to leave you for a while to greet a friend of mine who has just arrived," Ghilli Duh remarked.

"Who? Where? I don't see anybody."

"The Wulver. Look at him, right there at the edge of the woods. He doesn't like to show his face when mortals are around. Come on, let me introduce you," said Ghilli Duh, leading Hugh to the edge of the forest.

"You can come out of hiding," he called out, seemingly to no one. "Hugh is a good lad and doesn't frighten easily," he chuckled to himself as he searched the surrounding shrubs for his friend.

"If you say so, Ghilli Duh," a voice spoke from behind them.Hugh turned around and expected a horrid looking old fairy or elf but was not prepared for what faced him. He took a deep breath and tried hard to keep his knees from buckling as he saw a man with a wolf's head appear from the underbrush.

"Are you all right, laddie?" Ghilli Duh asked. "You look awfully pale."

"I am good, but I am starving. A handful of berries are not enough to keep me going, and that's all I had for the day. Will you please excuse me while l go and get some food," answered Hugh nervously and walked away.

"Aye right, I am hungry myself. Let's see what they have for us at the palace, come on Wulver," said Ghilli Duh, placing his hand on his friend's shoulder and steering him in direction fairy pond.

"We should all calm down," Asanopirh said. "No harm was done to William and Maighread, as the Laird still sees him as a friend,"

"Oh really?" Amanda said with sarcasm. "As a friend, would you throw your friend in a dungeon too?"

"They are not in the dungeon Amanda, relax. They are in the tower house with Julia, Anne, and Lucie. That is how we found out about their arrest, Nissa saw them there and informed Adelaide," replied Asanopirh.

"What will happen to them after Julia, Anne, and Lucie get away? Can we not get them out as well?" Amanda asked.

"No, their chambers are locked and guarded. But Nissa will remain at the castle to look after them and to keep in contact with us. She watched over William from the day he was born and would never leave him in such a situation," said Cait Sith.

"Thank your swift action Cait Sith," saidBilobeal. He got up and looked at the friends with a serious expression. You have to hasten your training as the situation is changing rapidly. We will do our part and work on your armours with heightened speed to get them ready in time."

"Dear friends it's time to get some rest and clear our minds so that we can come up a levelheaded to how to proceed. Sleep well. We'll meet in the meadow at sunrise," said Ralston. He was about to leave when Amanda grabbed his arm and asked.

"What about our training with Laratbogh and Oren? We haven't finished."

"Don't fret about your training Amanda. My sisters and I will accompany you wherever you go to advise you and make sure that you are safe," replied Oren, bowed and left. "So since that's settled, let's go and have something to eat before we hit the sack. I am starving," said Glen ushering his friends into the palace.

"I can't eat now, my stomach is in a knot," Ursula said, a troubled expression twisted on her face. "I'll go to bed and think about what can be done to free William and his mum."

"We will have a bite or two, and then put our heads together. We should be able to come up withsomething," answered Hugh.

"Well, you guys do that, I go to the fairy pond to talk things over with Ariana. Let's discuss what we came up with on our way to the meadow. Good night," said Amanda and walked into the garden.

Why is it that every time things seem to be going well something terrible happens? She thought as she dipped her pearl into the crystal clear water of the fairy pond.

"I am here, Amanda," a familiar voice spoke. "I stayed and overheard your conversation."

"Thank you, Ariana. What do you think about the situation?"

"Well, Lord Ralston is right. They are safe for now. But you should quicken your training so that you will be ready to free William and Maighread before the next full moon. Lord Ralston, Lady Sorcha and Lord Asanopirh are already devising a plan of action."

"What are they like Ariana, are they as fears as everybody seems to think they are?"

"Lord Asanopirh is the most fearless warrior I know. He is utterly ruthless when it comes to safeguarding his queen, realm or family. He and his warriors will never hesitate to use every trick at their command.

The dark princess Lady Sorcha is known for her slight recklessness and her evil temper. She most certainly will not hesitate to kill," said Ariana and rested her hands on Amanda's knees.

"Normally I would shudder at what you just told me, Ariana. But lately, I look at these vices as virtues. Have I gone bad?"

"No Amanda, you haven't. You and the ones you love are being threatened by something so venomous, that you must retaliate even though it horrifies and sickens you. Unleash your power and let them feel your fury. Don't think twice, as they would not hesitate to kill you. But please, don't worry about any of that now. You need rest so that you can focus on your training tomorrow morning. To fight with two swords is very dangerous and demands a high level of control and concentration. Go to bed Amanda, I will be here when you return," said Ariana. She held her gaze for a moment, then disappeared in the deep blue water of the fairy pond.

Amanda could not sleep and began to pace the garden. The thought of William and Maighread being locked up at Kilchurn Castle made her restless, but what troubled her most was that she could do nothing to get them out of the Laird's grip.

"Why are you not resting, Amanda? Don't you remember me telling you that you need all your strength and focus for our training," asked Ralston in a hushed whisper.

"Yes I do, but I can't close my eyes and pretend nothing's happened. I feel so helpless."

"I understand how you must feel, but you are not helpless. Very soon, you will be a fearless sword-yielding warrior, lightning fast and just as bright once you start spinning," he reassured her. "We never told you the second name your mother gave you. It is Evelyn, which in our world means the light. You have the power to create clarity and warmth, and erase everything that is dark and ruled by dark magic. Asanopirh has the gift of light too. His name means Death Shine. His light cannot create, he is the bringer of death to everything malevolent or treacherous."

"Is that why he is the only one wearing a silver armour?" Amanda asked.

"Yes Amanda, it is a gift from the Goddess Arianrhod. It magnifies his light and his power to blind, to defeat his enemies."

"This explains a lot, but it still leaves many questions unanswered. For instance, why are you here? I am sure that you did not come to me tonight to explain all of this," she said, raising her eyebrows.

"No, in fact, you are right. I came to ease your mind by bringing you news about a significant development," he replied.

"When I left you all tonight, I remembered that Nissa once told me about hidden passages in Kilchurn Castle. So I went to inquire if these passages could be used to get William and Maighread out. Nissa confirmed my suspicions and told me that these passages, in fact, lead out of the castle but have been flooded by the waters from Loch Awe many years ago. This, of course, does not present a problem for us, as we can ask the Goddess Coventina for help. Nissa agreed to guide William and his mum, through the passage up to the flooded part and call on Coventina to drain the waters which will allow them to reach the shore of Loch Awe where Asanopirh, Sorcha and I will be waiting to bring them to Inistrynich and onwards to Adelaide's cottage."

"When are you planning to do that? Can I come, please?" Amanda urged. "I have to see them to know that they are okay."

"We knew that you would ask," Ralston said, unable to hide his smile. "Yes we agreed to bring you along, but please keep it a secret this time. We are leaving during the night of the dark moon to make sure that all captives are freed and safe at the same time. Lady Arianrhod is going to wrap the castle in absolute darkness until we all reached the cottage after which it no longer matters."

"Oh, that is fantastic news!" Amanda exclaimed. "I'll be so happy to see Adelaide and all the others. Thank you, Ralston."

"Go and rest now, so you can focus on your training. And please, encourage your friends to do the same. Sleep well Amanda, I see you at sunrise," he said and left.

18 THE DARK MOON

Amanda leapt out of her bed bursting with energy and ran to wake her friends. It was as if a halo of joy had surrounded her since she had heard last night's good news.

"Good morning out of bed you guys! The sun isabout to rise, and a great adventure awaits us."

"Oy, miss sunshine what's up? Who scattered your thunderclouds? Not that I mind, but your change ofmood is spooky, to say the least."

"Nothing's up, Glen, but I realised last night that it is not an option to lose control if we want to set things right. We have to put all our energy into the training so that we can face each and every challenge that comes our way."

"Aye Amanda that's the spirit!" called Keelin from the garden.

"Good morning folks," Ralston greeted the friends. "I hope you are ready, come on pick up your gears and meet us in the meadow."

"Aye, but first I need some food. See you there in a wink," answered Glen as he washed his face.

The friends rushed through their breakfast, grabbed their weapons and raced each other on the way to the meadow. Out of breath but with fire in their bellies they reached the training ground where they were awaited by Ralston, Keelin, Aislinn, and Sorcha.

"Well, finally you are here, and all warmed up, I see, so let's begin. Hugh, you go with Sorcha and remember she doesn't speak your tongue so you will have to follow her gestures and movements closely," said Ralston with abig smile on his face

"Glen come on follow me, we will practice down by the river."

"Aye Keelin, I am coming," answered Glen eagerly

and followed Keelin down to the river.

"Ursula, we will climb up into the rocks to have a good view, plenty of targets, and enough ammunition," giggled Aislinn and waved Ursula to follow.

Hugh awaited his turn patiently and bowed to Sorcha to show her that he was ready to follow her where ever she chooses to take him. She acknowledged his readiness with a coy smile and gestured him to follow her into the woods.

"So that leaves the meadow to us, Amanda. And we will need it you have to have free reign while you practice handling your swords. Shall we begin?"

"Aye Ralston I am ready, tell me what I have to do."

"Draw your weapons and look at me," he instructed. "To fight with two swords, your movements have to be circular, fluid, evasive, and deceptive." He began to spin his arms, like the wings of a mill in a storm.

"The spiralling deflections will enable you to move lightning-fast and lead your opponents to anticipate a different attack entirely, thus making its reactions uncoordinated and leaving him to stumble. You never have to use smashing blows or, crushing strikes, because of the momentum you created by spinning. This motion also enables you to use elegant manoeuvers to deflect your opponents' blades while you drift back to score hits yourselves. Are you ready to give it a try?"

"Aye, but you better stand back," Amanda warned. "I don't know where I land once I start spinning. I might get dizzy and loose direction."

"That's okay, we have the entire heath to ourselves this morning so go ahead. Just make sure to hold your arms away from your body," he replied thought he lifted his swords as a precaution."

Amanda drifted like a whirlwind over the grassland, fast, and soundless, the blades of her swords reflecting the sun and flashing like lightning as she performed the dance that would bring certain death to any assailant. Ralston was stunned. He had expected her to discover her inborn gift of swordsmanship quickly but could not have dreamed of such a high level of mastery.

"What's wrong Ralston?" she said, seeing his expression. "What did I do wrong? Did I hold the swords at a wrong angle? Was my spinning uncoordinated? Shall I try again?"

It took him a moment to respond.

"No Amanda, you were unbelievable. Your speed, balance, and grace are unsurpassed. All that's left for me to do is to show you protective moves and how to fight with one sword in case you should drop one during a fight or get injured."

"Really?" Amanda said not quite sure how to take the compliment. "I never held a sword in my life before, but I always enjoyed dancing and spinning."

"Well, I see that your coordination and stance are flawless. Let's begin to engage in some actual combat training," replied Ralston. He bowed deeply, then raised his swords and opened Amanda's first ever sword fight.

Amanda spun around Ralston with swinging swords blocking all his attacks and even landing a few strikes. She felt strong and fearless, her breath was deep and even, her strides and spins fluid and without effort.

Meanwhile, Ursula and Aislinn stood perched at the top of the rocks, preparing their weapons.

"Ursula come on lass, pick a target. Start with something big if you like. I just want to see what you have to offer," Aislinn said.

"As you wish, Aislinn. What about the tree stump right next to Ralston?" giggled Ursula. Without waiting for approval, she lifted her slingshot and fired.

"Oy, what you think you are doing?" shouted Ralston as the pebble hit his sword. He turned around looking for the attacker.

"Sorry, I just wanted to get your attention, Ralston! I promise not to aim for you again," shouted Ursula and could not suppress loud laughter.

"Well, I guess you showed me," Aislinn remarked, impressed. "So let's try something a bit more demanding shall we?"

"Bring it on," Ursula replied in confidence. "What do you have in mind?"

"Try to knock an apple off that tree without bruising it," answered Aislinn with a broad grin.

"Aye, no problem. Any apple or do you have a favourite?" replied Ursula and winked at Aislinn with a mischievous smile. She aimed and hit the stem of an apple, sending it to the ground. Aislinn looked at Ursula with a dazzled smile and patted her shoulder in approval.

"Marvelous shot Ursula. I could not have done it any better myself. I believe the only thing I can still teach you is what ammunition to use, how to locate it and how to collect it. So let's have a look around for the right ammunition to mark, and finally, take out our targets."

"Certainly Aislinn, I am sure that there is a lot that I can learn from you about the right ammunition. Up to now I only used whatever I could lay my hands on."

"Good, so let's go down to the river and pick up some smooth, round pebbles. They are perfect for long- range targets," said Aislinn, signalling Ursula to follow.

"Wow Glen that was a good blow!" shouted Ursula as she stepped out from behind a large boulder onto the riverbank. But it is rude to take your teacher out on your first day of training."

"Oy, don't distract him, that could cost him dearly," replied Keelin. In an instant, he swung his staff and struck the back of Glen's knees sending him into the river with a big splash.

"Crivens Ursula, why did you do that?" Glen shouted.

"Well, you looked hot so I thought you could do with a cold dip!"

"Don't fuss, Glen that was a good practice. It showed you that you need to focus and not allow anything or anyone to distract you while you are in combat. This time you only got wet, but the next time it could cost you your life."

"Aye right, thanks Keelin for setting him straight, I only meant well," chuckled Ursula. She continued to collect river pebbles for her target practice when she suddenly heard the hissing sound of an arrow and felt it graze her boot.

"Who did that?" exclaimed Ursula, casting a startled look around her.

"I did. I had to stop you from bothering my brother!" Hugh laughed.

"Are you out of your mind, Hugh? You could have killed me!"

"Only if I had my eyes closed mo lennan."

"Oh I'll get you for this, you just wait! Where are you hiding anyhow? I can't see you."

"Look up. See me now? I am in the ash tree, right across the river from you."

"No!"

"Perfect, that means that our training with Oren and Faerydae helped me to improve my disguise."

"Aye right, can we all go back to our training now," said Keelin interrupting their conversation and raising his staff to continue the mock fight with Glen. "We don't have forever to get you ready for your quest," he reminded them.

By the time the light began to fade, the friends and their trainers had returned to the palace to enjoy a hearty meal, and wine while assessing their achievements.

"I have to say, you guys did very well. I've been truly surprised by your skills. We are now confident that you will be victorious in any combat and can successfully complete your quest. Slàinte mhath"! Cheered Ralston and lifted his chalice.

"Slàinte mhath!" responded the round of friends, lifting their chalices to drink to each other's health.

The friends celebrated their success late into the night

until they couldn't manage to stay up any longer and finally dropped exhausted but happy into their beds. Only Amanda stayed awake, she sat at the edge of the fairy pond gazing at the stars.

"Good evening, Amanda," Ariana's voice appeared beside her. "Why are you not in your bed? You should be exhausted after such an eventful day."

"I am far too excited to sleep," Amanda said, pleased to see her. "It won't be long now before we travel to Kilchurn Castle to free William, Maighread, and the others, and move them to safety in Adelaide's cottage. It will be a wonderful night for us all, we will be able to share our experiences and plans and most of all we can celebrate the first defeat of our enemies."

"Aye, that is a wonderful thought indeed. But nevertheless, you need your sleep, Amanda. Why don't you come and join me? The warm water, weightlessness, and silence will help you to relax."

"You are right," Amanda conceded, walking into the fairy pond. After only a few steps, she felt weightless and ethereal and began to float gently to the ground.

19 THE ESCAPE

This time, Amanda kept the promise not to tell her friends about the night's intervention, which was quite an achievement since she was not good at keeping secrets. Finally, the time had come to leave the realm of the Seelie Court and travel down the River Awe to Kilchurn castle.

"Is everyone asleep, Amanda?" Ralston asked.

"Aye, they'll sleep till late in the afternoon tomorrow. Laratbogh prepared an herbal tea that knocked them out like a bear in winter," whispered Amanda and could not stop giggling.

"Did you bring a dagger, Amanda?"

"Aye, Asanopirh I have one in each boot just in case."

"Good. Oh, and there is one more thing. We have to stay perfectly silent and use only hand signs when we enter Loch Awe until we return to the shore of Inistrynich."

"Aye," replied Amanda. She climbed into the boat and helped Ralston to push away from the shore and into the deeper waters of the River Awe. Soon, the boat was drifting swiftly downstream with the current, as if guided by an invisible hand.

Lady Arianrhod most certainly kept her promise the world looks as if it is cloaked in black shrouds, thought Amanda, feeling a cold shiver running down her spine. She had to shake off this eerie feeling and broke her silence.

"What do you know about Kilchurn Castle, Ralston?"

"Well, the castle was built on the small island of Kilchurn by the young laird's father, Sir Colin Campbell, the first Lord of Glen Orchy," Ralston explained. "At first, it was only a five storey tower house and courtyard with an outer wall which could only be reached by a low lying causeway. The causeway and the passages leading into the tower house were claimed by the water of Loch Awe soon after."

"So the tower house is where the laird is keeping William, Maighread, Lady Julia, Anne, and Lucy?"

"Aye. Luckily, William and Maighread are being held in the chamber with the hidden access to the passages. No one at the castle knows about it, the passages have not been used since before the birth of the young Laird. The Goddess Coventina flooded them to punish Sir Colin Campbell after he had abducted Lady Julia and forced her to marry him."

"Oh, I understand, so the Goddess is helping us because of Lady Julia."

"She is helping us because she wants the Laird to feel the same pain and sorrow, so many families had to endure because of his and his father's cruelties," Ralston said with a hard voice.

"Shortly after the death of his first wife Sarah Mac Dougal, Sir Collin Campbell attempted to gain control over the lands of the Mac Arthur clan. When the coup failed, he kidnapped Lady Julia Mac Arthur and forced her to marry him. He locked her in the tower house and only permitted her to walk in the courtyard under heavy guard. Their only child Duane was raised by his father, who poisoned his heart with hatred and fed him with lies so that he too would despise Julia."

"I see now why the Goddess is going to punish the young Laird," Amanda said. "He is just as cruel as his father. But what I can't understand is how my da, I mean William could be his friend. People even called them brothers, and now look what the Laird has done to his brotherly friend! He locked him and his mother in the tower."

"Aye Amanda but we are about to change all that. But let's stop talking now, we are almost there," said Ralston in a hushed voice, putting his hand over Amanda's mouth to feel her nodding in agreement.

Suddenly, the boat bumped into the stony shore of Kilchurn Island, making crunching, scraping noises as the waves pushed it up further.

"Hurry Ralston, push the boat back into the water. We can't afford to be discovered now," whispered Asanopirh.

"Aye, hand me the rope to pull you back in. I'll go and check the passage, William and Maighread should be there already."

"Right, here you go," replied Asanopirh handing Ralston the rope before the boat slipped silently back into the black water.

After Ralston had taken a few steps towards the passage, he saw the faint flickering of a torch upon parapet and pressed himself against the wall close to the exit of the tunnel.

"William, are you there?" whispered Ralston.

"Aye, we are coming. Who are you?"

"Never mind who I am, kill the light and don't talk. There are guards right on top of us. You are almost out."

There was no answer, and moments later the light disappeared too.

"We are out. Come on Mother, we are safe."

"Not quite yet," Ralston answered. "Keep low and make no noise," he instructed while pulling the boat back onto the shore.

"Climb on board and lay down," whispered Asanopirh, taking Maighread's hands and helping her to get into the boat. Moments later, as they reached the middle of the loch, Sorcha stood up, lifted her arms to the darkened sky, and called Lady Coventina.

The Goddess answered right away by sending high waves crashing against the walls of Kilchurn Castle, reclaiming the causeway and all the passages.

Ralston and Asanopirh lowered the oars into the water and rowed the boat on to the sandy beach at Inistrynich.

"You can get up now and make your way to the carriage so that we can get you to Adelaide's cottage," mumbled Amanda while helping Maighread across the beach and onto the carriage. Only after everyone was seated and the horses had pulled the carriage away from the beach did she take off her hood.

"Oh dear, Amanda it is you! I am so happy and relieved to see you well and unharmed," said Maighread, overwhelmed with joy. She could no longer hold back tears.

"Mum, why are you crying. This is a happy occasion. We are reunited, free, and on our way to safety. Thank you, thank you whoever you are," whispered William excitedly.

"You can thank us when we are inside the cottage. Until then, do not talk and cover yourself with these blankets," replied Asanopirh handing William the blankets Adelaide had made. No one spoke as the carriage travelled on over rough roads and sandy, trails until Amanda heard the familiar sound of the small brock in front of Adelaide's cottage.

"We are almost there," said Amanda, lifting her blanket to survey the surroundings. Just then, she saw the door of the cottage open and John, and Bhaltair came running out to welcome William and Maighread.

"Oy, Amanda what a great surprise! Come in, come in, hurry up," said John excitedly ushering Amanda and Maighread into the cottage where they were received with warm hugs and loud laughter.

"Oh, what a glorious moment! I am so relieved that you are here, Maighread, you have to tell us everything," Adelaide rejoiced. "Oh, my goodness, Amanda, I did not expect you! Oh my sweet lass, come here let me give you a hug."

"I had to come too, Adelaide. I could not remain in Elfame and let Ralston, Asanopirh, and Sorcha do all the work. I am so happy to see you all we have so much to talk about, but wait, where are Julia, Anne, and Lucy?"

"They arrived just before you and were drenched since they travelled by water. They are in your old room now to change and put wee Lucy to bed. Oh, I still cannot believe that you all are here! Let's go into the kitchen Annette, and Madge cooked up a storm."

"Aye, I can smell it," William said happily. "It smells heavenly, like mutton stew and fresh bread."

"Aye right, and we got some ale as well! Come on let's celebrate," cheered John and pushed them gently into the kitchen where Annette and Madge were waiting with tears in their eyes. After an emotional welcome, and once everybody finally sat at the table near the hearth, Adelaide lifted her cup up and spoke a toast of thanks to Ralston, Sorcha, Asanopirh, and Amanda.

"Slàinte mhòr agus a h-uile beannachd duibh!"

"Mòran taing, Adelaide," replied Asanopirh. He was about to take a sip of ale when he heard a noise at the front of the cottage. He made eye contact with Ralston, and Sorcha and rushed outside.

"Oh dear, I hope we didn't cause that," said Lady Julia as she and Anne entered the kitchen.

"I don't think so. Come on sit with us," answered Adelaide clearing space on the bench.

"How is Lucy?" asked Madge.

"She is sleeping soundly, I guess the excitement was too much for my granddaughter," answered Julia.

"Anne, why don't you take a seat near the hearth, you're still shivering, my love."

"Merci beaucoup, Adelaide," Anne said. "Please, tell me what you said when we came in."

"I made a toast of thanks to Ralston, Asanopirh, Sorcha, and Amanda, wishing them good health and every good blessing!"

"Let's go and see what's going on guys," whispered Amanda. She rushed out through the back door followed by Ralston and Sorcha.

"Oh dear, it's Harris, so no need to be alarmed," sighed Amanda, walking up to the carriage where Asanopirh and Harris stood talking in a hushed voice.

"Why aren't you coming inside? I am sure that it is not

all that safe out here, how did you even get here?" Amanda asked Harris.

"I am not malicious nor do I practise dark magic, so I have no problem coming here at all, but I was quite surprised when Asanopirh came out of nowhere and stopped my carriage. He was just giving me a rundown of all the happenings while I was gone when you showed up."

"Where have you been all this time, Harris?" she pressed.

"I went to France to stock up on some wine and visit Adelaide's brother my old friend the Earl of Douglas. You can imagine my surprise when Asanopirh told me that Archibald's daughter is not only alive but also has a child and is right here at Adelaide's cottage."

"Aye, I can well imagine how you must have felt. Adelaide will be so happy to hear from her brother, what a great night! Come on in Harris, don't make her wait," Amanda said with a smile

"Hold on, I need a moment to compose myself before can I face Adelaide," Harris said.

"What do you mean? You are her best friend, surely she will be overjoyed to see you."

"Aye, but the joy will be short-lived. I'm afraid I have very sad news to bring her, her brother is very ill and may not live to see the summer."

"Oh no, how terrible! We have to get Anne to him right away so that he can die in peace knowing that his daughter is alive and well and that he has a granddaughter."

"Aye, that is what Asanopirh and I were just talking about. Now let's go and continue inside. There is no way around it, I have to tell Adelaide and Anne," sighed Harris. He opened the door and stepped inside.

"Oh, good you are back. What was it?" called Adelaide as she entered the sitting room, looking anxiously at Ralston and Amanda.

"We brought you a visitor, Adelaide," said Amanda as

she stepped aside, revealing Harris behind her.

"My goodness Harris, how wonderful! Adelaide exclaimed in joy, embracing her guest.

"I have good news for you. You will never believe what happened since you left."

"I know Adelaide, Asanopirh filled me in. But I also bring news," he said softly. "Come, let's sit down and talk."

"Aye, I can hardly wait! Tell me, how is my brother? Is he finally coming to visit me this summer, or did he come up with another excuse?" Adelaide said with a laugh.

Harris sat down on the floor in front of Adelaide, took her hands and said, "Adelaide, I am afraid I have bad news for you. Archibald is very ill and does not have long to live, he wanted me to bring you home to spend the remaining days at his side."

Adelaide's face dropped. Her eyes were wide in terror and tears run down her cheeks.

"Adelaide, I am so sorry to bring you this dreadful news on a day that was supposed to be joyous and free of worry. Forgive me mo ghràdh," whispered Harris wiping away her tears.

"I am alright Harris, don't worry about me," she said, composing herself. "The day had to come. After all, Archibald is ten years older than me and has not been in good health ever since Margaret died. But it will be hard for Anne. We have to get her back to Touraine as fast as we can. You have to get her on a ship Harris, you know all the captains that sail to France."

"Aye Adelaide, but the Laird has armed men at all ports. He is still desperately looking for Amanda and Ursula, and you can be sure that all hell will break loose once he finds out that his captives are gone." Harris said solemnly. "We have to act quickly. Go and inform Anne, and I will see what can be done with the help of the elves." He got up, kissed Adelaide on the forehead and left the cottage to speak with the others in the barn.

20 THE REVELATION

Adelaide was devastated. The news of her brother's failing health had knocked the wind out of her and left her unable to speak. Streams of tears ran down her cheeks. She wished that she could stop the dismal mix of grief and frustration that was strangling her, but her anguish only intensified as she thought about how to deliver this heart-breaking news to her niece, who had already suffered so much.

She dried her tears and told herself that the time to grieve would come, but that she now needed to be strong for Anne. With that though she walked into the kitchen, where Anne was joyously celebrating her newfound freedom.

"Adelaide there you are! We were wondering where you went. What's wrong, you look pale?" Annette asked.

"I am fine," replied Adelaide. She cleared her throat to stop her voice from trembling. "I need to talk Anne alone. Would you all please excuse us? It will not take long."

"Of course, come on folks," said John ushering everybody out of the kitchen and closing the door.

"What's wrong Auntie? Did Harris bring you bad news?"

"Aye Anne, he brought news from Touraine, and I am afraid it is not good. Your father is dying and wants me to return to him and be at his side when his time comes," she said solemnly. "I would love to fulfil his wish, I but don't know how to get past the laird's men. All ports are being watched, and every ship is being searched. I am so sorry Anne."

"No, this can't be true," Anne said, shaking her head in denial. "I was hoping to return to Touraine with Lucy to live with him, and now you're telling me that he is dying and that I can't get to him?" her voice shook through her tears.

"Harris and the elves are in the barn discussing all the options, and will do everything to get you home in time, so please don't despair. If there is any way to get you home, trust that they will find it."

Anne was unable to speak and huddled in her chair. Her skin had turned pale, and her eyes glazed over like lifeless mirrors, reflecting nothing but the despair and hopelessness she felt. Harris entered the room a moment later.

"Adelaide, I need to speak to you and Anne," he said. "I believe we have found a way around the laird's men."

"Aye Harris, we are coming," answered Adelaide and rushed into the sitting room followed by Anne.

"We decided that I'll ride to Inistrynich before sunrise and make sure that Asanopirh's boat is well hidden, then I make my way to Dalmally to see what the Laird is up to. Amanda and the elves will return to Elfame and gather their friends to guard us on ourjourney."

Anne wiped the tears violently off her cheeks and gathered the strength to speak.

"What exactly did you plan Harris? And is it safe? Please remember that we have wee Lucy with us." We can't afford to lose her too.

"Aye Anne, it will be safe," answered Harris, leaning over to rest his hands her shoulders. "We thought that Lady Julia should come as well. She will not be safe here as long as her son rules over our land, and she has already been locked away for far too long to remain trapped at the cottage."

"You should not decide over Julia's fate. That is up to her and, as you know, there is another way to keep her safe," said Adelaide, looking at Harris with a nod.

"Aye, I know, I do agree that the time has come," replied Harris. He got up and disappeared into Adelaide's workshop.

"Well, now you all know the news that Harris brought

from my brother," Adelaide announced to the room. "We have to get Anne, Lucy, and Lady Julia out of here."

"Aye Adelaide and we want to help. But how? We can't very well leave the cottage when the Laird has placed a price on our heads," John said in despair.

"Don't worry, John I know you all have a heart of gold. We will be okay, and if things go well, Anne, Lucy and Lady Julia will be on their way to France by next full moon."

"Aye Adelaide, that's right," said Harris who had just reentered the sitting room with a roll of parchment in his hand. "You all know that I have many friends in the maritime business, so I will be able to find a small cargo ship to take us to France soon enough. I will arrange for the ship to anchor in Loch Etive to take the lassies and me on board and to the port of Rochelle. If the winds are with us, we should be able to get to Archibald in time so that he can go in peace with his daughter and grandchild at his side," he said, handing a parchment to Adelaide.

"Thank you, Harris. I know that you will do your utmost best to reach him before his time has come," said Adelaide. She began to unroll the parchment.

"You might be wondering what this is all about," said Adelaide to the group, holding up the parchment. "Well, I think that the time has come to reveal a long-held secret and to release Harris, Maighread and myself from an ode we swore to Lady Sarah Mac Dougal thirty-five years ago." She took a breath, looked to Harris and Maighread with firm eyes, and continued. "Lady Sarah asked us on her deathbed to keep the existence of Lord Collin's firstborn son secret until he was old enough to claim his land and title as heir of the Dukedom of Glen Orchy."

"But why? Bhaltair asked. Didn't the child die together with his mother that night?"

"No the child did not die. Please hear me out, I'll tell you what happened on the night of the winter solstice in the year 1187. Lord Collin insisted that he did not want a

Dougal to inherit his land and commanded Marianne the midwife to kill the boy as soon as Lady Sarah was dead. He ordered me to take care of his body. You may remember that this was a forced marriage after the Campbell clan had lost a land dispute with the MacDougal's. Anyhow, we could not bring ourselves to kill this child and vowed to Lady Sarah to hide and take care of him. She wrote a sworn testimony that the child is Lord Collin's rightful heir and sealed it with her ring before she died. This document cannot be challenged as Lord Collin had ordered the ring that bore her seal to be destroyed moments after she died," said Adelaide. After she had finished, she placed a roll of parchment on the table.

"So whatever happened to the boy?" asked John, after a moment of silence.

"He sits right here," said Maighread and pointed to William. "The midwife, Harris, and Adelaide brought him to me in the night of the Winter Solstice, just after my own new-born son had died and asked me to raise him as my own and not to reveal who he truly is."

"Mum, are you saying that I am not your son?"

"Yes William," said Maighread with quivering lips. "You are Lady Sarah's son the Laird's heir and elder brother of Duane."

"He is not," said Lady Julia with gritted teeth. "Duane is not Collin Campbell's son, he is the son of the one you all call The Stranger," she whispered.

"Hold it, are you telling me that you knew all along that Duane is not the rightful Laird? Interjected John angrily, studying her face with caution. "And you did nothing, all this time?"

Julia shrugged her shoulders and spoke with a broken voice. "I could not tell Collin the truth, he would have killed us both. I did not care for my life I have lived locked up behind the tower's walls from the day he had abducted me, but I could not risk my son's life, so I kept silent."

"How on earth could you have fallen in love with such an evil man like Lord Dougal and have a child for him?"

"He was the only one that dared to visit me," Julia replied weakly. "He treated me kindly, and with respect, he took care of my injuries and bruises whenever Collin had beaten me for not giving him an heir. He brought me flowers and messages from my family. So I fell in love with him. Then, one day, Collin grew suspicious and sent him to the mines of Wemyss. I never saw him again, and when Duane was born eight months later, Collin told everyone that I had died in childbirth. Dougal's heart was broken, and he swore to take revenge on all members of the Campbell clan until his last breath. He does not know that I am alive and that Duane is our son."

"Oh dear, please forgive me, Julia, how painful for you to live locked up and without love for so many years," apologised John.

"I am so glad that we were able to free you Julia and I promise to keep you safe from here on," Adelaide said.

"Thank you, Adelaide, and thank you all, I never thought that the day will come when I could leave Kilchurn as a free woman."

"Well, we better make sure that you will stay free and unharmed, by removing Duane from Kilchurn castle and our lands," Bhaltair said, rising up defiantly.

"Slow down Bhaltair, we have to get Anne, Lucy and Julia to France before we can reveal William as the rightful Laird," Harris said.

"Aye, and we have to ask William if he wants to claim his title," John said.

"Thank you, John," William said softly, speaking for the first time since all had been revealed. He picked up the parchment delicately and began to examine it.

"You will see that your lineage and claim cannot be

disputed. The document was registered and certified by the Third High Stewart of Lothian, Walter Fitz Alan, shortly after he was instated in 1214. And here is your mother's ring," said Adelaide as she handed William Lady Sarah's ring that bore the seal of the MacDougall clan.

"How is that possible? You said the laird ordered the ring to be destroyed?"

"Aye just as he ordered to you kill you, but we saved you and your mother's ring."

"So with all that settled my dear friends, let's focus on our task at hand to take our three lovelies to France," said Harris trying to lift the mood.

"Aye, Harris and to do all that we will need a clear head. So let's call it a day and go to bed," said Adelaide.

"I agree, let's go to bed. Guit nuit to you all," replied Harris kissing Adelaide before leaving the cottage.

"Where is he going? And where are the elves, and Amanda?" asked Anne.

"He is sleeping in the barn so not wake us when he is leaves in the morning, Amanda and her friends left already, so you go and get a good rest. Guit nuit," said Adelaide and kissed Anne on the forehead.

21 HOPE AND SORROW

Amanda had not spoken a word since they left Adelaide's cottage. Too many thoughts tumbled through her mind. The guys will never believe half the things that happened tonight, it's just mind-boggling. But I am relieved that we were able to get everybody out of the castle unnoticed, she thought, as she stumbled sleepily through the forest of Elfame.

"It's been a long night Amanda you better go and take a rest. You look as if you are sleepwalking. We'll be back later to discuss our journey," Ralston said as they reached the great hall of the palace,

"Aye, Ralston, I am absolutely exhausted. I hope that the tea has not lost its effect as yet so that Ursula and the lads are still sleeping, see you later," she replied, as she shuffled into her bedchamber. With her last bit of strength, she managed to kick off her boots just before she dropped dead-tired onto her bed. She slept like a log until Ursula shook her awake late in the afternoon.

"Wake up, Amanda! I can't explain what happened, but we slept through most of the day and missed our training."

"Never mind about the training today. We have more important things to take care of."

"More important than our training? You have to be kidding, what could be more important?"

"You're about to find out. Just get the lads out of bed and meet me in the garden, I'll explain everything to you there."

"Aye right, if you say so," answered Ursula and left to wake Hugh and Glen.

"Oh man, why do we have to get up this early? It's still dark!" Glen grumbled as he stumbled drowsily out of the palace.

"Oh dear Glen, it is not still dark, it is getting dark

again," replied Amanda with a mischievous smile.

"Blimey, what's up with all the excitement? What could possibly have happened while we were sleeping?" Hugh asked through a yawn.

"Well, not all of us were so lucky to sleep till now Ralston, Sorcha, Asanopirh, and I got William and Maighread out of Kilchurn Castle last night and brought them safely to Adelaide," Amanda explained.

"Why didn't you wake us? I thought we agreed to do everything together, especially as it involves our parents! And what about Anne, Lucy and Lady Julia?" asked Hugh angrily.

"Aye Hugh you are right, we did agree. But this time, it was safer to go in a small group. And you can relax, it all went smoothly, everybody is safe and in good spirits. But we received some troubling news last night which makes it necessary for Anne, Lucy, and Lady Julia to sail to France as soon as possible."

"I don't understand anything anymore. Wouldn't they be just as safe at Adelaide's as our parents are?"

"Of course they would, but that's not the reason Hugh. I am afraid Anne's da is dying, so you will understand that we have to act quickly. Harris left for Dalmally this morning to get hold of the captain he sailed with from France. His ship is due to return to Rochelle soon. If he is willing to take them, we will have to guard them on their way to Loch Etive where they are going to board the ship."

"Good finally some action, so when are we leaving?" Hugh asked.

"As soon as Cait Sith comes to get us. I hope it will be soon since there is another issue we need to tackle once the three are safely on their way to France."

"Aye, we know, we have to free your father and all the girls," Glen said.

"Right Glen, that's part of it," Amanda nodded. But we have to unseat the young Laird before we can do that."

"Hang on, do what? How are we going to topple the Laird? Do you want the sheriff to come for us?"

"The sheriff might even help us! Duane is not the rightful Laird, William is. Let me tell you the whole story right from the beginning." Amanda said and began to tell her friends what she had learned during the night at Adelaide's cottage. Her friends were just as bewildered by what they heard as she had been. It certainly was hard to believe that everything they thought to be true turned out to be an elaborate deception. The friends were still busy discussing Lady Julia's revelation of the Lairds true ancestry when Ralston arrived, accompanied by Asanopirh. "By the looks of your puzzled expressions I gather that Amanda told you about last night's events, I understand that it must have come as quite a shock to you, but you have to shake it off so we can focus on our journey to Loch Etive," said Ralston wasting no time.

"Aye right Ralston, what's the plan?" Hugh asked looking at him in great anticipation.

"You guys must secure the river banks to make sure that we won't be ambushed by the Laird's men on the way to Loch Etive," Ralston explained.

"Aye, no problem at all. So how soon will we be leaving? And have you considered the sea change?" Glen asked.

"Aye, Glen, we are hoping to make the journey during the night of the next full moon, so we can catch the high tide," Asanopirh nodded.

"That sounds good, but won't the bright moonlight make you an easy target once you row out to the ship?" Hugh asked with a look of concern.

"We thought of that. That's why we asked the Selkies to pull the dinghy through the Loch and to Oban's outer harbour, where the ship will be waiting for them with set sails. So even if they're seen by the Laird's men, there is no way that anyone could catch up with them."

"So if all goes well, they should be on their way to

France before sunrise," Hugh said, satisfied with the plan that had formed. "Now then let's hear what exactly you want us to do?"

"We need you to guard the rugged river bank on the right, together with Sorcha, Ursula, and Aislinn, while Amanda, Glen, Ghilli Duh, and the Dryads protect the wooded shore on the left," Asanopirh explained. "We have to be extremely vigilant since we have no idea what to expect. Always keep in mind that Lord Dougal commands not only the Laird's men but also a group of Red Caps, and I am sure that you know what to expect of them," he warned.

"Aye we do, but tell me how you expect us to keep up with the boat? The river runs faster than we possibly can, especially on the stony riverbanks and through the thickets."

"Aye right Hugh, but you don't need to worry, the boat will be pulled and controlled by a group of Ashrays, and they will make sure to keep in line with you."

"Brilliant, then let's not waste time with discussions, let's go to get more combat practice. It would be good to learn how to move and fight in total darkness," suggested Glen.

"Aye, nothing wrong with that, but keep in mind that we will be out there during the full moon. I asked Oren and Bilobeal to show you how to disguise yourself. Oh, and Bilobeal is going to bring your armours so that you can train fully fitted by tomorrow."

"Oh wow so he kept his promise, that's brilliant, I can't wait to try it on," Hugh saidexcitedly.

"Aye, neither can I, my dear brother. But before we get too excited let's look for some food. I am starving I haven't had any food all day," replied Glen, rushing inside.

"Do you ever think of anything other than food, goodness gracious!" shouted Ursula as she followed Glen into the palace.

"Oh dear, Glen loves food far too much, I better go

and help Ursula stop him from stuffing himself again," said Amanda with a sigh and left.

"Hugh, can I have a word with you please?" Ralston said, making a gentle sign for him to stop before he joined the others.

"Sure Ralston, what is it?"

"I would like Ursula and you to meet Bilobeal at Ben Lomond so that he can show you to how to move fast and safe on rugged terrain, and how to signal the others if it becomes necessary. You will have a better perspective to observe the wooded bank. Your group will be watched by our beloved Goddess Arianrhod. She is going to circle above you in the shape of a large owl and trust me when I say that she doesn't miss a thing. She can even see the darkness of the mortal soul."

"Crivens, I did not know that she could become visible for a mortals eye," Hugh said in wonder.

"Oh, you had seen her before, at the lake, when she guided us as the Northern Light."

"Wow, that was Lady Arianrhod? Well, she is truly magnificent. Alright, I am ready to go let me get Ursula. What about Aislinn and Sorcha?"

"They'll join you later," said Ralston. He walked into the palace to talk to Amanda and Glen while Hugh and Ursula picked up their weapons and left to meet Bilobeal.

"Good night Hugh and Ursula my bonnie lass, it is nice to see you again," Bilobeal greeted them as they arrived. "I heard that the time for some action has come, at last, so let me begin by giving you some important information about the art of disguise."

"Aye Bilobeal. That be great we haven't had the chance to practice between rocks yet," replied Ursula.

"But I am sure that Laratbogh and Oren would have told you that you mortals have a distinct shape by which your enemies can easily recognise you. So I will show you how to obscure your shape by tucking grass and bramble into your hair and clothes, and how to cover your hands, and face with charcoal, ash, or mud so that you blend in with your surroundings."

"Yikes, must we do that? My hands are okay, but I really don't like mud or charcoal in my face and hair."

"Oh come on Ursula it will look good on you! In fact, why don't we test it out?" said Hugh and picked up a hand full of stone dust.

"Don't you dare Hugh, or I kick your behind up and down the rocks," she threatened.

"Well, in case she does, it most certainly would be good to know what you have to do when you meet an obstacle," said Bilobeal, laughing as he slapped Hugh on the shoulder.

"Well, let me tell you what to do in such a situation. Always try to avoid climbing over the obstacles by all means. But if you have no choice then you must keep your body in line with its top to prevent showing yourself against the sky," said Bilobeal and turned around to face Ursula. "And as for you, Ursula, my bonnie lass, I'm afraid you will have to cover your face. But you can use wood ash instead of mud. It's almost as if you were powdering your face. Here you go," said Bilobeal and reached her a small satchel filled with ash.

Ursula looked at the satchel with disgust and reluctantly covered her hair, face, and hands.

"I like that look on you, Ursula, you should do that all the time from now on," said Hugh cracking up with laughter.

"Oh that did it," yelled Ursula. She dropped the satchel and chased him up and down the hillside until she suddenly tripped and fell.

"Are you okay, Ursula?" shouted Hugh in shock, rushing over to help her.

"Aye I am okay, but what did I trip over? I placed my steps so carefully," wondered Ursula and began to search for what had caused her fall. "I found it!" she exclaimed, picking up a shiny object. "But what the heck is a water flask doing here between the rocks?"

"A flask? Let me see lass," said Bilobeal and hurried over to where she stood.

"Aye, that is a flask carried by the Laird's man. So they were here, and might even still be around. Let's be careful and only communicate by hand signs," whispered Bilobeal. He signalled Ursula and Hugh to crouch low and follow him.

The three advanced slowly, hidden by the shadows of passing clouds and behind large boulders when Ursula suddenly noticed smoke rising from a campfire close to the shoreline of the loch. She tapped Hugh and Bilobeal on the shoulder and pointed to what she had discovered. Bilobeal nodded and signalled for her to stay hidden behind a boulder, while he and Hugh moved closer to the shore.

Ursula's heart was pounding like a blacksmith's hammer, and her hands began to shake. *Crivens, we could have stumbled right into them,* she thought as she started to collect small pebbles for her slingshot while glancing over the top of the boulder now and then to make sure that Bilobeal and Hugh were safe. But she could not see them and was about to leave her hiding place to take a closer look when suddenly she heard stones sliding down on the slope behind her. She loaded her slingshot and positioned herself to fire when Sorcha appeared silently in front of her, followed by Aislinn.

Ursula placed a finger on her lips, signalling them not to speak, and pointed to where Bilobeal and Hugh had disappeared. Sorcha nodded, readied her bow, and rushed with lightning speed down to the shore without making the faintest sound, while Aislinn, loaded her slingshot and signalled Ursula to follow. Aislinn and Ursula moved cat-like, gracefully down the slope until they were able to see seven men sitting around a fire at the shore of Loch Lomond.

"What are you doing here? Didn't Bilobeal tell you to

stay hidden and wait?" whispered Hugh from behind a nearby boulder.

"Oh hush Hugh why should you have all the action?" mouthed Ursula and began to walk further when a strong hand gripped her wrist and pulled her back.

"Ursula, my bonnie lass, didn't I ask you to wait?" Bilobeal said in a hushed tone. This is not the time to get reckless and take unnecessary risks, you hear? We have to get back to the palace now and change our plan, come on."

"Aye Bilobeal, alright. But don't we have to wait for Sorcha? She went down to the shore to look for you."

"I know I saw her and asked her to return the palace to alert everyone, so let's go. Hugh come on lad lets hurry, we need to act swiftly now."

"Hugh, what happened? What did you see?" asked Ursula nervously.

"It's not what we saw, it's what we heard, Ursula. It makes me extremely sad and furious at the same time. Let's not talk about it now, we have to hurry back and tell the others, come on," said Hugh. He took Ursula's hand and started to run. As they reached the palace, they were surprised to see that everybody had already assembled and was awaiting their arrival with heightened anxiety. Ursula could not imagine what Hugh and Bilobeal could have overheard down at the loch to merit all this excitement. She shook it off as an overreaction, but as she walked to the table to get some water, she noticed that everybody was fully armed, as if they were ready to storm out at a moment's notice.

"What did you hear Hugh? I am getting anxious now. Did anything happen to our parents? Come on tell me, tell me now." she urged.

"Sit down Ursula, Bilobeal is about to share what we heard with all of you," Hugh said trying to calm his voice.

"Where is he, I don't see him anywhere? Where did he go Hugh?" said Ursula and looked around the hall nervously. Moments later Bilobeal entered the Great Hall accompanied by four other Drows that carried large and obviously heavy bags.

“Dear friends, you might be wondering why I send Sorcha to call you to arms. But as it seems, the day to fight has come earlier than we anticipated. Sorcha surely told you that we discovered a group of the Laird's men at the shore of Loch Lomond and were able to overhear their conversation. I am afraid what we heard is very troubling indeed.”

“Oh for goodness sake what did you hear, please Bilobeal spit it out.”

"Aye Amanda I will, but please brace yourself for some truly terrible news, the same goes for you Ursula, my bonnie lass,” he said before continuing. “At first, we thought these lads were boasting about their romances, but we soon recognised the names and realised that they were talking about Marianne the midwife and her Brownie Nissa.”

“What did they say, and how could they have known about Nissa?” ask Laratbogh.

“Well, according to one of the men, Nissa was discovered at the castle shortly after a chambermaid alerted the Laird to the disappearance of Anne, Lucy, Lady Julia and the other two captives. All guards were called to search the castle grounds immediately, but all they found was a strangely coloured rooster in the courtyard."

“Oh no, please tell me that they were unable to catch her,” Laratbogh said, a look of despair washing over her face.

“I am so sorry, Laratbogh, they were. One of the maids knew that Brownies shapeshift into a rooster if they are in danger of being seen by mortals, and she knew that this rooster was Marianne’s Brownie. They killed her and brought the beheaded rooster to Marianne, who collapsed at the sight of Nissa.”

“So what happened to Marianne?” asked Amanda.

"They took her to the castle and tortured her until she told them that they were at Adelaide's cottage. The Laird sentenced her to hang in the market square by next full moon, he then readied himself and a group of soldiers to raid the cottage by nightfall," Bilobeal explained solemnly. "So you understand the urgency for action."

"Aye Bilobeal you are right we have to act swiftly even though the cottage is impregnable, but it is high time to show the Laird that he is not all-powerful. Amanda, Hugh, Glen, Ursula put on your amours and let us pick up our weapons we will show the Laird his boundaries."

22 THE FIRST ENCOUNTER

Normally, Amanda was able to hide her emotions well by keeping her face blank. But today was different. The anger and fear that welled up inside her began to show. Her eyes were narrowed, and cold, and her lips had tightened. A chill of apprehension washed over her, as she stepped out from under the small bridge to make her way to Adelaide's cottage and deliver the heartbreaking news.

"Are you all right, Amanda?"

"I am fine Ralston, it's just the lack of sleep. You don't have to worry about me."

"I am worried. You look pale, and you are trembling. As soon as this is over, you have to rest."

"Asanopirh, Oren just saw a group of soldiers rushing through the glade. We have to act swiftly now. We can't afford to hesitate," shouted Bilobeal.

"Aye, we're coming. You best stay at the bridge, I'll send you Hugh and Glen to observe the situation," replied Asanopirh.

"Are you ready, Amanda, or would you rather secure the cottage?" whispered Sorcha in a soft and measured voice.

"No Sorcha, I am ready to face the Laird and his men. After all, this is what we trained for," said Amanda with cold determination, signalling her friends to follow.

We have chosen the right time to return to the cottage, she thought as she watched the evening mist spreading over the cottage. The land around it provided a perfect cover for the elves as they took position around the cottage and on top of the barn. Ghilli Duh, Oren, and Laratbogh had lined up at the edge of the forest and were ready to take on any intruder who dared to approach the cottage.

"Amanda and Ursula, please go inside and brief everybody about the latest development. And please make certain that they sit tight. Tell them to keep up their routine so that our visitors remain unaware of our presence," Asanopirh instructed.

"Aye, but what about Hugh and Glen? Shouldn't they accompany us?" Amanda asked.

"No the lads are securing the brook and the bridge with Bilobeal and his men. Go, go now," said Asanopirh and sank back into the mist.

Amanda and Ursula heard Adelaide talking to Annette as they approached the cottage.

"This is the strangest weather. How can we have such dense fog after all the sunshine we had today?"

"You are right, Adelaide, it is very unusual, and it appeared out of nowhere. I've never seen anything like it before," Annette remarked.

"Shush, hold it," Adelaide stopped her. "Did you hear that?"

"Hear what?"

"It sounded as if the back door was opened. Is that you, Madge?"

"I am right here," Madge replied. "I just put the kettle on the fire for some tea. What's the matter?"

"Where are John and Bhaltair?"

"They went to the barn to check on the animals."

"Well then we have a problem, I could swear that I heard the back door open. Let's hope the enchantments haven't been compromised," whispered Adelaide. She walked up to the fireplace, picked up the poker, and lifted it over her head, ready to strike.

"You can put the poker down, it's just us," said Amanda as she walked into the sitting room.

"Goodness, you gave us quite a scare, Amanda. How come that you are back so soon, and who is that with you?" Adelaide asked.

"We are all here, Adelaide, Ursula is at the back door,

and the lads are down by the brook. The Drows, the Elves, Ghilli Duh, and the Dryads came as well."

"What happened? I thought we took care of everything and covered all of our tracks?" Annette said worriedly.

"Unfortunately, we didn't. It looks as though our worst fears have come true. The Laird and his man are on their way to storm the cottage and capture anyone they find," answered Amanda trying to avoid Annette's frightened stare.

"Why? What has caused him to do that?" asked Anne in a trembling voice.

"Nissa was recognised by one of the chambermaids as she was trying to leave the castle. They killed her and then went to Marianne's home, arrested and tortured her until she gave you all away. The Laird accused her of treason and condemned her to hang on the eve of the next full moon," said Amanda biting her lip to stop herself from crying.

The women were paralysed and stared at Amanda with wide eyes as they heard the news about Nissa and Marianne.

"Say it isn't so, please. She can't be dead," pleaded Anne, reaching out to Amanda for support.

"I am so very sorry, Anne," said Amanda. She embraced Anne, who was shaking violently with grief.

"This is terrible news, yes, but we cannot allow ourselves to fall apart now. The Laird and his men are on their way to get us too, but we will not let them succeed. Annette, you go and call the men in from the barn. Best tell them to bring more firewood to not look suspicious. Madge, continue making the tea, we all could do with some calming lavender," said Adelaide in a surprisingly calm and collected voice.

"Don't worry about us, Amanda. We have prepared ourselves for all eventualities. Annette and Madge have braced themselves for a moment like this and should be able to stop John and Bhaltair from flaring up. You just focus on what you have to do and do not forget that the cottage is protected by many enchantments."

"Aye Adelaide, I hope that they are as strong as we all think they are since we will be under attack soon," said Amanda.

"I think we got a message from the elves. The smoke from the kitchen fire just turned red!" called Madge from the hearth.

"Aye, that's a sign from Sorcha. It means that the Laird and his men have arrived. Goodness, where are John and Bhaltair? They should be in here now," shouted Amanda and ran to the back door, through which Annette and the two men appeared.

"Crivens, Amanda, you came back quickly. Oh Ursula, my bonnie lass, you are here too. How wonderful! Come here, give your old da a hug," laughed John and embraced his daughter.

"Bhaltair was asking Amanda and Ursula about their heavy amours but stopped mid-sentence when he saw flaming arrows soaring towards the cottage."

"We'll explain later," Ursula said in a rushed voice. "You all better go into the kitchen now. Stay there and lock the doors until we come back to get you."

"But Ursula!"

"Da please we know what we are doing, and we are not alone. Ma come and hold da," said Ursula as soon as they had safely entered the cottage, she slammed the door closed and leaned against it with all her weight. The day they had feared had finally come. *Please, Lady Coventina, protect this house*, Ursula thought while she exchanged a look with Amanda. Both girls nodded and took position behind the windows.

Hugh climbed onto the parapet wall of the small bridge. He stood upright, with his bow drawn ready to fire while Glen had poised himself in the middle of the bridge's arch prepared to charge, but nothing happened after the first flaming arrows failed to reach across the brook.

"Why are they just standing there staring at us?" Hugh asked cautiously. "Are they afraid?"

"No, they can't see you. The Cottage and the land surrounding it is protected by powerful enchantments." Bilobeal reminded them. "Did you really think that I would have you two standing there if they could see you?"

"Oh, I hadn't thought of that. But if that is so then why did we even come? I thought we were needed for protection."

"We came to show the Laird and his men that it is unwise to interfere with anyone under the protection of the Queen of Elfame," chuckled Bilobeal.

"You can lower your weapons lads, you are up here to observe and to listen to their conversation. It would be good if you could get a little closer, but under no circumstances step off the bridge. Do you understand?"

"Aye Asanopirh, alright. Let's go and listen to their bramble my dear brother," whispered Hugh. He jumped down from the parapet wall and relaxed his arms.

"What is wrong with your men?" they heard an angry voice say. "They are useless drunkards, all of them."

Even though they had never seen him, the brothers recognised immediately that this was the Laird.

"But my Lord, it wasn't their fault, its magic. Remember that the people in the village say that the weaver is using magic," another man pleaded, trembling with fear.

"I'll show you magic. Hand me my bow, Sean," shouted the Laird. He pulled an arrow from the fire and aimed it at the cottage. Everybody's eyes followed the arrows high arch expecting it to land on the cottage's roof setting it on fire. Instead, it disappeared into thin air just as all the others before.

"That's impossible, hand me another arrow," the Laird said in denial. Hurry don't just stand there!" the Laird was screaming now, his face red hot as he kept trying to set fire to Adelaide's home. Yet he couldn't manage to even get one of the arrows to cross the brook.

"Blood bas! He screamed throwing the bow into the fire. He mounted his horse in raging fury and galloped right through a crowd of his men, injuring everyone who couldn't get out of his way fast enough.

"What a brut! Oh I would love to pull him off his horse and give him a few gentle touches with my staff," said Glen bursting with anger.

"Glen, look, one of the soldiers stopped his horse," Hugh interrupted his brother, "He is either extremely brave or damn stupid."

"Aye, but it seems that he has a message for the Laird. Can you hear anything?"

"No…, let's watch them close, maybe we will be able to figure out what he had to say."

Glen and Hugh didn't have to wait long. Moments later, one of the Lairds men broke out of the brushwood pushing and shoving an elder man in front of him.

"Crivens, that's Harris!" Hugh exclaimed. "Why did he come here, he should have known better! Damn, what was he thinking?"

"Maybe he didn't know. I am certain that the Laird did not announce what he was up to. It doesn't matter either way we have to get him out of there," said Glen. He was about to step off the bridge when Hugh grabbed his tunic and dragged him frantically back across the bridge.

"Glen, are you blooming mad! Have you forgotten what Asanopirh said? We can't leave the bridge!" shouted Hugh. "Let's tell the others, there must a way to free Harris."

"For a moment I thought you had gone mad? What on earth's name were you thinking, lad?" shouted Bilobeal.

"That's just it, Bilobeal, he wasn't thinking," Hugh said. "He saw Harris being pushed around by the Lairds men and lost it."

"Aye, but one more step and you would have been

pushed around too. You have to keep calm and controlled and not allow your rage control you, Glen. Let's go up to the elves and see what can be done," said Bilobeal signalling his men to surround Hugh and Glen to make sure they wouldn't do anythingreckless.

"What's up, why did you leave your posts?" Asanopirh asked when he saw Hugh, Glen, and the Drows approaching the cottage.

"The Laird just took Harris hostage, and will surely use him to pressure Adelaide we can't let that happen," Bilobeal said resoundingly.

"Aye, and we won't. You go inside and talk things over. I'll be right back to join you, I just want to have a quick talk with Ghilli Duh," said Asanopirh and was gone in a blink of an eye.

"Ghilli Duh, I need your help, where are you, my friend?" Asanopirh said after the others had gone inside.

"I'm here, Asanopirh. I saw what happened, there is no need for explanation. I informed the Dryads and asked them to block all escape routes. Now you can drive them away from the cottage and into our arms. We will teach them a lesson they'll never forget, that is if they survive," said Ghilli Duh. In an instant, he swung his cloak around him and disappeared.

"Hugh, Glen, what happened? What is all the commotion about?" asked Amanda as they entered the cottage.

"I'll tell you, but first tell me, where are the others?"

"They are all in the kitchen. What is it, Glen? Tell us," whispered Ursula, bending over to peer out of the window.

"You won't see anything from here, Ursula. The Laird and his men have backed up into the woods," said Glen as he opened the door to the kitchen.

"Brilliant, so they have given up," hailed John as he entered the sitting room.

"No, they haven't, John. They've captured Harris. It

will not take long before they use his life as leverage against everybody inside the cottage," replied Glen in a hoarse whisper.

"Well, what are we waiting for, we have to get him out of there!" replied Amanda as she headed for the door.

"Where you think you're going, Amanda?" Ralston jumped up to stop her." What are you planning to do, walk up and shake the Laird's hand?"

"Oh come on, we have no time to talk, Harris needs our help."

"Ah, and it would do what for him when you get caught? No, we have to devise a new plan of action to give them a surprise they will not easily forget," said Ralston with a big smile.

Soon everybody was in deep discussions about what approach to take. Everyone except – Adelaide, who stood trembling and with clenched fists at the window. After a heated deliberation, Asanopirh gave orders.

"Bhaltair, Hugh, and John, I would like you to remain and defend the cottage should it come to that. I am going to leave Keelin and Sorcha with you. Ursula, you take a position on the roof with Aislinn. Cover our backs and signal us when it is safe to leave cover. Ralston, Amanda, Glen, and Hugh, you come with me. Bilobeal you and your men, must guard the brook and bridge."

"Aye Asanopirh will do, no one is going to get past us," said Bilobeal and left to position his men.

"Well, then all that's left to do till sunset is to check our weapons and keep an eye on our enemies. Has there been any movement Adelaide?" Asked Asanopirh stepping closer to the window.

"Aye the soldiers are busy collecting wood; I assume that they are planning to hold their post throughout the night."

"I am not so sure that that is what they have in mind, but I will ask Faerydae to take a closer look," said Asanopirh. He was about to turn to leave through the back door when he heard Adelaide scream in terror.

"What happened, Adelaide?" John asked, running to the window. He barely managed to catch her as she collapsed.

"The Laird is going to burn him! The soldiers have piled wood and straw on top of the carriage and tied Harris to a stake. Ralston, Asanopirh, you have to safe him!"

There was no answer from the elves, only a whirl of wind as they flew past John and out of the door.

"That bastard will not succeed," hissed Asanopirh through his clenched teeth. "Ralston you go to the brook and ask Lady Coventina for help. Meet me with Amanda on the other side," whispered Asanopirh and vanished.

Ralston rushed to the edge of the brook, dipped his hands into the water and called out to the River Goddess, *"Lady Coventina, please come to me. Show your fury and aid us to set this innocent free."*

He barely had time to step back from the shore before the water of the brook began to rise flooding the land where the Laird and his men stood.

The laird shouted at his men in the commotion.

"No one moves! Stand your grounds, we are not afraid of a bit of water," he shouted as he mounted his horse and picked up a torch to light the pile of wood. As he closed in on Harris, the water began to rise, forming a towering wave that crashed and ripped away everything in its path. The soldiers struggled desperately to stay afloat and reach dry land but were washed away by a second wave. The stake Harris had been tied to broke in the surge. In an instant, he was freed and able to swim across to Adelaide's land.

Adelaide stood waist deep in the ice-cold water, frantically searching for the man she loved. She desperately fought against the raging current and the cold that was slowly making it harder for her to breathe. Her hands were turning blue, and her legs felt as if they would give in at any moment. *Please, Lady Coventina don't let him die, return him to me,* she thought. That's when she saw him bobbing in the current, struggling to hold on to the very stake that he had been tied to. She launched herself into the raging water, caught his tunic and pulled him onto the shore before she fell exhausted to her knees clenching him in her arms.

"Mo ghràdh, I was so afraid!" She said between heaving breathes. "Why did you come? Surely you must have known what the Laird was about to do."

"Aye mo chridhe, I did, but I had to come and make sure that you were safe. I would not be able to live on if anything should happen to you," answered Harris and kissed her hands.

"Crivens you two, you really know how to get an old man's heart beating," Bhaltair said.

"Aye, there is never a dull moment with these two. Come on, let's get them up to the cottage," said John with a heavy sigh. Julia and Annette came running towards them with large towels in their hands ready to wrap Adelaide and Harris in warmth.

"Let's get you into the house, and out of these wet clothes Madge and Anne have some hot broth waiting for you," said Annette as she wrapped her arm around Adelaide to support her on the way up.

"Did you see that guys? Harris is safe, and half of the Lairds men were washed away by the brook!"

"Aye, Glen, but that is not good enough he. Has to pay for his malice, let's go and make sure that he is not about to try again," said Ralston. He hurried to the Rowan tree followed by Glen and Amanda.

"I can't wait, to pay him back for all the suffering he has caused," Amanda said through gritted teeth. "Let's teach him the meaning of fear."

"Aye, let's chase him back into his castle. Lock the door, and throw away the key! Are you ready?" Shouted Glen, raising his staff and looking expectantly at Ralston.

"Aye, let's go. Be fast, be strong, and be safe!" shouted Ralston and took off running.

Amanda and Glen followed him into the woods, ready to fight anything or anyone that crossed their path. In no time at all, they had reached the edge of the forest where Laratbogh and Oren stood guard and gave them a headcount of the men at arms.

"There are around fifty men out there, twenty of them lined up at the brook, a dozen surrounding the Laird, and about eighteen in the forest," Oren informed them with military precision.

"Why would they split up, does that make any sense to you?" asked Glen, and looking puzzled.

"Makes perfect sense. The men at the brook serve as a distraction so that the second group can approach the cottage unnoticed. At least that what they have planned," mocked Laratbogh and giggled quietly.

"Blimey, it will be hard to fight with a staff in the underbrush," Glen remarked, looking down at the cumbersome weapon in his hands.

"Don't bother yourself with the group in the forest, Glen, Ghilli Duh is looking forward to giving them a good thrashing. You will be fighting alongside Asanopirh," Ralston explained. "He is waiting for you behind the blackberry bush which, by the way, is Faerydae in disguise. She'll make sure that you are not ambushed. Her thorns will rip everyone to shreds before they can get close."

"Brilliant, see you on the other side, Ralston. And please, look after Amanda," called Glen before he disappeared into the thickets.

Meanwhile, Ursula and Aislinn sat on the cottage roof, keeping a close eye on the Laird and his men so that they could alert their friends to any danger and give the signal when it was safe to leave their cover to attack.

"Aislinn, I think it is safe now. The Laird is addressing his men, and not one of them is checking on the surrounding."

"Aye, these fools feel absolutely safe. I think it is time to give Amanda and Ralston the go ahead."

"Yup, let's do it. Ursula nodded in agreement. She loaded her slingshot with a ball of red candle wax, aimed at Amanda's shoulder and released the sinew.

"Are you sure she'll get your message?" asked Aislinn, concerned.

"Oh yes most certainly. This is her favourite way to send signals," answered Ursula with a big smile.

Amanda and Ralston were standing silently hidden behind a large oak tree awaiting the signal to attack when something struck Amanda's shoulder.

"Damn, what was that?" she exclaimed. She passed her hand over her back and smiled as she wiped the red wax from her shoulder.

"What's wrong, Amanda?" Ralston asked. "Did you get hit?"

"No, I just got the message from Ursula that is time to attack," giggled Amanda pointing to the red wax on her jerkin.

"Aye Amanda let's lash out against injustice and black magic," he replied firmly. Amanda nodded and felt a rush of strength and courage as she drew her swords. She began to run alongside Ralston Through the thick green forest before they finally broke free of the brush and into the enemy lines. They immediately spiralled through the surprised armed men, cutting them down like weeds. Glen had also reached the Lairds guards and began swirling his staff masterfully through the air, sending the Laird's men flying. Meanwhile, Asanopirh had mounted a horse in pursuit of the Laird, who had fled the scene and raced back to the castle.

The screams of the terrified men alerted their comrades at water's edge and in the forest, sending them into a frantic run towards the cottage. Arrows hissed through the air and struck the lairds men without a warning just as Bilobeal and his men came running across the bridge with raised staffs and axes, lashing out at anyone still trying to get to the cottage. The band of soldiers in the forest flung their weapons into the bushes and scattered in all directions in terror, making them easy targets for Ghilli Duh. Laratbogh and Oren sat in their trees and watched as Ghilli Duh tripped and bush-whacked the terror-stricken soldiers as they stormed through the woods.

It was over as quickly as it had begun. Dead soldiers covered the blood-soaked ground. The few survivors that had the strength to stand ran for their lives.

Amanda felt exhausted and nauseated as she looked around. Throughout the fight, she had been able to maintain a cold detachment from her opponents by keeping her mind numb and empty. But the sight of the dead men made her feel distressed. She lowered her eyes and saw that her boots and jerkin were drenched in blood. Not hers but the blood from the men she had slain and wounded.

"Amanda, are you alright? You look like a ghost," asked Ralston as he walked up to her.

"Aye, I am alright," she said in a dead voice. "But I have to get away from here I can't breathe. The smell of blood sickens me. Let's go to the brook and wash off."

"Right, Glen and Bilobeal's men are already there. But stop a moment, where did you get this?" asked Ralston and pointed to her breeks, which were covered with yellow ashes.

"I have no idea…" she said looking down and noticing the ashes for the first time. "Wouldn't that mean that there were Red Caps in the midst of the soldiers?"

"Aye, and that you killed some of them. But I am certain that there will be more around, so we have to return to the cottage as fast as we can. They'll have surely tried to get to the cottage," Ralston said, lifted his arm to signal Bilobeal and his men to follow him. Amanda and Glen had a hard time to keep up with the charging elf and only caught up with him after he had crossed the bridge and stopped to speak with Bilobeal.

“Bilobeal we have to search the forest and the fields for Red Caps. I am sure that they tried to break through to the cottage.”

“They didn’t, nothing got past us relax Ralston. But if they were here, that means that Lord Dougal is not far,” Bilobeal said.

“You are right. We have to set off as soon as Asanopirh returns and get William to his family and Anne, Julia and Lucy on a ship to France. The MacDougal clan owns a huge fleet of galleys. – Surely they be willing to take care of them,” Ralston said.

“Aye, and Clyde MacDougal will be fuming when he finds out what Colin Campbell had planned for his grandson while his daughter lay dying. You guys better return to the cottage to get our travellers ready. My men and I will take the fallen soldiers back to Dalmally,” said Bilobeal.

“Let me come with you and talk to the members of the Guild. I am certain that they will help us to free Marianne,” said Bhaltair as he approached Ralston and Bilobeal.

“We’ll use any help we can get,” Bilobeal conceded. “But you must remain in the Guildhall, you cannot be seen in the streets of Dalmally.”

“Agreed. Let’s go and load the bodies onto Harris’s carriage,” replied Bhaltair.

23 THE GUILD

Morning broke over the small village of Dalmally. Its streets began to fill with people, rich and poor, young and old, all headed to the market square to make their purchases. At first glance, it appeared to be a typical market day. But instead of the usual hustle and bustle with merchants excitedly shouting to sell their wares, the air was pierced with palpable grief.

The wooden stalls, where the villagers would meet to exchange news and listen to the latest gossip, were eerily silent. Even the pick-pockets and beggars stared petrified at the grim sight in the middle of the market square.

The Lord Dean of the Guild had been called to read out the writing on the carriage on which the fallen soldiers were laid. It was a sombre moment for the community. The slain men were the husbands, fathers, brothers, and sons of many of the villagers.

Angus McNell was walking around the carriage for the fifth time, trying to gather strength to read the inscription out loud. Finally, he spoke.

"Here lay the men that were led astray as all they had learned was to obey,
Blindly accepting injustice and cruelty,"
his voice began to falter as he read the second paragraph.

"Cailleach Mother of the mountains, withered, aged and older than time,
Embrace these men forgive their crime,
Guide them back to your womb,
beloved mother, and crone."

After a long silence Gavin the baker said. "Let us lay

these men to rest and then meet at the guild hall to mourn their death."

"Aye Gavin, let us bury them and notify their families," said Angus. He led the procession out of the village.

Late in the afternoon after the fallen soldiers had been laid to rest, the guild members of Dalmally and the surrounding villages had assembled in the dimly lit Guildhall to pay their final respect with a prayer. Their voices rang solemnly through the hall.

"If ever there is a tomorrow,
We'll meet again without pain or sorrow,
When it will be a dinna ken,
may you sleep well in the arms of the Morrigan."

The hall which usually echoed with laughter and heated discussions lay silent. Only the fire's soft crackling sounded through the room, and the reflections of its flickering flames danced on the walls.

"I've enough of this slaughter!" shouted Gavin, breaking the painful silence. Too many have died for the Lairds crimes. We can't sit by any longer and allow this to continue."

"Aye I agree, enough is enough!" shouted the butcher Ross, slamming his fist on the table. His eyes blazed with rage, and his chest heaved ominously.

"You are right Ross, but there is little we can do. We owe the Laird our allegiance as we had sworn when he was instated," Angus said, shaking his head in defeat.

"You're wrong. Angus," Bhaltair announced as he entered the Guild Hall, Duane is an impostor. The rightful Laird is William. It is to him we owe our allegiance."

"Crivens Bhaltair, we thought that you and your family were dead."

"We would have been had we remained in our homes. But because of my wife's foresight, we were able to flee and find refuge before the laird's murderous gangs came for us."

"I am so glad that you are safe," Ross said. "But tell me, how can the innkeeper be the rightful laird? He is merely a commoner like us."

"No, he is not, Ross. He is the son of Lady Sahara and Lord Collin Campbell." Bhaltair said, raising his voice for all in the hall to hear.

"Nonsense, how can he be?" Angus protested. "We all know that their only child died soon after its birth."

"That is what we were lead to believe, Angus, but the truth is quite different indeed. Lord Campbell ordered the midwife to kill the child immediately after Lady Sahara had passed on and demanded Adelaide to bury his body in the courtyard. But the women did not obey his cruel order but swore an ode to Lady Sarah on her deathbed to keep her son safe until he was ready to reclaim his birthright. The midwife knew that Maighread's son had died the same night shortly after his birth and asked Adelaide to take him to the castle grounds to bury him instead. Maighread took William and raised him as if he was her own. Now the time has finally come for him to claim his inheritance," he concluded.

"Is there any proof of what you say, Bhaltair? And either way, how could we if we ever depose Duane? We are no soldiers, and our sons are in the Laird's service, that means they would have to fight us! How could you expect us to take up arms against our own flesh and blood?"

"No, Gavin, no one expects you to fight, William is on the way to his grandfather Clyde MacDougal as we speak to ask for support and protection. All we have to do is to provide food and shelter for him and his men when he returns."

"He has my support," shouted Peter the cobbler and looked encouraging at his fellow guild members.

"Aye, I will give him my support and feed his men!"

"Thank you, Ross," said Bhaltair. He turned expectantly at Angus.

"Aye, I think that the Guild give William its support

and protection. What say you?"

"Aye," hailed the guild members and raised their tankards.

"Well then, it's settled. Let's just hope that William returns before the next full moon," said Bhaltair sighed and sat his tankard down.

"Why, what is so special about the full moon?" asked Peter.

"The Laird sentenced Marianne to hang on the eve of the next full moon," answered Bhaltair in a low and sullen tone.

"Blood bas, what could she possibly have done to deserve that? Is he trying to silence her so he can remain in power?"

"No Angus, Duane is not aware that he is not the rightful Laird. Neither does he know that his father is the one we all call the Stranger."

"What! So he is responsible for the disappearance of our daughters? Let's go for him now, we cannot allow him to kill Marianne."

"We certainly won't!" Bhaltair said. "With your help, we will be able to free her the moment they walk her out of the castle and over the bridge. I think the best place for an ambush is right outside your forge, Douglas."

"Aye right, I will create some billowing smoke and have a boat ready to move her out one time," Douglas agreed. But what about the Laird's men? They are not going to give her up without a fight."

"Oh don't you worry, we are going to get help from the Queen of Elfame and the Drows. No one would be able to stop us."

"Brilliant! So let's make haste and prepare for the return of William and his men," Angus proclaimed to the hall.

"Aye Angus," cheered the guild members in a chorus, clinking their tankards once again.

"Let's go Bhaltair, we don't want the lamplighter to see

you. He will give you away in a heartbeat, that spineless bastard," whispered Bilobeal from behind the guild's flags. "Aye, you are right, let's hit the road, I am dead tired.

And anyhow, Madge will be worried by now, the sun is setting again. Where did you hide the carriage?"

"Behind the blacksmith forge. I wanted to use the time to check the planned escape route."

"And are you satisfied?"

"Aye, it's perfect. The elves will block the bridge by pretending to be a group of quarrelling drunkards, which will keep the guards distracted while my men get Marianne into the boat. She will be gone before they even have time to look around," laughed Bilobeal and slapped Bhaltair on the shoulder.

"Oh I can hardly wait to see their faces," replied Bhaltair with a broad grin.

"I'm sorry my friend, but I am afraid won't be seeing that. This was your last visit to Dalmally until William has been officially instated and accepted by all clans."

Bhaltair looked at Bilobeal with raised eyebrows and was about to flare up, but stopped himself when he thought about the danger that his presence in Dalmally brought, and how fortunate he had been today.

"Aye right Bilobeal, I should not push my luck," he conceded. Let's head back."

*

"We can't wait for Bhaltair, and Bilobeal to return," John decided. "William has to reach his clan before morning and we have to get the lassies on their way to France."

"Aye, I agree, Madge and Annette are already helping me to get them ready. The elves want to leave shortly," replied Adelaide, as she walked into the kitchen were Anne sat all curled up near the hearth and glared lifelessly into the fire. Her beautiful blue eyes were red and swollen from crying all night.

“Anne my love, you have to ready yourself for the journey. I’ll take care of Lucy. Come on, mo lennan,” said Adelaide gently as she ran her hand over Anne’s golden blond hair.

“What’s wrong with Anne, Julia? Do you think she has the strength to make this journey?” asked Annette.

“Aye she will be fine, she is a very strong young lass. But the news of Nissa’s death and Marianne’s capture has hurt her deeply.”

“Indeed, it shocked us all. But Marianne will be fine, the elves, and the Drows are going to free her, don’t you worry. Let’s get the food ready for Lucy. It’s best that she eats something before you head out. With any luck she will fall asleep as soon as the boat starts rocking,” said Adelaide placing some bannocks, cheese, and a flask of ale in a travelling bag.

“Very well, but where is she?”

“She is outside with Glen. He is showing her how to fight with a staff. She loves it so much that she already broke three of my new broomsticks,” chuckled Adelaide.

“I’m not surprised, she is a feisty wee lass, I’ll go and fetch her,” answered Julia and left the cottage.

“Can I have a word with you, Adelaide?” Harris asked after Julia had left. “It is rather important.”

“Aye Harris, I hope it’s not more bad news.”

“Not at all mo ghràdh, in fact, it’s good news. I tried to tell you the night I arrived, but with all the dreadful events I could not find the right time.”

“Oh, what is it? I most certainly could do with some good news for a change.”

“It has to do with the Count of Anjou. You see he died last winter. Your brother was able to persuade the King to dismiss all charges of witchcraft laid against you. Adelaide, you are no longer in danger. You can return to Touraine with me Adelaide,” he said his eyes open wide with hope.She stared at him for what felt like forever before speaking. “This is wonderful news indeed. Harris,” she said with a soft smile. “I would love to come with you. But I am needed here, at least until Lord Dougal is defeated and Amanda is reunited with her parents. I hope you understand.”

“Aye,” he replied in a hoarse whisper. Adelaide’s answer had taken the sparkle from his eyes and wiped away all happiness he had felt moments ago. It is not the answer I hoped for, but I understand,” he turned his head and looked out the window trying to hide his pain fighting back the tears that began to well up in his eyes.

“It’s time to get ready. The sun is about to set, and the elves are waiting for us at the shore of Inistrynich. I better get to the barn and span in the horses,” he said after a moment.

Adelaide watched Harris with tears in her eyes as he entered the barn to get the carriage ready. She thought her heart would burst into a thousand pieces, and felt a searing pain spreading through her chest that made it hard for her to breathe. It was the same dreadful feeling of loss she had felt all those years ago when she had to leave her home in Touraine and flee to Scotland to avoid being burned alive.

Why is it that people fear what they can’t explain? Why aren’t they willing to open their minds and welcome the great mysteries that nature has to offer? She thought. *It is sad that they choose to stay ignorant and destroy everything that is different. Many years ago they ruined my life, and now once again I have to bid farewell to the man I love. I would have wished for nothing more than to return home to Touraine, to see Arthur one last time and spend my remaining years with the man I love.* She squeezed her eyes shut, trying to stop her tears from falling.

“Adelaide where are you? We are ready to leave,” called Amanda as she entered the cottage.

“I’m here mo lennan,” answered Adelaide wiping away her tears and forcing herself to smile.

"We are ready to move, but Anne doesn't want to leave without saying goodbye."

"I am coming Amanda," answered Adelaide and followed her to the carriage.

"I cannot leave without saying goodbye, Adelaide, and thank you for everything you have done for us. I will carry you in my heart forever and hope to see you again one day."

"Have a safe journey, Anne. Give my love to your father, tell him how desperately I wished to be with him and that I try my utmost best to come soon," whispered Adelaide and kissed Anne goodbye.

"Lady Julia, please get in the carriage. It is time to leave," called Glen reaching out his hand to help Julia into the carriage.

"I am not coming," Julia stated firmly. "Scotland is my home, and it is my duty to help William to set things right. After all, I am the rightful Lady of Kilchurn Castle," she said and stepped away from the carriage. Her face was ashen, and tears streamed down her face.

Everyone looked at Julia in bewilderment. Their eyes filled with sadness, but they also knew that they had no time to argue over her decision. They had no choice than to leave now if they wanted to use the Lairds shock over his defeat for their getaway. Harris turned around and looked at Adelaide one last time before he cracked the whip in the air. The two brown horsed broke into a trot and pulled the carriage away from Adelaide's cottage.

24 THE JOURNEY TO DUNOLLIE CASTLE

Ominous dark clouds loomed above Loch Awe, blocking out the sun turning its water jet black. The silhouette of Kilchurn Castle appeared from the mist like a menacing spirit.

The young Laird had taken refuge in his bedchamber after his failed attempt to overrun Adelaide's cottage. Unable to eat or sleep, he began to drown his desperation and fear in wine, hoping that Lord Dougal would remain unaware of what happened. He had forbidden his servants and guards to speak about it under the threat of death to prevent Lord Dougal's spies from learning of his defeat.

An eerie silence filled the castle. The castle's servant spoke only in hushed voices now and then when orders needed to be passed and hustled through the halls and passages barefooted. No one dared to provoke the Laird's anger. He was well known for his violent temper and brutal outbursts, which had only gotten worse after his dreadful defeat last night. Even the kitchen lay silent since the cook had ordered the maids to only use wooden bowls and keep the chopping to a minimum.

"Blood bas, how many men had to die last night because of the Lairds ignorance? Didn't he know that no one with ill intent is able to cross that bridge?"

"Too many and many more will die because of his insatiable lust for power. He should have known better than to anger the Seelie Fae. Mark my words, Alan, this is only the beginning. Dark times lay before us," whispered Kenneth the Laird's stable hand wiping the sweat from his bald head. He was a frail old man, his face hardened from livelong servitude. His eyes were pale and lifeless, and his once strong hands were now stiff and deformed from arthritis.

"Lust for power, nay Kenneth that's not it. He is

desperate to get Lucy back and hand the two lassies over to his wicked master. You know of whom I speak," hissed Alan and tightened the grip on his clay tankard so hard that it shattered in his hand. He had once been a soldier himself but resigned to working as a servant since he had lost a hand fighting for the young laird. He knew how wicked and bloodthirsty his master was and how much he feared Lord Dougal.

"Aye, you're right Alan, the grief over losing Lucy and the fear of Lord Dougal's wrath have made him wild. But you are going to join him soon, look at what you have done!" said Rhona, the kitchen maid, as she picked the tankards broken pieces off the ground.

"I hope you get a grip of yourself, me lad when you bring the laird his wine. I would not like having to wipe it off the floor, my knees are not what they use to be," said Rhona and looked sternly at Alan. She was a lovely, motherly woman, with greying hair and a warm smile for everyone. She had worked at the castle all her life and often spoke about the good old days when Lady Sarah was still alive. Every morning before she started the kitchen fires, she would go to the small graveyard behind the castle to place fresh flowers on her Lady's grave, and the one of her son.

"You know Rhona, the wine looks like the blood of the men he sacrificed last night. I hope that I am going to see the day when he will be punished for all his wickedness."

"Be careful what you say, Alan the walls of the castle have ears," Kenneth warned. "You don't want to end up in the dungeons like the ten guardsmen that failed him."

"Failed him? It wasn't their fault that the captives got away, they had help from the Seelie Fae! There was absolutely nothing they could have done," Alan insisted.

"Stop tempting your faith, you two, and keep quiet. Come on Alan, go and bring the Laird his wine before he loses his temper again and breaks more furniture. Just leave it by the door and knock," whispered Rhona and pushed the men out of the kitchen.

*

The rain had started to fall, gently at first, then torrential and unforgiving on Kilchurn Castle and the loch, drenching the guards on the castle's walls to the skin and obscured their view of the loch and its shores. The men felt cold and weary. It had been two days and nights since they'd slept. The laird had not given them a chance to rest ever since the escape of the captives and had forbidden them to light any fires, meaning the men had to find shelter in turrets.

"I hope that the rain continues for a while so that the guards wouldn't see us," whispered Amanda.

"Let's hope so. We could do with some blessings from the clouds. But you better check that our travellers are comfortable. They are so quiet, I can't even hear little Lucy," said Harris in a hushed voice as the carriage rolled down to the shore.

"Aye Harris, they are snuggled up under Adelaide's blankets and look very sleepy. I am sure that they will fall asleep as soon as the boat starts rocking."

"Fall asleep? It's just past midday, how can anyone sleep at this hour?"

"With a little help from Laratbogh! We added a handful of herbs to their broth, trust me, it is better for them and easier for us. Oh, look, Harris! Asanopirh and Sorcha got the boat ready! Could you get the horses to walk a little faster? I don't want to have to carry these guys to the boat!" giggled Amanda and blushed.

"Aye, giddy up, my sweets!" shouted Harris. He made a kissing sound and slackened the reins. It worked like a charm, and a short while later everyone was safely seated in the boat.

"Well then, let's get the boat into the water," Ralston said, satisfied. Come on Harris, help me push."

“Hang on a moment, I don’t see the oars anywhere. I know that they were here when I checked the boat yesterday,” said Harris looking around nervously as the boat began to float.

“We don’t need them. Come on Harris you should know that by now! Jump in so that we can get on our way,” replied Ralston and pointed to the water, from which three Ashrays appeared, picked up the rope, and began to pull the boat away from the land and out to the middle of the loch. Soon, the shore disappeared behind shifting sheets of steel-grey rain that floated over the loch.

“We will find shelter here behind the islands until Ioroth gives us the all clear,” whispered Ralston and dipped his hand into the water to signal Ariana. The boat slowed immediately and drifted gently through the calm waters between the wooded islands. The rain had slowed by now, and the sun began to break through the branches in long slanting silver rays.

“You should take the opportunity to rest a bit and have some water. It wouldn’t take very long till we hear Ioroth’s call to leave the shelter and continue on our way across the loch,” murmured Asanopirh, scanning the sky for the golden eagle. Amanda began to feel nauseous from the bobbing of the boat. She turned her head to the breeze trying to calm her churning stomach with long deep breaths until she heard Ioroth’s high-pitched sound, the eagle’s call was like no other and could be heard miles away. *I hear you Ioroth, thanks to you for being our eyes in the sky*, Amanda thought as she climbed over William, Anne, and Lucy, who lay curled up in the back of the boat fast asleep. She took the pearl from her neck and dipped it into the water to tell Ariana that it was time to move out of their green shelter, cross the loch, and get on to the river. The rain had stopped completely now, and the sky above the loch was clear and blue, which meant that the boat was now visible to the guards on the castle walls. The Ashrays knew the danger they were in as they left the islands and soared across the loch and up the river, until the boat disappeared under the green cover of the wooded riverbanks. Soon the river's current had gotten so strong that the Ashrays were able to release the rope and allow the boat to float freely like a swan, past the grassy river banks and through patches of tall reeds that swayed gently in the afternoon sun, before coming to a stop in an ancient forest.

"Pick up your weapons guys, it's time to step on land. Watch your steps on the smooth rocks and take cover between the reeds whenever you can," Ralston instructed.

"Aye, don't worry, we know what to do. I just wish we had time to fish! Did you see the size of the silver carps and river trout?" uttered Glen excitedly pointing to the fish that rushed out from under large river stones and shot through the crystal clear river water like arrows.

"We'll come back for them as soon as we are done with all of this, I promise. Let's go, my dear brother, grab your staff and head for the bushes," chuckled Hugh as he waded through the shallows of the river to the opposite bank where Ursula and Aislinn were waiting

"Come on Amanda, let's go," Glen urged. "Oren and Ghilli Duh are waiting for us."

"Just give me a moment, Ariana is calling me. Go on, I'll catch up with you," replied Amanda as she bent down to listen to Ariana.

"Amanda, I have disturbing news. I saw Lord Dougal's banner being hoisted over the turrets as we left the islands, signalling his presence at the castle."

"Thank you, Ariana. That is truly troubling news indeed, did you tell the others what you saw?"

"Aye, Harris and the elves know, so you just have to inform your friends about the new situation. I have to go now and get the boat with your charges out of here. We don't know if we have been seen, it would be wise not to waste time," whispered Ariana and disappeared.

Amanda bent down picked up a small river pebble and aimed carefully, throwing it at Hugh's back, he instantly spun around and looked Amanda quietirritated.

"I have some important news for you," she mouthed and waved excitedly.

"Bullocks Amanda! Since when do you throw rocks at me? Why are you so agitated," asked Hugh as he returned to the shore.

"Never mind, it most certainly did not hurt you, and I had to get your attention before you reached the other side," she brushed his complaint aside. "Ariana just told me that Lord Dougal is at Kilchurn Castle. You know what that means."

"Aye I do," Hugh replied, a look of seriousness washing over his face. So we can expect that things will get pretty ugly soon. We can only hope that we weren't seen by his spies, thanks for the warning, Amanda," he said hurrying back to Ursula and Aislinn.

Terrible visions swirled through Amanda's mind as she hurried into the woods to meet Glen, Oren and Ghilli Duh to tell them about the latest development.

"Damn, we should have foreseen this. We only have three nights till full moon, so let's speed things up a bit," murmured Ghilli Duh. He walked up to a large oak tree and began to drum on his massive stem.

"Who are you calling," asked Amanda scanning the surrounding shrubs and trees for any sign of movement. Suddenly, a group of tall highland stags broke through the underbrush. They trotted up to Ghilli Duh and lowered their heads in respect and reverence.

"Thank you for coming to our aid so quickly myroyal friends," said Ghilli Duh. He bowed to the group of stags before he turned to Amanda, Glen, and Oren. "Make haste my friends and mount the stags so that you can keep up with the boat and protect it. The river has swollen from the heavy rain and runs very quickly now," instructed Ghilli Duh as he helped Glen, Amanda, and Oren climb onto the backs of the mighty creatures. He then whispered an enchantment and stepped back. The stags reared high in the air and took off with such giddying speed that the three friends had to hold on to their antlers with all their might not to fall off. As soon as they left the forest and galloped along the river bank, they noticed that the boat was far ahead of them and began to worry if Bilobeal, Hugh, Aislinn, and Ursula would be able to catch up with them.

"Oy, what are you trying to do, break your legs running like this over the rocks?" shouted Bilobeal from the top of the stony river bank. Out of breath and soaked with sweat, Ursula stopped and leaned onto a large boulder to take a breath.

"We have no choice if we don't want to lose the boat! Don't you see the speed it is going? The river is so strong that not even the Ashrays can slow it down."

"Well, yes, I can see that, but there is still no need to risk injuries," answered Bilobeal rummaging through his sporran. He withdrew a silver whistle, blew it releasing a high-pitched whiz that echoed through the glen.

"Blimey Bilobeal, have you gone mad! You can be heard twenty miles away," shouted Hugh and looked at Bilobeal quite perturbed.

"I bloody well hope so! After all, we are in need of some transport," said Bilobeal pointing to a herd of large mountain goats coming over the hilltop. "Welcome, my lovely furry friends. I greatly appreciate your coming," cheered Bilobeal and patted the heads of the large black and white mountain goats.

"Climb on, you guys, we have no time to lose if we want to catch up with our friends."

"Crivens, you can't be serious! They stink, Bilobeal, how should I ever get that stench out of my clothes?" exclaimed Ursula as the goats came closer.

"Hm, so tell me what you would like to do instead? Break your legs and bruise your pretty face, or catch up with the boat comfortably on the back of a goat?"

"Well, if you put it that way, I'll take the stench," Ursula conceded.

"I knew that you were a smart lass. Are you ready, Hugh?"

"Aye Bilobeal, I am. This will be quite an experience, I have never ridden a goat before," giggled Hugh. He jumped onto the back of one of the goats, holding on to its horns for dear life as it began to run and jump from rock to rock.

Meanwhile, Ralston paced on the boat in alarm.

"I can't see Amanda anywhere. It was a mistake to leave them," Ralston muttered, scanning the river bank nervously. "The lads, are not ready to fight up on their own."

"Calm down, they are not alone," Sorcha reassured him. "They have Ghilli Duh at their side, what could happen to them as long as they are under the protection of the most powerful spirit of the forest? I am more worried about our friends on the rugged river bank. I hope that Bilobeal will be able to keep them safe."

"He is doing just that," Asanopirh said. "Didn't you hear his whistle a while ago? I am certain that he called his herd of mountain goats to carry them over the rough terrain. Knowing him, they are well on their way and might even show at any moment."

"I can't hear a thing over the rushing waters, but I certainly hope that you are right, Asanopirh."

"Aye, I am, just look! There they all are," chuckled Asanopirh and pointed at the two groups offriends riding along the river banks ahead of the boat.

"Now that is a sight to behold!" Harris exclaimed in wonder. "Who knew that you could travel on the backs of stags and goats."

"You can if they are your friends," replied Sorcha with a broad smile on her face.

The following hours went by without a sign of danger.

The rushing river had soon slowed and was meandering along fallen trees and swamp-like pools that were filled with green water which sparkled like stars in the afternoon sun. *I wish that we could stop and stay here for a while, forget about all the horrors and make time stand still,* Amanda thought, as she watched Oren following the boat through an archway of branches and soft green leaves high above the river.

Ursula was relieved and extremely grateful when she was finally able to get off that goat. Seemingly unable to get rid of the creature's horrible smell, she kept sniffing her tunic while stumbling along the rugged river bank. Distracted, she tripped and had to grab on to a branch over her head to stop herself from plunging into the river.

"Yuck, what is that?" she screamed and looked at her hand in disgust.

"What, what did you do this time? I swear you cannot walk alone for more than five steps," teased Hugh.

"Ha, ha, how amusing," she sneered sarcastically. "Just take a look at this mess! My right hand is covered in some smelly green gunk."

"Oh come on Ursula, let me see. It can't be that bad, I am sure that you are overreacting again," he replied and turned around with a cheeky smile on his face.

"Yikes, I take that back! It stinks worse than the bock I sat on. Come on, let me hold your other hand so that you can wash that green stuff off without falling into the river."

"Hugh, you are such a good friend, let me shake your hand," said Ursula, lurching forward and reached for Hugh.

"Don't you dear!" shouted Hugh, barely escaping her grip by running into the river.

"What are you guys up to this time? You will give us all away with your silly games!"

"Sorry Bilobeal, but Ursula was trying to smear my face with the nasty smelling green slime she picked up from one of the branches over there." Bilobeal stopped in his tracks.

"Green slime?" he said. "Hold it, that's not a laughing matter. Ursula, my bonnie lass, don't wash it off before I've had a look at it."

"Oh but Bilobeal, it stinks and burns terribly! Hurry up, I can't stand it much longer." He rushed over to examine her hand.

"Blood bas, that is what I feared it would be," he said in a sombre voice. Go quickly wash it off completely, and cut off that sleeve! We cannot afford to take any chances," he said signalling Ralston to bring the boat ashore.

"What's the matter Bilobeal?" Asanopirh asked. Why did you stop us when we are so close to Taynuit, couldn't you wait until we'd arrived?"

"We could all be dead by then. Ursula, my sweet lass, let me have that sleeve. Then take out your medallion and signal Amanda to stop. Do you recognise this, Asanopirh?"

"Aye, of course, I do, it's saliva from a Boobrie. That beast must have been flying above us for quite some time," said Asanopirh while scanning the treetops for any sign of the bloodthirsty beast.

"And it's obviously drooling looking down at you guys," hissed Ghilli Duh as he appeared from the bushes.

"We can't risk continuing our journey on the river," Ralston declared. "Let's wake William and Anne. I hope they'll be able to walk."

"They will be. Let me handle this, it will not take long," said Ghilli Duh. He bent over William and Anne, placed his hands on their eyes, and murmured an enchantment."

"I heard everything, Lord Ralston, and thought it best to ask my sisters Laratbogh and Faraday to join us. They should be with us in no time," said Oren before she disappeared in a weeping willow on the edge of the forest.

"The sun is going to set soon, and if you are right about the Boobrie, then there is no doubt that the Red

Caps will be on your trail as well. So I think that it would be best if the Ashrays and I take the boat back to Loch Awe to give them a false lead."

"Aye right, Ghilli Duh. It may not fool them for long, but hopefully just long enough for us to get to the forge," Asanopirh said. He pushed the boat back into the river before turning to the willow and shouting up to Oren. "Oren, tell me, what do you see? We should be close to Taynuit."

"Aye, I can see the forge! It's about two miles ahead of us," replied Oren.

"What's going on? Where are we? Please don't tell me that I slept the whole way!" asked William as he found himself lying next to Anne and Lucy.

"Never mind William, there is no time for long explanations," Harris said. "It would be best if you could pick up Lucy and head into the forest I fill you in on the way. Glen, come on me lad, go and help me to get Anne on her feet. You heard Asanopirh, we have to get away from the river as fast as we can," he whispered and splashed some water on Anne's face before he and Glen pulled her up and helped her to keep her balance as she walked her first few steps.

It took Anne a while to shake off the sleepiness and open her eyes, Laratboghs herbs were very potent and meant to be effective throughout the entire journey. But when Amanda and Glen told her about the Boobrie and that he was circling above them, she lit up like a candle and begun to run behind William. Soon, all of them had reached the forest and were walking over moss covered grounds and along large patches of ferns and clumps of hazelnut trees. Laratbogh, Faraday, and Oren were rushing through the treetops, dropping branches and pine cones to mark a safe trail, until the forest opened up to a meadow. It looked like a sea of tall waving grasses, deep purple thistles, and brilliant gold wildflowers.

"From now on, we have to continue without the

Dryads protection, so I think that it would be best if we wait until the sky has darkened before we leave the tree cover," Ralston asserted.

"I don't think it will be necessary to wait that long, we should be able to make a run for it. I go out to take a look before I give you all the go ahead, but to stay on the safe side, you and Amanda should take position in the middle of the meadow. I would feel a lot better knowing that I have your blades at a ready in case any Red Caps are around and willing to take the chance to attack us," Asanopirh said. "Hugh, you and Sorcha should position yourselves at the opposite edge of the meadow. Have your arrows ready and your bows drawn in case the Boobrie tries to attack. Ursula, you, Glen and Aislinn should remain at the edge of the forest and cover our backs we cannot be sure that we weren't being followed. Go, go, and be safe my friends," he said in a hushed voice before he left the tree cover of to search the glade and the surroundingshrubs.

Amanda and Ralston stepped out of the forest, crouched low, and dashed through the high grass to a group of flowering elder shrubs in the centre of the meadow. They pulled the swords from their scabbards and scanned the sky for the Boobrie. Hugh and Sorcha made their way to the other side of the meadow and readied themselves to secure the sky.

"I hope he shows, I would love plug that bastard like a chicken."

"Be careful what you wish for, Hugh. Many men and even elves have lost their lives to this beast. He is extremely fast and powerful, and remember that he can shapeshift into a horse. So do not take any chances I would not like to lose you," replied Sorcha and looked straight into his eyes with an intense expression of concern.

Ursula, Glen, and Aislinn had taken their position at the edge of the meadow and stood staring into the darkening forest.

"How are we supposed to see anything in this darkness?" exclaimed Glen shaking his head in frustration as he leaned on his staff.

"You will be able to, just close your eyes and stand still for a moment while Laratbogh and I give you the sight," replied Aislinn before she and Laratbogh pulled Bella Donna stems from their hair and blew the flower dust towards Glen and Ursula.

"Open your eyes now and tell us what you see."

"Wow, yes, yes, Laratbogh I can see clearly! As if the sun was shining through the treetops," replied Glen, rubbing his eyes in disbelieve.

"I have no idea how you did it, but thanks! Now they can come I am ready," replied Ursula and loaded her slingshot.

All of a sudden, they heard Asanopirh's voice echo from across the meadow.

"Run, Run! Don't look up and you will be okay!" he shouted.

Anne held on to Harris' arm, picked up her skirts, and took off running as fast as she could, stumbling over the rutted ground. She staggered through the waist-high grass and weeds while keeping an eye on William who was carrying wee Lucy tightly wrapped in one of Adelaide's blankets. The three of them were just steps away from the elder shrubs in the middle of the meadow where Ralston and Amanda waited with outstretched arms ready to pull them into the cover when they heard Oren's voice.

"Drop to the ground and don't move."

Harris, William, and Anne dropped like stones to the ground and looked terrified up to Amanda and Ralston, as the Boobrie circled above them and darkened the sky with his broad black wings. His head and his black piercing eyes were caught by the fading light of the sun as he whizzed over the heads from Harris, William and Anne, ready to attack.

At that moment Hugh and Sorcha broke through the

thickets with their bows drawn and aimed at the Boobrie's head. The arrows soared through the air and pierced the beast's neck but did not slow it down. The Boobrie shook his head and threw the arrows off like dewdrops before he returned for another attack. The enormous creature sailed through the air, then tipped his wings and went into a steep dive with his sharp talons fully extended to grab his prey.

Amanda let out a scream that could freeze blood as she rushed out from the elder shrubs and charged the attacking beast. Her initial shock had given way to burning fury that raged inside her like a blazing fire. She darted across the meadow with raised swords that flashed like flames as she leapt up in the air and slashed one of the Boobrie's wings, sending black feathers flying and spraying the grass with his blood. He turned around wildly flapping his massive wings in pain knocking Amanda to ground before he disappeared into the clouds.

"Amanda, mo ghràdh are you okay, did he hurt you?" whispered William,

"I think I am okay Da, but my shoulders are killing me," replied Amanda with a forced smile and flinched.

"Stay down Amanda, he's coming back," said Ralston. He swung his cloak over her and placed his hand on her chest to stop her from getting up.

"William, you all have to take cover under the blankets so that the beast will not be able to see you. We can't make another attempt to cross the meadow until the sky has completely darkened."

"Aye Ralston, I would like to agree with you, but I am afraid that it is too late for that, look up," replied William and pointed to a gathering of shadows that swept over the sky like a flock of starling

"The Sluaghs are here, blessed be! They are the only thing this beast fears more than death. He will not return tonight we are safe," Ralston breathed a sigh of relief. He lifted Amanda off the ground as if she was weightless, closed his cloak over her and carried her into the forest to recover from the battle. Amanda was trembling and felt as if all energy had been drained from her body as she desperately clung to Ralston with her last remaining strength. She could hear his heart pounding under his heavy armour and felt his warm breath on her skin as he lowered his head and gazed into her eyes.

"Don't ever frighten me like that again, *mo ghradh*. I would not be able to bear it if anything should happen to you," he whispered. He pulled her closer and kissed her before he lowered himself to the ground, holding her in his arms.

"William, my dear friend, I think the time has come to ask for your grandfather's help. I suggest you write him a short message and send your ring along with it. Ioroth is going to take it to the castle before nightfall. Tell him to meet you at the stone circle of Strontoiller by sunrise," said Asanopirh and handed William his dagger. "This will be your quill, William. The Boobrie's blood should make a fine ink."

"Aye Asanopirh, let's hope he will recognise the ring and will be curious enough to meet his dead grandson," replied William. He took off his necktie wrote a short message on it, knotted it around the ring, and he tied it to one of Ioroth talons.

25 LORD MACDOUGALL

The Laird stood on the high stone wall of the castle's tower and watched as the sun's golden orb slowly disappeared behind the hills and valleys in a haze of copper and purple making way for the fast approaching night sky. He was a man of extraordinary stature and strength in spite of his age. His eyes were as blue as the summer sky, gentle and bright. His thick wavy hair had lost its golden hue and shimmered like spun silver in the evening sun. The Laird had seen and fought many battles and had lost the two women that had meant everything to him. His young wife had died of a high fever many years ago, and his beloved daughter lost her life in childbirth. He was still mourning their deaths and despised the silence that surrounded him. He knew that he would die alone, and without an heir, leaving his land and people without protection.

"My Lord, you have to take a look at this eagle, isn't he just magnificent?" whispered his servant Dunbar in admiration as the bird passed through the rays of the evening sun and revealed a flash of gold on its neck that gave him his name.

"Aye, I see him, Dunbar. You are right he is breathtakingly beautiful. It has been a long time since last I have seen such a majestic golden eagle," replied the Laird in a husky drawl.

"If I didn't know any better my Lord, I would say that he is heading straight for the castle."

"You are right Dunbar, it most certainly looks that way," replied Lord MacDougall, following the flight of the bird with great interest.

"Oh dear, my Lord, I don't want to be a spoil joy, but it looks as if he is going to attack! We better return to the tower."

"Calm down Dunbar, don't get your knickers in a knot! He has no cause to attack us, but it looks as if he is carrying a message. Look, there is something tied to one of his talons."

"Well, I am not comfortable with this, since when do eagle deliver messages? Please, my Lord, let's take cover," replied Dunbar in a high pitched voice ducking behind a rampart to get out of the way of the approaching bird.

"Would you look at this? I was right, he is carrying a satchel!" exclaimed the laird, trembling with excitement. The closeness to this majestic bird of prey made his heart beat so loudly that it echoed in his ears.

"Is the message for me, my friend? May I take it off you, or would you attack me if I do?" Asked the Laird as he walked closer to Ioroth, who had perched himself on one of the ramparts with his enormous wings fully spread.

"Thank you, my noble friend, I am sure that this is a very important message and the way you look at me tells me you expect an answer for your master," said the Laird in a soft, soothing voice as he untied the bundle from Ioroth talon.

"Dunbar go to the kitchen and fetch a juicy piece of meat for my friend so that he can refresh himself before he returns to his master."

"But my Lord I can't just leave you, what if he attacks you?"

"He will do no such thing, don't be silly! If that were his intent, he would have done it already. Now go and do as I say, or would you like to offer him a piece of your flesh?" chuckled the Laird as he began to unfold the piece of cloth.

How strange, who would send me a ring? He thought and froze when he recognised the ring's seal as the one of his deceased daughter Sarah. His hands began to tremble, and his breath quickened as he proceeded to flatten the scrap of linen on which a message was written in blood.

Dear Grandfather,

This message must be bewildering for you, as you were lead to believe that my mother and I had died during the night of the winter solstice thirty years ago. The truth is that my father Lord Collin Campbell ordered the midwife to have me killed immediately after my mother's passing. She did not obey his order but made a pledge to my dying mother to keep me safe me and hold the ring as proof of my identity. Now a member of the Campbell clan is once again, attempting to take my life, so I must reach out to you and ask for your help and protection. My companions and I will await your response by sunrise at the stone circle of Strontoiller.

Sincerely yours

William MacDougall

The Laird stared at the message in shock and disbelieve! Could it be true, had the boy survived? He felt torn between hope and doubt and had to sit down on the tower's steps to contemplate his next move.

"My Lord, what happened? Did the bloody bird attack you?"

"No, Dunbar he did not. The message he brought was from my grandson William, help me up, will you? We have to get our men armed and ready to make our way to the stone circle at Strontoiller. My grandson is in need of my help!" shouted the Laird, grabbing hold of his servant's hand pulling himself up.

The thought of his grandson being alive and asking for his help gave him a rush and made him feel energised, fearless, and purposeful.

"Come on Dunbar, tell the commander to assemble the

men and then go and get my armour it's time to bring my grandson home," shouted the Laird joyously, crossing the oak-cladded Great Hall with long, fast strides.

"But my Lord, your grandson is dead, remember? He died the night he was born," said Dunbar in a trembling voice running behind the Laird with his green damask cloak flapping behind him like a pair of limp wings.

"Well, we now know that he is not. The boy survived and is on his way here. Hand me my sword and take my dagger up to the eagle so that he can take it to my grandson. Go and do as I say, I can't wait to bring him home," shouted the Laird in jubilation.

"You want me to go near that bird?" Dunbar said with hesitation. "But my lord, what if he attacks me?"

"Don't be such a coward, he is not going to attack you! Just rest the dagger on the rampart so that he can take it to my grandson, go on," said the Laird and burst into laughter.

*

I use to love the full moon and its magical silver light, but lately, it has become an impending omen of death and oppression, William thought as he sat on a large boulder near the edge of the meadow and listened to the gentle rustling of the grass and the sounds of the forest. The ground was still damp from the rain, and the evening mists had begun to rise and spread the rich fragrance of the wildflowers, leaves, and loam across the glade and the surrounding forest. The group of friends rested on the moss-covered ground under a large old fir tree and stared silently into the fire, trying to calm the anxiety that had built once they began to comprehend how close they came to losing William, Anne, and Lucy. Anne had withdrawn from the group and sat huddled under the low branches of the tree clinging to Lucy.

"You're trembling, Anne you must be cold my love,

why don't you come closer to the fire and take a blanket?" asked Harris in a hushed voice. He picked up a blanket and placed around Anne and Lucy.

"Thank you, Harris, that is very kind of you, but I think it's my nerves that are making me tremble. This was a close call today, I truly thought that the Boobrie would kill us all."

"Aye Anne, it was truly terrifying, and I am sure that everyone is now painfully aware of the dangers we will have to face. We can only survive if we stay close and act as one," muttered Harris got up and added a large log to the fire. The fire hissed softly as the wood shifted and sent a shower of sparks high up in the air.

"Oh, Mummy look, fireflies!" shouted Lucy excitedly, throwing off the blanket jumping up down in delight.

"No my love they are not, fireflies. Fireflies would not come so close to the fire they would burn. But come, on let's look for some in the bushes, they love to hide there," said Anne took her daughter's hand and walked away from the fire to some nearby hazelnut shrubs.

"I don't think that's a wise move," Glen whispered. He looked across to Ursula picked up his staff, and followed Anne and Lucy.

"Wait for me Glen, I am not going to let you go alone," said Ursula, strapping her slingshot onto her wrist. She ran into Hugh as she followed Glen into the forest.

"Where the heck are you coming from? I've been looking for you everywhere," hissed Ursula pushing him out of her way.

"Well, I was standing right behind you for quite a while, which you would have noticed if you weren't so busy with your slingshot."

"So and where were you before?"

"I had a talk with Sorcha, Asanopirh, and Bilobeal near the rowan tree, right over there."

"Oh yes, is that so? Why couldn't they come over to the fire and talk to all of us?"

"Oh come on Ursula, what does that matter?"

"Oh quite a lot my dear brother," Glen interrupted, overhearing the conversation as he returned with Anne and Lucy. "You were with Sorcha, which is enough to drive our bonnie lass Ursula crazy with jealousy," whispered Glen teasingly and took cover behind Hugh when he saw Ursula picking up a large branch.

"Ah, what, what are you talking about Glen? Anyhow they told me that Cait Sith brought a message from Ghilli Duh that makes it necessary for them to return to the cottage tonight."

"Oh well, and what was the message," asked Ursula impatiently?

"Well, she told them that Lord Dougal had ordered the Laird to sentence ten of his guardsmen to death by drowning, and the spineless coward obeyed and had them thrown from the tower."

"Crivvens, how could he do that! And why?" asked Ursula and looked wide-eyed at Hugh.

"Because he is gutless bastard that will do anything the so-called Lord tells him to do. But don't worry they were saved by the Ashrays and taken to the cottage by John and Bhaltair. You can imagine how indebted they felt for their rescue and how stunned they were to see Lady Julia at the cottage. They now know the whole story and have sworn their allegiance to her and the rightful Laird."

"That's bloody brilliant but how do they all fit into the cottage? Isn't it getting kind of crowded in there by now?

"Oh, Glen have you still not realised that the cottage is a place of magic? It will always have enough room no matter how many people Adelaide takes in," said, Ralston, as he and Amanda appeared right next to them.

"Blimey, I feel like a fool now," mumbled Glen and blushed.

"Never mind we still love you," giggled Ursula and ruffled his blond locks.

"Well that's nice, but you don't have to mess up my

hair, me bonnie lass," replied Glen mockingly and reached for Ursula's hair.

"Oh stop it you two!" Hugh said. "Let's go back to the others and tell them before Williams grandfather arrives with his men."

"If he arrives, that is," Ralston clarified. We can't be sure of that. Remember that he believed up to today that his grandson died some thirty years ago. Let's all go back to the fire and wait for Ioroth return," he said as he walked back to the fire.

"Come on over you guys, hurry, hurry! Ioroth has returned and brought me my grandfather's dagger, that means that he is coming," exclaimed William jubilantly and held up a richly decorated dagger that bore the MacDougall's coat of arms.

"That's fantastic news, William! We should leave right away, we can rest once we reach the stone circle."

"Aye Ralston, I agree. I would feel much better knowing that we are all safe," replied William. He lifted Lucy onto his shoulders and placed one arm around Anne to support her.

"Hugh, Glen, Ursula, you better join the Dryads and secure our flanks. I am not yet certain that we are out of danger, so please keep your eyes open and your weapons ready."

"Will do Ralston," answered Hugh and signalled Glen and Ursula to spread out and join Laratbogh, Oren and Faerydae.

The walk through the forest was peaceful and very quiet all that could be heard was the chirping of the crickets and the whisper of small leaves dancing in the breeze.

"We should be close, don't you think, Ralston?" inquired Glen as the trees thinned and the first fragments of the rising sun began to filter through the treetops.

"Aye Glen, look at the meadow right in front of us," answered Ralston and pointed to an opening in the underbrush. With their last remaining strength, the friends rushed out of the forest and reached the meadow just in time to watch as the rising sun's dazzling gold and orange hues spread over the mountains and the stone circle of Strontoiller that stood in the centre of the meadow.

"Are we safe here, Ralston?" asked Glen as he rested his staff on the ground.

"Aye Glen, the stone circle is a place of pure white magic. It will not allow anything dark near it so you can rest."

Exhausted but relieved that they had made to the stone circle, the friends sunk down onto their blankets and enjoyed the spectacular display of the radiant colours which had replaced the dark blue and purple of the twilight sky and bathed the valley in a golden glow.

"Don't fall asleep now you guys, look up to the hill crest. Do you see the riders? I am sure that it is my grandfather with his men," shouted William excitedly.

It was a spectacular sight as the group of armed men came closer. Each and every one was clad in the bright red and green MacDougall tartans and right in front on a white stallion rode Clyde MacDougall proudly holding the banner with his coat of arms.

"Fàilte mah, my brave men and noble ladies. Tell me, which one of you is my grandson William?" shouted the laird as he approached.

"It's me, my Lord," replied William. He stepped forward and bowed to the Laird.

"Stand up William, a MacDougall bows to no one. Grab your things and mount your horses, I can't wait to hear your story over a good hearty breakfast."

"As you command," answered William and helped Anne and Lucy onto the back of the massive warhorse before he swung himself effortlessly up behind them.

"Oh am I relieved that we have horses. I'll be glad if I don't have to see any more goats for the next ten years."

"There is nothing wrong with goats, Ursula! I love

them roasted on a spit over an open fire basted with red wine, herbs, and garlic," replied Glen with closed eyes and an expression of delight, as if he could taste the roast already.

"Well said, my dear brother. Let's hope the laird means it when he says a hearty breakfast, I am starving," shouted Hugh and began to laugh.

"I hope that you all are comfortable and ready to leave!" shouted the Laird as he gave the signal to move away from the standing stones and over the hill towards Dunollie Castle.

Amanda enjoyed the ride on the broad back of the warhorse. They rode along a small brook that meandered through pastures with grassing cows and sheep and through acres of pale green wheat that moved gently in the warm breeze like waves in the ocean. Everyone had remained silent and savoured the beauty that surrounded them and the feeling of safety between the Laird's armed men. They were quite startled when Dunollie Castle appeared before them high above the busy harbour of Oban. The horses broke into a gallop as they came closer to the castle as if they could smell their stables and the fresh hay. It did not take not long before they passed through the massive gates of the Castle.

"Welcome back, my Lord," shouted Dunbar as he came running out of the castle to take hold of the stallion's bridle. He began to address William, but the clatter of hooves on cobblestones muddled his words so that William looked at him with a puzzled expression.

"Speak up when you address my grandson, Dunbar," the Laird commanded incensed as he dismounted his horse. The castle's servants must have heard their master's voice since they all came running out of the stables, kitchen, and pantries to see the laird's grandson William MacDougall.

"Ah, I see curiosity got the better of you. Well, come closer and welcome your young Lord and Master. Sir

William MacDougall," shouted the Laird and pointed proudly at William.

The servants bowed deeply and only chanced a quick glance at William's face before they begun to whisper excitedly.

"Aye, he looks like his mother, my beloved daughter Lady Sarah," the Laird said, a trace of nostalgia in his eyes. "But enough with the talking we are hungry! Hurry and bring us food and wine, we must celebrate William's homecoming," he cheered ushering William and his companions into the Great Hall. The Hall was an impressive sight, with its high loft ceiling, whitewashed walls with oak wainscoting and elaborate tapestries. Countless torches spread their flickering light over a massive oak table that was covered from end to end with the most delicious foods and large jugs filled to the brim with ale and red wine. On the flagstone floor lay large red and green coloured rugs, and the long wooden benches were covered with sheepskins.

"Don't just stand there, my friends! Sit down, eat and drink with me to celebrate my grandsons return."

"Aye, my Lord let's celebrate the homecoming of Lord William!" shouted the commander and lifted his beaker in a toast to William. The feast lasted long past sunset with music and dance before the servants showed everybody to their respective bedchambers. William, Ralston, and Amanda remained in the Great Hall to tell the Laird about, everything that had happened ever since the so-called Lord Dougal had appeared at Kilchurn Castle and in the surrounding villages.

"Wait a moment," the Laird paused after hearing their story. "The man that you refer to as Lord Dougal sounds like an orphan I had taken in more than forty years ago. He had accompanied your mother to Kilchurn Castle after her wedding, and he was the one who brought me the message of her death and the death of her son William. He used to be a very quiet and humble servant... Iwonder what happened to turn him into such a wicked man. But that is nothing we should concern ourselves with right now. We have to get Harris, Anne, and Lucy out of here before we can make our way to Kilchurn Castle to unseat Lord Campbell's bastard son."

"Aye, Grandfather, how soon would you be able to put them on a ship to France?" asked William. He walked up to a large window and looked down to the harbour where five galleons lay on their anchor.

"The high tide will come in tomorrow around sunset so that we should aim to get them out of here before midnight. But do you really think that Lady Anne will be strong enough to make that journey after all that she has gone through in the last few days?"

"I'm certain she will be. She wants to be with her father when he dies, and there is not much time left. And besides little Lucy will enjoy this great adventure. I'll go to their bedchamber right now to bring them the message, if it is alright with you, my Lord," said Amanda as she got up from the table and looked expectantly at the Laird."

"Very well Amanda, go and tell her. The earlier she knows, the better. I'll get my servant to deliver the message to the captain at sunrise tomorrow so that he can get the ship and crew ready to lift anchor around sunset."

"Thank you, my Lord," replied Amanda excitedly. She ran out of the Great Hall to bring Anne the excellent news.

"Well, William, me lad, I think it is time for us to retire. We have lots to do before we can pay Lord Campbell a visit. Guit nuit, my dear grandson. My servants will show you to your bedchamber. See you tomorrow morning bright and early," said Lord MacDougal in a hushed voice He smiled and left the Great Hall. *My grandson doesn't that sound wonderful,* he thought as he walked through the long corridors to his bedchamber.

26 THE FAREWELL

The halls of the castle felt as bleak and cold, as during the darkest days of winter. All candles and torches had been extinguished on Lord Dougal's orders, and fires were limited to the kitchen and the Laird's private quarters.

"Wickedness can only dwell in darkness," mumbled Allan under his breath as he left the kitchen with a basket of bannocks and a pot of tea for the Laird. He had contemplated many times leaving the castle as numerous other servants had done since the arrival of Lord Dougal. But he had nowhere to go, so he made his way through the dark corridors to the Laird's bedchamber, as he had done for many years, knocked twice and announced himself.

"Come in, you fool, or do you expect me to open the door for you?" shouted the Laird in a hoarse voice.

"Aye my Lord," replied Allan. He rested the tea on the ground opened the door and entered. The bedchamber looked like a battlefield, broken pieces of furniture and shards of pottery were scattered around the fireplace, and the neck of a broken jug stuck out of theashes.

"Place it on the table near the fireplace I will help myself to it when I am ready. Now get your crippled arse out of here."

It's crippled because of you, you noble vermin, thought Alan as he left the bedchamber fuming with rage. The Laird enjoyed it immensely to make fun of the men that had been disfigured or maimed in the countless battles they fought for him. Instead of being honoured for their sacrifice, they had to labour as serfs for no more than their daily crust of bread and a place to sleep in stables. Alan tried to control his anger with the thought of the bacon and eggs that Rhona had prepared for him as he hurried back to the kitchen.

"Bring me to the wounded so that I can find out who or what thwarted the attack on the weaver's cottage. And get this blasted inbreed out of his bed, my patience is running low," shouted Lord Dougal so loudly that his voice echoed through the corridors and halls of the castle.

"As you wish, my Lord, please follow me. I'll show you to the place where we keep the wounded," replied the commander of the guards in a trembling voice and bowing so low that he almost lost balance.

"Please my Lord, place this silken handkerchief over your nose when we enter the stables the stench of the decaying flesh is horrific," whispered one of the Lord's servants, handing him a perfumed handkerchief.

Alan could not believe what he had just witnessed. The proud commander of the guards trembling in fear and the Laird hiding in his bedchamber. He ran straight back to the kitchen and told Rhona what he overheard.

"Goodness gracious, what does he want with the wounded men? Haven't they suffered enough? You better eat quickly so that you can follow them, we must know what they are up to," said Rhona in a hushed voice. She filled Alan's tankard with ale before she returned to the heard.

Alan gobbled his breakfast down as fast as he could, swung his old cloak over his shoulders as he snug into the barn, and hid in the straw just as Lord Dougal and his servants made their entrance.

"Shame on you. Commander, for letting these brave men lie in their own faeces. And what is this, is this supposed to help the men to gain back their health? This is appalling!" shouted the Lord, kicking over a bowl with watered down broth before he bent over one of the wounded soldiers.

"Now tell me, my good man, how you sustained these injuries. You don't have to fear me, I am on your side."

Yea, right you are, you are the one who brought all the

grief and loss on us, thought Lucas as he stared into the Lord's dead grey eyes.

"Forgive him, my Lord, he lost his voice during the fight in Eredine Forest. We hope that he will recover fully so that he can return to his father," mumbled the commander.

"Who is his father?"

"It is Ross MacDuff, the butcher my Lord."

"Very well then, who can tell me what happened in the forest?"

"I can," whispered a badly wounded soldier as he tried to sit up. "Stay down my son and tell me what you witnessed."

"Well my lord, it was no army that defeated us, it was magic. The trees came alive and battered us with their heavy branches, and the thorn bushes ripped the flesh from our bones. Only when we could do no more than crawl did it stop,"

"Commander, I demand that these men be moved into the Great Hall without delay, and the fire is lit and well-tended so that they can rest in comfort while my servants attend to their injuries," the Lord demanded before he returned to the castle's gallery, where Duane awaited him red-faced and fuming with rage.

"Get out of my way, you preposterous shadow of a man," hissed Lord Dougal and pushed Duane out of his way before he sat down in front of large painting picturing Lady Julia on her wedding day. Her long copper coloured hair was held together with a glittering net of gold and pearls and on her shoulder rested a tartan sash in the colours of the Campbell Clan. "My Lord, all men are now in the Great Hall, what would you like us to do with the old stained bedding?"

"Burn them and get the men bread and wine so that they can gain some strength, and recover, we need every man if we want to free this land of magic," ordered Lord Dougal.

Alan made it back into the kitchen without raising anyone's suspicion over his long absence. He was in the middle of telling Rhona and the cook what he had witnessed when Lord Dougal's servants bolted into the kitchen demanding bread and wine for the wounded.

"Very well my good men. You can return to your duties, while we take care of everything."

"Damn you woman who do you think you are, giving me and my men orders? Get the wine and the bread and crawl back into your hole," sneered the lead servant and pushed Rhona so hard that she fell to the ground. The cook's eyes flashed with anger as he tightened his grip on the cleaver in his hand. He was about to teach the men some manners when Alan stepped in front of him with a large wicker basket of freshly baked bread and blocked his way.

"Would you like me to take the bread to the Great Hall for you sir?" Alan asked Lord Dougal's lead servant.

"Very well, you go and do that, but we'll take the wine. Go on then, move it, don't stand in our way!" the man replied pushing Alan out of the kitchen.

"There is something very fishy going on I swear," said Rhona as she dusted herself off.

The ground of the Great Hall was now covered with piles of straw on which the injured men were laid and lovingly cared for by the castle's maids.

"My brave soldiers, I am deeply troubled to see how little the Laird values the sacrifices you made and promise that I will change that, starting right now. From now on every one of you will receive double rations, and my servants will attend to your injuries while the women that cared for you thus far will return to Dalmally and spend two days with their families," declared Lord Dougal. He bowed to the maids and signalled his servants to lead them out of the castle, before raising his chalice in a toast to the men. "Let us share this special wine as I solemnly swear that your suffering will come to an end today."

"My Lord, we have to talk," hissed Duane from the entrance of the Great Hall, "I will not tolerate these filthy men in my Great Hall drinking my best wine while your servants turn my courtyard into a cabbage field."

Lord Dougal walked out of the hall and stared at Duane with an expression of disgust as he ordered his servants to close and lock the doors.

"Make sure that these doors stay locked and that the women are on their way to Dalmally to spread the good news. The villagers will be happy to know how well we look after our injured men," he instructed his men.

"And now to you, my dear Laird Campbell. Don't fret you do not have to trouble yourself about any of that much longer. My men are preparing graves, not a cabbage field. Did you honestly think that I would waste time with these worthless men, did you? The wine they are enjoying right now will be the last that passes their lips as their wretched lives will end with the setting of the sun," replied Lord Dougal with an ice cold sneer as he left the castle accompanied by his armed men.

"Where are you going, my Lord?"

"I have a forest to burn, Duane. Go back to your bedchamber and enjoy the spectacle."

*

"Do you have everything, Anne? Adelaide's letter to your father, your blankets, and Lucy's staff?"

"Aye Amanda, Harris took care of everything when he boarded the ship with Lucy, all that's left for us to do is to say goodbye," whispered Anne. Tears fell steadily down her cheeks as she hugged Amanda and Ursula, before boarding the ship that would take her, Lucy, and Harris home to Touraine. The dockworkers removed the gangway, untied the ropes, and gave the boatswain the all clear as soon as Anne had reached the ship's bridge.

"Raise the anchor and set the sails," ordered the

Captain before he welcomed his three passengers aboard. The anchor winch creaked as the heavy rope tightened and began to pull the anchor from the muddy harbour bed. The breeze caught the unfurling sails, and the galleon started to move slowly away from the harbour and out to the open sea.

"Come on you guys, it is high time to get back to the castle. I am sure that my grandfather and his men are ready to ride out," said William

"You're right William, let's not waste time standing here and mourn. After all, we have things to do and places to go," cheered Hugh as he mounted his horse.

"Race you to the castle!" shouted Amanda. She picked up the reins, squeezed her horse gently, and galloped out of the harbour with thundering huffs.

"Oh, do you truly believe that you will get their first Amanda? Well, let me show you how it is done."

"Aye Hugh keep on dreaming," chuckled Amanda as she reached the ramparts just as Lord MacDougal and his armed men crossed the drawbridge.

"Oh good, you are back," he greeted them. "I gather you are all ready to leave."

"Aye my lord," answered Amanda. She turned her horse around and took one last look across the sea as the sails of the galleon slowly disappeared behind the island of Jura.

"Now that's how I like to travel," Glen remarked. "Let's hope we will be able to do that for all our journeys from now."

"You are right, and it's a lot faster too," Hugh agreed. "We should be able to reach Adelaide's cottage before sunrise. That is, of course, if you don't get too comfortable. We are already falling behind, look at Ralston, Amanda, and Ursula they've almost reached the forest."

"Well, you go, keep up with them if you like, Hugh. I'll stay with the Lord and his men."

"Aye see you later," laughed Hugh as he pulled away

from Glen and galloped after Ursula, Amanda, and Ralston. The four friends enjoyed the silence of the woods, the smell of the trees and the damp forest floor as their horses ambled past moss covered rocks and trees, through patches of tall ferns and blueberry fields, below the lush green canopy of the trees and the star-studded night sky.

"It is nice to see you back in the forest," called Oren from a nearby tree.

"It is great to be back in the woods! I'd choose the glades and the forest over a castle's Great Hall any time," Amanda laughed. "Are you alone Oren?"

"No Laratbogh and Faerydae are way upfront to make sure we don't meet any unpleasant surprises again. But I'll go and get them if you like so that we can continue the journey to Adelaide's together while you tell us about William's grandfather," replied Oren and disappeared.

Shortly after, Laratbogh and Faerydae broke through the underbrush on the backs of the beautiful stags that had carried Amanda and Glen earlier.

"Goodness, you startled me! I expected to see you in the treetops," chuckled Amanda.

"Well, Oren secures our path from the treetops while we check the underbrush. I am so happy to see you all back in the forest and that we have the chance to spend some time with you," said Faerydae and smiled at Glen who had just caught up with his friends.

"I am delighted to be back with you," answered Glen with a warm smile. He could not take his eyes of Faerydae, whose waist-long green hair shimmered like emeralds in the moonlight as she leaned over to take his hand. The friends were sharing their adventures and plans with the Dryads when Hugh noticed an orange tinge in the night sky.

"Look up guys, I wonder what is causing that glow. Could it be a Northern Light?" Exclaimed Hugh and pointed to the sky.

"Certainly not, it is flickering so it must be a fire in the distance. Oren, can you see anything?" Ralston shouted up to the treetops. He sped to a clearing nearby closely followed by Amanda and her friends.

"Eredine forest is on fire!" screamed Oren and looked at Laratbogh in terror. "Where is Faerydae, where is our sister?"

"She was right next to me not a moment ago," replied Glen, turning his horse around and galloping back to where he had seen her last. He jumped off his horse and began to search in the thickets for a sign of Faerydae. His heart began to race, and his breath became quick and laboured as he fought his way through a field of tall ferns. All of a sudden Faerydae's stag appeared in front of him.

"Where is she did you throw her off, did you hurt her?" shouted Glen in desperation and grabbed the stag by his antlers.

"Leave him be, it's nothing that he has done, Faerydae is dying," whispered Laratbogh and parted the ferns next to Glen revealing Faerydae as she lay motionless on the mossy ground. Her skin and beautiful hair had lost their colour and shine and looked ashen.

"Glen, mo ghradh, I have to leave you much too soon," whispered Faerydae. "But I beg you to let me go and not to mourn my passing, I will return to you one day. So please, be happy, cherish every day of your life and the company of your friends. Take this acorn home to the land of Elfame and plant it under the tree where I showed myself to you for the first time. I loved you from the moment I saw you and I always will," she whispered with her last breath.

"No, no, don't leave me!" screamed Glen in agony. He fell to his knees and took Faerydae in his arms.

"Oh no, what has happened!" Amanda and Ursula exclaimed in horror as they saw Faerydae's lifeless body in Glen's arms.

"Her tree died in the fire and so did she. We have to take her home to Elfame, bury her, and plant the acorn she carried so that she can be reborn," replied Oren in a hushed voice.

Amanda's heart beat echoed in her ears, and a dreadful feeling of emptiness washed over her as she looked into Faerydae's lifeless eyes. Ghilli Duh passed his hand gently over her eyelids and closed them forever. He then took her out of Glen's arms and carried her to the river's edge to call his sisters Arianrhod, Coventina, and the Queen of Elfame.

Amanda, Ralston, Hugh, Lord MacDougal and all his men silently pulled their swords and raised them towards the sky in a salute to Faerydae. The river slowed to a gentle flow. Its soft curls gleamed like jewels in the moonlight as a silvery mist rose and enveloped the forest like a mourning veil. Glen followed Ghilli Duh to the river's edge with his hands clenched in trembling fists, trying to battle the grief that tore him apart. Tears welled up in his deep blue eyes as he listened to the Dryad's beautiful mourning song.

Ghilli Duh strode into the river with Faerydae's body raised into the moonlight just as the Queen of Elfame broke through the mist on a raft that glowed as brightly as the full moon.

"Ghilli Duh, my dear brother, you called me to take your beloved daughter Faerydae home. And so I will. We will plant the acorn that holds her life's essence and wait for the day when she returns to us."

Ghilli Duh bowed to his sister and lowered Faerydae gently onto the silver raft. He passed his hands over her body covering her with a shroud of flowers before he returned to Glen to lead him to the float.

"You have to full-fill Faerydae's last wish to remain at her side during her last journey through the realm of the living." Ghilli Duh gently whispered to Glen. The friends watched as Glen and the float disappeared in a cascade of brilliant shooting stars.

"We have to avenge Faerydae's death and bring Lord Dougal's reign to an end," whispered Ralston. He embraced Amanda and held her close to his chest as if he feared to lose her too.

"Aye, let's make haste my friends to put an end to all this cruelty," said William in a trembling voice before he turned to Oren and Laratbogh. "I pray that you and your sisters will remain safe."

"They will William," replied Ghilli Duh. "Faerydae was the only one that had chosen a home tree in Eredine Forest, as she wanted to remain close to Glen. So it is right that he will be the one to take her home to Elfame and replant the acorn she carried. You mustn't dwell in darkness and sorrows my friends, Faerydae will return to us in time. Go now and continue your quest under the guidance and protection of our beloved Lady Coventina."

Everyone had lost the energy to speak. They felt as if their hearts were bound and shackled as they rode through the remains of the ancient forest that had provided shelter to Amanda and her friends countless times and had been home to so many creatures. The once verdant forest was reduced to smouldering ashes, blackened tree trunks, and lifeless sticks of charcoal that reached for the sky like lost souls. The voices of the wildlife that once dwelt there had been silenced, as many of them had perished in the blaze. After a seemingly endless ride, the lingering smoke lifted reviling Adelaide's cottage as it stood untouched on the small knoll above the gurgling brook, like a promise of a better tomorrow.

Amanda slid off her horse and ran to the cottage, where she embraced Adelaide and broke into tears "We lost her, Adelaide, we lost Faerydae," she cried burying her face into Adelaide's shoulder and clinging onto her tightly, as if she was drowning in the grief over the loss of her friend. "I know, I know, mo chridhe," Adelaide comforted her. "Ghilli Duh told us what happened. I can't even begin to tell you how sad we all are over the senseless death of

Faerydae, but I am so glad that you all have returned safely. You should rest, my love, you look exhausted. Come on, I'll get you some food that will help you to calm down."

"That is a marvellous idea, do you have enough food for all of our men, Adelaide?" William asked as he stepped into the cottage.

"Aye, William I do, Ross brought enough meat to last for weeks, and Peter filled my pantry with enough bread and scones to feed two armies. I'll ask Madge and Julia to set up the food for you and your men in the barn."

"Thank you so much, Adelaide. Tell me, is that Marianne I saw as we came over the bridge?" William asked.

"Aye the guild members freed her just after you all left. The Laird's guards brought her out of the castle to hang her in the market square two days earlier than planned. I guess Lord Dougal was eager to get rid of her, but she'll tell you all about it herself, come along. Maighread can't wait to see you," said Adelaide. She took William's hand and pulled him into the kitchen to greet to Maighread.

"Oh William, my love I was so worried about you! Where is Amanda?"

"I am right here, Granny," shouted Amanda as she came running into the kitchen.

"Amanda, my bonnie lass, I am so happy that you are unhurt! But you look tired, come over here and rest while I get you a bowl of the stew you two love so much.

"Aye mum," William agreed. "You do that, but then you and Adelaide have to come with me so that I can introduce you to my grandfather, Lord Clyde MacDougal. He is waiting in the barn for you. So please give Amanda her bowl and come along," he placed his arms around Maighread and Adelaide and led them to the barn, where Lord MacDougal was engaged in a lively conversation with John and Bhaltair.

"Grandfather, please excuse the interruption, but I would like you to meet the two women that saved my life,

raised me, and made me the man I am today,"
William said with trembling lips.

"I am honoured to meet you, Maighread and Adelaide. I will be forever grateful for your selfless devotion to my daughter, and for raising my grandson with love and tender care. He has truly become a righteous young man," said Lord MacDougal, kneeling before Adelaide and Maighread and bowing his head in gratitude.

"I thought a MacDougall bows to no one," whispered William in his grandfather's ear and smiled.

"Oh no my Lord, please get up, we are honoured that your daughter entrusted William's life and wellbeing to us. We love him dearly, and we are so grateful that you are finally united," answered Maighread taking the Lords' hand and pulling him up.

"What a glorious day, let us give thanks and celebrate! Lift our tankards in honour of the friends that are here with us today, the ones we lost and to a new beginning. Slainte mhath shouted Bhaltair as he lifted his tankard.

"Slainte mhath, my dear friends and companions! Let us all enjoy this special day and thank our generous hosts for their hospitality, good food, and wine. But let us also not forget why we came and that our mission is not yet complete. So eat, drink, and rest for a while!" cheered Lord MacDougall, pointing to the large table in the middle of the barn that had been stacked with the most sumptuous food wine and ale. "Tomorrow, we ride on to Kilchurn Castle to put an end to the torment that was brought over these good people."

Amanda and Ursula had found a cosy place in a pile of straw, away from all the excited laughter and heated discussions. The girls were lost in thought.

"Amanda, do you remember the cold morning when we first met Ralston right here in the barn?"

"Aye, I do. Look how much has happened since," answered Amanda sleepily. She closed her eyes and tried to forget about all horrors they had met since that day in the barn, the loss of Nissa and Faerydae were fresh in her mind.

"I am so relieved to see that the fire did not reach the cottage and that you all remained unharmed," sighed Hugh as he poured some red wine for Adelaide.

"Aye Hugh, the enchantments protected us from the blaze, but it consumed Eredine Forest and claimed the life of Faerydae which is an act of unspeakable cruelty."

"Do you know what happened, Adelaide?"

"Aye, we all do. We saw Lord Dougal and his troops at the edge of the forest and overheard as he ordered a group of Red Caps to set fire to the forest. I believe he intended to flush us out of the cottage, but little did he know that the charms that protect the cottage are by far more powerful than anything that he could muster. He was furious when he realised that his plan had failed. "

"Do you know where he is now?"

"Aye, we do. Two of Julia's guards, followed him to Kilchurn Castle and found out that he brought the Laird to Dalmally, to speak to the peasants and guild members," said Bhaltair, who had overheard Hugh and Adelaide.

"And have they done so?" Hugh asked.

"Not yet, as all of them were busy in the fields and in their workshops. But the lamplighter was sent out to invite them to a general assembly at the Guild Hall around sunset today, and they will be there, you can be sure of that. The guild members know what Lord Dougal has done to the injured soldiers, and they will not let the opportunity pass to make him and the coward Laird pay for it."

"What are you talking about, Bhaltair?" inquired William with concern.

"I am talking about the vicious murder of twenty soldiers. Ross's son Lukas was the only survivor. He had gotten suspicious of the Lord's sudden generosity and did not drink the wine they were served which saved him. Not long after the men that had the wine they began to tremble, curl up in pain and had trouble breathing. Lukas knew what that meant, as he had seen these symptoms in cows and horses before. He burned his pile of straw and hid behind the banners next to the doors just before the Lord's servants entered to collect the bodies. While he waited for the opportune moment to make a run for the drawbridge, he overheard them mocking the deceased and discussing what they would do to the maids before they are sent off to the caves of Wemyss."

"These vile acts will have an end. I will make sure of it!" William declared, outraged. "But it will be me who will put an end to this, not the guild members. Grandfather, we have to ride to Dalmally now to prevent a massacre. Lady Julia, you have to return to Kilchurn Castle to claim your place as the rightful Lady of Glenorchy now that Duane has left. We have to cut him off from all supplies and refuge!" William declared. He got on the back of his horse and galloped across the bridge with flying huffs. Lord MacDougal and his men dropped everything, flung themselves on their horses, and dashed behind William.

27 THE CAVES OF WEMYSS

Amanda was not in the mood to celebrate. The excited chatter and laughter were more than she could handle right now, the grief over Faerydae's dead and the destruction of Eredine forest still felt too raw. Instead, she hid in a large pile of straw, curled up in her blanket and fell into a deep sleep. In her dreams, she relived the escape from Kilchurn Castle, the Boobrie's attack, Nissa's and Faerydae's death but also the happy moments when William embraced his grandfather and the elation on Anne's face as the Galleon pulled out of Oban harbour.

"Amanda, wake up, there is no time to sleep right now. We have to make our way to Wemyss," whispered Ralston and shook her gently. He deeply regretted having to wake her, her face was so relaxed, and a faint smile lingered on her lips. But he had no choice. They had to seize the opportunity to take possession of the Sapphire and free the captives while Lord Dougal focused on Dalmally.

"What are you saying, Ralston? We're riding to Wemyss now?"

"Aye, that is exactly what Ralston was saying, Amanda," Ursula confirmed. "Come on, you sleepy head, you missed all the excitement."

"How long have I been asleep? What excitement have I missed? You are not referring to all ruckuses you guys made while I was trying to get some sleep, right?" asked Amanda as she sat up and rubbed her eyes open?

"Oh dear Amanda, that's exactly what I am talking about! Come on, stretch your legs, we have to go," cheered Ursula. She picked up Amanda's scabbard and handed it to Hugh before she rushed out of the barn to help Ralston with the horses.

"Damn, what's the great hurry? Why are you all acting so crazy?"

"Don't fret Amanda, I'll explain everything, come on, grab my hand, I'll help you up," chortled Hugh, pulling her to her feet.

"Thanks, Hugh. I am feeling kinda stiff, it's not very comfortable to sleep in the armour," moaned Amanda. She stretched and looked around. "Where is everybody?"

"Well, William and his grandfather left for Dalmally, Lady Julia rounded up her guards and is on her way to Kilchurn Castle, and you already know where we are heading," Hugh explained.

"Aye, that part I know, and trust me when I say that I can hardly wait to get there, but the rest of it needs some unravelling, which I hope you'll do once we are on our way."

"I will Amanda, but we have to get going, Ursula, and Ralston just left to check something out," urged Hugh and helped her in the saddle. Amanda and Hugh took one last look at the cottage before they forced their horses into a quick trot. They dashed through the woods, past Dalmally, and caught up with Ralston and Ursula in a small birch grove overlooking the River Lochy outside of Tyndrum.

"What are you looking at, Ralston? Are you contemplating passing through Tyndrum?" asked Amanda.

"No, we stopped so that I could take a closer look at the group of boats heading for Dalmally," Ralston explained.

"Why, what is so special about them? Don't you think that the men are just eager to get an early start in setting up their wares for the market tomorrow? After all, it's Beltane, and the market will be crowded with vendors from all the surrounding villages."

"Aye, right, and for the special celebration of Beltane they are selling wood axes and swords made of scythes, right?" replied Ralston with sarcastic laughter as he pointed down to the passing boats.

"Goodness, I did not see that! What do you think they are planning to do with these primitive weapons?" Amanda asked clearly disturbed by what she saw.

"I suspect they plan to join Lord Dougal to fight side by side with his men and the Red Caps. He lures prisoners and peasants into his service with the promise of freedom and land and these desperate fools fall for it, leave their families and run into their own demise."

"This is horrible, they haven't got a chance against well-trained soldiers, they will be slaughtered like cattle!"

"Aye Amanda it is high time to end this. But to do that we might have to fight men like these in the caves of Wemyss and on our way to the Blue Glacier. You must promise me not to hesitate or show mercy to these men, they don't deserve your pity, they are driven by bloodlust and greed," insisted Ralston looking sternly at Amanda, Hugh, and Ursula.

After a moment of contemplating the grim fate of these men, the friends turned their backs on Tyndrum and continued their journey. They trudged determinedly through woods, across valleys covered with heather, and along fields of barley and rye. A balmy breeze caressed their faces and ruffled their hair as the sun began to set over Ben Lomond.

After an arduous journey throughout the night and over rugged terrain, the horses and the travellers were exhausted. The friends decided to take a rest and began to scan their surroundings for shelter. As soon as the first rays of the rising sun lit up the valley, the friends noticed a dreary old cottage behind a group of large oak trees.

Exhausted and hungry, they slid off their horses, and tied them on a small pasture behind the crumbling cottage. Hugh walked up to the weather-beaten door and knocked gently before he opened it ever so slightly to peep inside. Judging by the cottage's neglected outer appearance he expected to see broken furniture and rats rushing around. But to his great surprise, the cottage was clean and cosy. Bedding made of fresh hay had been placed along the walls, a large cauldron hung over brightly glowing embers, and a basket with bannocks and bread stood on a table near the fireplace.

"Now that's a surprise, I could have sworn that the cottage was abandoned. The way it looks, its owner must be close by why else would there be a kettle on the fire? " exclaimed Amanda as she slipped past Hugh into the cottage.

"Oh dear, the mutton stew seems ready to eat, what do you think folks would they mind if we have some?"

"Aye, young Master Hugh, go on," replied a soft voice. "I prepared it for you all, have as much as you like. And then make yourselves comfortable in the hay."

The friends took a step back and scanned the cottage curiously to see who had spoken.

"Oh dear, come on and show yourself! My friends will not harm you," laughed Ralston. He lay down his weapons and stretched comfortably out on a pile of hay.

"Aye very well Lord Ralston as you wish," stammered the delicate voice. A shy Brownie girl, dressed in a long brown and green dress, appeared from behind the door and lowered to a curtsey.

"My goodness! Please forgive me for staring at you, but you are the first Brownie I've met, my name is Amanda, and I am delighted to meet you," beamed Amanda. She bent down to shake the Brownies tiny hand.

"My name is Nala, and I am honoured to meet you all," whispered the wee Brownie and dropped another curtsey

"Did you do all this by yourself?" asked Ursula in admiration.

"No, not really," replied Nala. She turned around and pulled two other Brownies out of the shadows. "These are my brothers, Ben and Fen. They cleaned the cottage and brought the hay, but I did all the cooking, just as Lord Asanopirh asked me to do. He and Lady Sorcha await you at the edge of the dark forest, and Master Bilobeal will join you near the cave's entrance."

"Thank you for the message, Nala. And thank you of course for all the hard work you and your brothers have done," said Amanda. She took off her scabbard and sat down next to Ralston.

"You three have done a marvellous job. The cottage is spotless, and the stew smells heavenly my mouth is beginning to water, I can't wait to try it," exclaimed Hugh and rubbed his palms together in high expectation.

"Blimey, you sound just like Glen," giggled Ursula and patted his shoulder.

"What about a shot of ale before we serve the food?" suggested Fen as he handed each of them a tankard filled to the brim with refreshing ale.

"That's a brilliant idea me wee lad, but you should drink with us!" replied Hugh and smacked his lips.

"Sorry sir, we have to decline. We'll take care of the horses and then leave so that you can rest. We'll return by nightfall with provisions for your journey to Wemyss and make sure that all traces of your presence have been removed," said Ben as he filled four large wooden bowls with steaming hot stew.

Well-fed and content the friends rolled up in their soft blankets, closed their eyes, and fell asleep. Their breaths slowed, and the expressions on their faces gave way from strain and stress to peace.

The day passed, and soon its golden light began to make way for the deep blue night sky when the friends woke and started to stir.

"Oh, that felt good," sighed Hugh, gave a big yawn and stretched like a cat. "All I need now is a wee bit of stew before we head out what about you folks?"

"Same here. And while you go for the stew, fetch some water, will you? I am really thirsty," said Ursula. She got up and brushed the hay from her jerkin.

"No need to trouble yourself, master Hugh, we placed

food and water in your satchels." Fen appeared. "Your horses are fed and saddled so that you can continue your journey without delay," the Brownie bowed and pointed to his brother Ben, who held the door open for the friends.

"That's very kind of you! Although I'll admit it somehow feels as if you were trying to get rid of us…" Hugh said with a cheeky smile.

"Oh no, not at all Master Hugh!" replied Fen nervously and blushed. "But we got word that about twenty armed men left Dalmally for the caves of Wemyss around midday, so we thought it would be wise to act swiftly."

"You are right Fen, thanks for the warning, but tell me, where is Ralston?" asked Amanda as she left the cottage.

"He is waiting for you behind the cottage, take good care and be safe we will see you and your friends again soon," answered Fen with a bow.

Hugh, Amanda, and Ursula run the last check on their weapons. As they walked around the cottage and stumbled into Ralston, who had just appeared out of the darkness right in front of them.

"Sorry, I did not intend to startle you, but we have to make haste. You heard Fen, we must cross Ben Lomond while the moon is high in the sky," said Ralston, handing them their reins mounted his horse and sped away from the cottage.

It was almost midday when the friends finally reached the edge of the dark forest. The journey across Ben Lomond had been extremely challenging the trail was steep and narrow, with straight rock walls on one side and an almost vertical drop on the other. The friends had decided to dismount and lead the horses across by foot.

"Crivens, that was a grind. I hope we don't have to use the same trail on our way back," remarked Hugh as he dismounted his horse.

"I don't think we will," Amanda said. "It would be faster if we take one of Lord MacDougal's galleons to return the sapphire."

"Aye right, I had completely forgotten that we have a fleet of ships at our service!" he replied with relief. But we have to get it first, has anyone seen Sorcha or Asanopirh?"

"I haven't seen Sorcha yet, but Asanopirh is right behind you, turn around," declared Amanda as she pointed to a bright, blinding silhouette on a wooded bluff.

"Blimey! Now I truly understand the meaning of his name. I most certainly would not want to be his enemy, that gleaming armour will surely be the last thing you ever saw," remarked Hugh through squinted eyes.

"Our horses will not enter the dark forest, so we have to leave them with Ben, Fen, and Nala," whispered Sorcha in Hugh's ear.

"Crivens, Sorcha, you startled me!" exclaimed Hugh with a shudder, placing his hand on his heart.

"You better calm your nerves before we enter the forest. It is not a place for the faint-hearted," laughed Sorcha squeezing Hugh's shoulder.

"Come on Sorcha, I am not faint-hearted, and you know that," protested Hugh, and handed his reins to Nala.

"Very well Hugh, we all know that you're not don't worry. But before we enter the forest, I have to caution you all not to touch anything the forest has been poisoned and is dying," Asanopirh instructed. His voice was hard as metal, and his eyes mirrored the anger that roared inside him.The friends felt as if they stepped into icy waters as they entered the dark forest. A dense and pungent mist rose from the ground, obstructing their vision and burning their throats and nostrils with every breath.

"Blood bas, I can't breathe," mouthed Ursula, dropping to her knees in a violent cough.

"Oh Ursula, I am very sorry! We forgot that you are mortals," whispered Sorcha as she ripped strips of cloth from her cloak and handed them to the three friends. "Here, take this and place it over your mouth and nose our cloaks block dark magic and poison, but I would still advise you to wear your gloves and to pull the blankets over your heads," she added in a hushed voice as she made sure that the strips of cloth had been tied appropriately.

"Let's use hand signals from here on, we don't want to alert the guards," mouthed Ralston after he got the all-clear from Sorcha. The friends rushed through the doomed forest like fleeting shadows, without making a sound or leaving a trace. There was no sign of life anywhere no bird's song or chirping crickets not even the sound of rustling leaves. The forest floor was sodden and covered with decaying limbs, dead, twisted vines hung from the trees like snakes. Noxious black and yellow lichens encrusted the trees and shrubs, draining them of their last drops of life's essence.

"Stop," hissed Asanopirh. He pointed to the cave's entrance. It was framed by massive roots of a huge oak tree that towered on a massive rock before them.

"Majestic, isn't she? You should have seen her when she was healthy and strong now the ancient one is fading away," whispered Ghilli Duh as he ran his hands gently over the trees gnarled roots.

"We did not expect to see you here, Ghilli Duh. It must be tough for you to see what has been done to these woods," whispered Asanopirh as he greeted the almighty spirit of the forest.

"Aye, Asanopirh, it makes me shudder. But I had to come and see if there was anything the Dryads or I can do to set things right again we have not given up hope yet."

"Did you bring Laratbogh and Oren with you?" Amanda asked searching the trees for any sign of her friends.

"I'm afraid that would be too dangerous at this point in time I wouldn't risk their wellbeing. But rest assured, they will nurture the forest back to life once you have driven the murderous scum out of here."

"Oh that we'll Ghilli Duh, you can be sure of it," insisted Bilobeal as he stepped out of the cave.

"How lovely to see you Bilobeal we were just about to enter," whispered Amanda and bowed to Bilobeal.

"Are you on your own, or did you bring your brothers?" Ralston asked as he embraced his comrade.

"Aye, Sabaltalab and Phaervlon are inside scoping out the passages leading to the inner caves. They should return at any moment - that is, if they haven't been discovered…"

"Discovered? By who? You are not talking about us, dear brother?" joked Sabaltalab in a hushed voice as he and Phaervlon appeared in the cave's entrance.

"Och, what happened to your beautiful amber coloured armour Sabaltalab? And your emerald green jerkin Phaervlon? Why are you dressed in black today?" giggled Sorcha.

"We thought it would be wise not to stick out like a sore thumb. After all, we will be dealing with some truly nasty vermin here."

"Aye you are right, Phaervlon, your copper hair is bright enough. But tell me, what did you see?"

"About thirty Red Caps overseeing the mine workers, and another fifteen armed men are guarding the Sapphire and Gregor's cell," Phaervlon informed them. But to tell you the truth, Sorcha, they are easy targets."

"What makes you think that?" asked Ralston as he stepped closer to the three heavily armed Drows.

"Because they are wasted, Ralston! All these fools do is sit and drink while boasting what they will do with the riches they made guarding the caves."

"Let's not waste precious time then! Bilobeal, since you and your brothers already know the tunnels, you should go ahead and clear the way for Ralston, Hugh, and the lassies," Asanopirh declared. "Sorcha and I'll take care of the guards, get the Sapphire and free Gregor."

"Aye, Asanopirh," replied Bilobeal before rushing with his brothers into the caves, closely followed by Hugh.

"Be safe, Hugh. Please don't do anything stupid," whispered Ursula wiping tears from her eyes.

"I will, I promise," replied Hugh and threw Ursula a kiss as he ran after the three Drows.

It only took Hugh a few steps into the cave to realised how thankful he and his friends should be for their soft suede boots the loud clatter of their old boots would have echoed through the caverns and given them away in a heartbeat.

"Stay close to the walls, Hugh. The guards could hear you when you walk through the puddles," muttered Sabaltalab, pointing to the shallow water-filled holes in the cave's floor.

"Aye, but tell me what's that sweet smell?"

"It's arsenic, in other words, the smell of death. No one would be able to survive in here for long, but Lord Dougal does not care, he just roams the land and abducts strong, young men, and women for the work in his copper mines," replied Sabaltalab in a hushed voice pointing to the green veins in the cave's walls.

How many of the lassies will still be alive and able to make the journey back home? He wondered. *What did Ralston say about mercy for the Lord's servants? Well, they will not get any from me, that's for bloody sure they gave up the right to live when they agreed to guard these caves,* he thought biting his lip so hard that he broke through the skin. Small drops of blood trickled down his chin and were about to drop.

"Blimey, Hugh are you bonkers!" hissed Bilobeal when he saw Hugh's bloodied chin. "The Red Caps can smell blood from miles away! Here, take this, it will stop the bleeding let's just hope they are not hungry today."

Hugh looked ashamed at Bilobeal when he realised that his anger could have cost them their lives. *You have to get it together you eejit, calm yourself and breathe slowly just as Faerydae taught you,* he thought, taking the leaves from Bilobeal and pressing them between his lips.

Amanda followed close behind and suspiciously scanned the tunnel walls for holes or narrow spaces in which Red Caps or armed men could be lurking. She was surprised to see elaborate drawings and strange markings all over the tunnel walls. She turned to Ralston and whispered, "Have you ever seen anything like that before?"

"Aye, these are drawings from my ancestors that used to live in these caves. But you should not allow yourself to be distracted, keep your eyes fixed on the tunnels for any shadows," mouthed Ralston and walked ahead of Amanda.

It is so quiet, too quiet for my taste, she thought, holding her breath and listening harder. *Someone or something is close... it cannot be Ursula, as she is further behind.* She could hear breathing close to her. She steadied herself and pretended to be unaware of her pursuer. She stopped to bend forward as if she were fastening the laces on her boots. In a swift movement, she gripped the dragon tooth handles of her swords and drew them with a deadly whistling sound from her scabbards. She extended her arms and whirled through the narrow cave like a lethal Blizzard.

She was swirling so fast that it was hard to make out her form. Her blades flashed like lightning as she slashed everything near her. Sparks sprayed as the blades hit the cave's walls, while a blinding white light emanated from her and illuminated the tunnels. She had a deadly focus on anything that moved and remained ice cold, but there were no more shadows, the air was stifling hot, and the smell of sulfur and blood filled her lungs. Yellow ashes had tinted the walls all around her, confirming that her intuition had just saved their lives.

The eerie silence returned. There was no other breathing than hers, so she decided to wait for Ursula, leaning against the wall to calm herself. *This is taking too long, what is she doing? Did she fall or...* Amanda did not dare to finish that thought and ran back to look for Ursula. The most horrific images flashed before her eyes, and a singular, cold fear filled her chest.

"Ursula, where are you?" she whispered. She held her breath and listened into the deserted tunnel for a reply.

"I am here Amanda I can't walk, you'll have to go on without me. I'll be okay."

"Damn you, Ursula, how could I go on when I know that you are hurt? Where are you? I can't see you," replied Amanda in a trembling voice. She hastened towards Ursula's voice. She nearly choked on her own breath when she saw her best friend lying on the ground in a puddle of yellow tinted water, her jerking wrapped around one of her legs.

"Damn, damn, what happened Ursula? How bad is it?"

"A bloody Red Cap came out from nowhere and slashed my leg! But I got the bastard. He must have thought he'd finished me and leaned right into my dirk. He looked very surprised just before he dissolved into this," whispered Ursula and tried to smile.

"We have to get you out of here, can you walk?"

"I don't know, I'll try. But we have to be careful that no blood will soak through, you heard what Bilobeal told Hugh."

"Aye, I think we will be okay. Your jerkin seems like it's holding up. Come on, lean on me." Amanda and Ursula made it back to the cave's entrance where they were met by Ghilli Duh.

"Hurry back in, Amanda, I'll take good care of her, don't you worry," said Ghilli Duh. He wrapped his cloak around Ursula and disappeared. Amanda took a few deep breaths before she ran back into the cave to catch up with Ralston. There were yellow ashes and pikestaffs everywhere. *Blimey, we must have wiped out half of them already. I wonder how the lads are doing,* Amanda thought as she rounded one of the last corners and ran straight into Ralston's arms.

"Crivens Amanda, you had me worried. Are you all right? Where is Ursula? Come on, we have to hurry back, Bilobeal is waiting on us."

"Aye Ralston I am sorry, it was not my intention to worry you, but Ursula got hurt, so I had to get her out. I'll tell you later what happened, let's get back to the guys."

"It's about bloody time," Bilobeal exclaimed when the duo reappeared. "Come on you two, we have to make a move while half the group of Red Caps is gone. We should be done and out before they return."

"They will not return, don't worry Bilobeal, Amanda and Ursula took care of them. Let's finish the rest and then get everybody out of here," replied Ralston.

"Brilliant. But wait, where is my bonnie lass Ursula?" inquired Bilobeal. He walked three steps back into the tunnel,"

"She got hurt, so I had to bring out, Ghilli Duh took her to safety. Come on, let's go and finish these bastards off," hissed Amanda as she pulled her blades and walked over to Hugh who stood in the middle of the cave like a rock in human form fearless and ready to kill.

Hugh held two arrows between his fingers, pulled the bowstring and took a deep breath before he aimed at two Red Caps facing each other in a deep conversation. *They won't even know what hit them,* he thought as he released the sinew. The arrow's hissed through the air and hit the two Red Caps with such a force that the cloud of yellow ashes sprayed in all directions. He quickly placed another arrow between his fingers and scanned the cave for the next target. His rage over Ursula's injury had grown like a fire in a furnace all he wanted was to make them pay.

"Blimey Hugh, now that was a nice shot! Leave some for us will you," laughed Sabaltalab. He ran towards a group of Red Caps, swinging his axes with such a force that he severed their heads from the bodies with one strike.

"Ralston, you go on and take Amanda to her father. Phaervlon and I will get the other captives out of here Sabaltalab and Hugh are having so much fun cleaning up that I think we can leave the rest to them. See you outside," Bilobeal smirked as he ran off towards the cavern where the captives were held.

"You heard him Amanda let's go! According to Sabaltalab, your father's cell is next to vault with the Sapphire. I am sure Asanopirh and Sorcha have taken care of the guards by now," said Ralston. He took Amanda's hand and pulled her through the labyrinth of tunnels. They reached the cavern just as Asanopirh and Sorcha were about to unlatch the door to Gregor's cell.

"Please let me," Amanda asked, breathing fast. She took a moment to steady herself, and then removed the heavy cast iron bar form the door with trembling hands. The door swung open and gave way to total darkness.

"Ralston, hand me a torch. I can't see a thing," shouted Amanda looking fearful.

"I'll come in with you, Amanda. I am sure he is okay," said Ralston in a calming voice. He placed his arm around her shoulders and walked with her into the pitch black cell.

"Father, it's me, Amanda, where are you? I have come to bring you home. Please, show yourself." Amanda called out, trying her best to keep her voice from trembling.

"Amanda, mo ghràdh I am here. You came to free me, everything will be fine now."

Amanda listened hard and tried to follow the voice. She lowered the torch and saw a frail man with long matted hair leaning against the wall trying to stand. She could not move or speak. Tears streamed from her eyes, and she began to shake violently.

"Sorcha, take Amanda out of here while Asanopirh and I take care of Gregor. We don't know how many of these wretched men are left in the caves," Ralston instructed, releasing Amanda into Sorcha's arms before he addressed Gregor.

"We have to place something over your eyes, Gregor, so that the light will not blind you. Give me your hand, we will get you out of here," whispered Ralston. He placed his cloak over Gregor's head and shoulders before he and

Asanopirh carried him out of his cold and callous prison.

Slowly, they made their way out of the caves, emerging into the light to meet Ghilli Duh and the others, who had been waiting for them.

"Well, it appears to me that you got all the captives out. Let me make certain that no one followed you or spread the word of what happened here today. You better step back," Ghilli Duh said. He looked up to the mighty oak, raised his arms, and whispered an enchantment.

The oak began to moan and creak as she loosened her grip on the granite rocks beneath her towering stem. Soil and gravel began to trickle through her roots like grains of sand through an hourglass, counting down the last moments of her long life before she finally fell with a deafening roar taking the massive boulders with her and burying the cave's entrance.

As the last boulder came to a rest and the cloud of dust and debris finally settled. Amanda breathed a sigh of relief. She appeared calm and composed, but deep down her emotions of triumph and horror battled for dominance. Her hands were trembling, and her heart thumped so loudly that she was sure everyone around her could hear it.

After she had steadied herself, she looked at the group of captives again. Their eyes were half open, and glassy. They appeared to look past her. Their hollow cheeks, boney forearms and hands showed Amanda that they have been starving for a long time. Their once rosy skin was now red and covered with lesions andwarts.

"I can't make out any of my friends, Ralston. I don't know these lassies, and my father might not have the strength to make the journey," cried Amanda and closed her eyes.

"Give it time Amanda. Nala, Ben, and Fen will take them back to the cottage where Lady Brigid will help them to regain their health and strength. You have to trust that everything will turn out well," whispered Ralston as he pulled her into his arms.

28 THE CHANGE OF TIDES

William urged his horse into a gallop and dashed through the forest with flying huffs closely followed by his grandfather and his men. He was hoping to reach the Guildhall before things got out of hand. He knew the guild's members would not stand a chance against the Laird's heavily armed men and Lord Dougal's dark powers. Shortly before they reached Dalmally, his grandfather caught up with him and signed for him to stop.

"William, me lad, let us rest for a moment to plan our approach. We cannot afford to take chances if we want to avoid casualties. I suggest that two of our men ride into Dalmally and check the situation before we enter."

"Aye Grandfather, whom would you like to send?"

"Seamus and my commander James they are getting ready right now and could be in, and out of Dalmally before nightfall. While they do what they must, we can get the horses' hooves wrapped with cloth so that we can ride in without making a sound."

"That's a bloody brilliant idea!" Well then, let's send James and Seamus in and get to work. We have quite a few huffs to wrap, but what are we going to use?" laughed William as he slid off his horse.

"Well James thought of that and brought a bale of sackcloth, after all, this is not our first takeover, me lad," chuckled Lord MacDougall, giving his commander the sign to leave.

"Perfect, I am ready to start wrapping when you are."

"My men will take care of the horses, we have more important things to do. Let's walk up that knoll while we talk, I need to stretch my legs a bit I am getting to old for long days in the saddle," remarked the Lord resting a hand on William's shoulder for support.

They walked over a tree-covered knoll on to a flowery meadow, where countless tiny fireflies glittered like a shower of sparks in clumps of blossoming hawthorn and rowan trees.

"Grandfather, I think we should split the men into two groups and enter Dalmally from both sides. That way, we can gain control of the two the gates and the market square before the Laird's troops even know what hit them."

"Ayem that is a bloody brilliant idea, William! That's precisely what we shall to do, we must avoid any confrontation that could harm unarmed villagers," replied the Lord. He was about to return to his men when the commander's servant came running towards him.

"My Lord, the commander has returned and would like to speak with you."

"By all means, send him up, my good man. Tell me is Seamus back too?"

"Aye my Lord, both of them have returned and strapped back on their armours," answered the servant as he bowed and backed away.

"Sir William, my Lord, I am happy to report that we should be able to unarm the Laird's men without a fight, as they are presently going from house to house pillaging and have their hands tied up carrying their plunder."

"Bastards! Men, get in the saddle and put an end to that," He addresses his soldiers. "Seamus, you enter through the North Gate and make sure that no one slips through your fingers. And James, you know what to do, I want the village cleaned out, while William and I attend the gathering in the guildhall. Meet us there with a handful of your men once you're done."

"Aye my Lord, it should not take long. See you at the Guildhall," responded the commander bowing briefly before he rounded up his men and hastened towards

Dalmally. William and his grandfather mounted their horses and cantered slowly towards the village to give Seamus and his men time to take control of the north gate before they entered the village.

"This way Grandfather. We best use the backroads and enter the Guildhall through the cellar. That way we can remain hidden and observe what's going till the right moment presents itself."

"Aye right, go on then and lead the way, me lad."

William slowed his horse and guided his grandfather through the meandering narrow alleys to the back of the Guildhall.

"Here we are," whispered William and gestured his grandfather to dismount. They tied their horses behind some heavy-laden carriages before he lifted the trapdoor to the cellar. The two men lowered themselves with the pulley and begun to inch their way through the dimly lit cavernous basement past piles of barrels and unstable looking stacks of crates.

The beaten earth floor was soggy and covered with broken glass forcing the two men to step gingerly so as not to make any noise or risk nasty cuts. It took them quite a while before they reached some narrow unstable-looking steps that lead up to the guild's Great Hall. William climbed up first and silently pushed two floorboards apart to listen to the conversation.

"William, me lad, be careful. Don't push them too far we don't want to be discovered before the opportune moment has arrived," whispered the Lord as he tried to find a secure footing on the narrow steps.

"Don't worry, we are behind the counter. The only one that might notice the planks being out of place is Marisell, and this will tell her to keep quiet about it," replied William as he slipped a red scrap of cloth through the narrow opening.

"What did you do that for? Do you think she will understand the meaning of it?"

"Aye, she will, Grandfather. I learned that from Amanda, this is how she messages her friends, and Marisell is one of them," replied William with a broad smile and signalled his grandfather to listen.

"My dear Laird, we are deeply honoured by your visit today," exclaimed Angus as he raised his tankard. "It has been a long time since last you shared a drink with us, so please allow us to toast to your wellbeing, *Slainte mhath*!"

"Thank you, Angus, my good man, and thank you all for being here tonight. But before we announce the reason for this gathering, I would like to present to you my counsellor and fatherly friend, Lord Dougal," announced the Laird bowing to Lord Dougal.

Angus bent his head ever so slightly to Lord Dougal in acknowledgement but did not address him nor raise his tankard to salute him. He noticed how the tension was building. The Guild members were shifting restlessly on their benches, so he decided to stop the pleasantries and ask straight why the Laird had come and why he thought it necessary to bring an advisor.

"Ah, I can see that you like straight talk and I respect that. So then let me tell you why we are here today my honourable Guild Master," replied Lord Dougal with a nasty sneer. "We are here to solicit your help. Aye, you heard me correctly we need your help. As you most certainly know, your noble Laird has been attacked

His wife and daughter were snatched from Kilchurn Castle and are presently being held against their will. Many of our brave soldiers lost their lives in an attempt to free them. You all will agree I am sure, that we can't remain idle and leave their death unavenged. But with your help and that of your sons, we shall put an end to this lawlessness and reunite the Laird with his Lady and his beloved daughter."

"William, we have to act. The room is ready to explode."

"Aye Grandfather, I believe I just saw Seamus and

James enter the hall, let's go."

William pushed the two planks further apart, lifted himself up and hid under the counter before he gently tugged Marisell's skirt to alert her of their presence. She dropped her towel and stooped down pretending to pick it back up.

"I saw your message, and I am glad that you are here to put an end to this," she whispered. "The members have heard more than enough and are ready to strike. Each and every one is armed and ready. Best stay behind me while I check out the six men that have just entered the hall."

"Never mind them, they are our men. You best get out of the way, I would not like to see you getting injured me, bonnie lass," said Lord MacDougall and helped Marisell climb down into the cellar. William slid the planks back into their place and stepped out from behind the counter, closely followed by his grandfather.

"You are a liar and impostor Duane, and you Sir, are no Lord. You are a cold-blooded murderer anddeceiver," shouted William to the hall. He drew his sword and walked up to the platform where Lord Dougal and Duane were seated.

"How dear you threaten me, William!" screamed the Laird on top of his voice, jumping up from his seat. "You are an escaped prisoner, guards, take hold of the innkeeper and throw him back into the dungeons where he belongs."

"You are the one who belongs in the dungeon," roared Lord MacDougall, jumping on to the platform. "You are a bastard and a fraud of a man. Look at your wretched father right beside you, the self-proclaimed Lord Dougal. He was called Douglas when he came to my castle begging for food and shelter, which I granted him. He worked as a stable hand at my castle in Oban until my beloved daughter Sarah wed Lord Colin Campbell of Glenorchy. I ordered him to accompany her as her envoy to Kilchurn Castle, and he deserted her." He grabbed the false Lord by his tunic, lifted him up and spit in his face before he threw him off the platform.

At that moment all hell broke loose in the guild hall. The Laird pulled his dagger and tried to attack Lord MacDougall but was stopped by Seamus with a nasty blow to his face. Two of the castle's guards made a feeble attempt to fight the commander back but realised quickly that they would not survive that mistake and made a run for the door where they were met by Lord MacDougall's men. William and Angus had their hands full trying to stop the guild members from ripping Duane to shreds and did not notice that Lord Dougal had used the turmoil for his escape. Only after the false Laird had been tied to his chair and the men had returned to their benches did they notice that he had fled.

"Blood basm where is that depraved creature! Did he get past you, Seamus? James, can you see him anywhere?"

"No my Lord, he must have slipped out through the cellar," shouted James. He flung himself over the counter and disappeared in pursuit of their target.

"Seamus, I need your help. That cowardice slime has stabbed the lassie, come and help me to bring her up."

Seamus and James lifted Marisell out of the cellar and carried her to the large table in the centre of the hall, They carefully rested her on a pile of cloaks the members had spread out to comfort her. She had a deep stab wound in her right shoulder which bled profusely.

"Lukas, come me lad take our carriage and get Marianne and Adelaide. We have no time to lose if we want to save her life," shouted Ross and pushed his son out the door.

"Angus, we leave the situation in your hands while we give chase to Lord Dougal. I am sure that he is on his way to Kilchurn to take over the castle and if he succeeds, he would most certainly try to kill Lady Julia. Please look after Marisell and don't let Duane escape!" exclaimed William before he and his grandfather stormed out of the Guildhall followed by their men.

*

Lord Dougal was fuming with rage, as he left Dalmally. *Did this stupid lass honestly believe that she could stop me? Could it be true that that weasel of a man, is, in fact, my son,* he thought as he crossed the drawbridge of Kilchurn Castle.

"Up the bridge and take your positions on the wall-walk, I hereby order you to kill anyone who dares to approach," he commanded.

The guards were not brave enough to ask for the whereabouts of the Laird, nor question Lord Dougal's orders. They hurriedly lifted the massive bridge before they took positions on the castle's walls, wondering who would be bold enough to attempt an attack.

Lord Dougal stormed across the bailey and into the Great Hall, with his cloak flying behind him like a raven's wings. He was determined to claim Lordship over Glenorchy when he saw Julia in the Lairds chair at the end of the Great Hall. He could not believe his eyes and had to draw a deep breath to suppress his fury over her sudden resurrection.

"Oh blessed be, you are alive, mo chridhe!" he forced himself to say. "Colin told me that you had died in childbirth, I am overjoyed to see you alive and well."

"Do not insult me with your lies sir," shouted Julia as she rose from her chair and stood towering over Lord Dougal. "You wished me dead so that you could snatch the Lairds throne and his land as you did with the caves of Wemyss. But mark my words your reign will come to an end."

"Who is to end it?" the Lord replied, dropping all pretences in an instant. "Surely not you, you gullible wench! You clung to me like a wet cloak and were oh so willing to believe that my feelings for you were pure and deep, while all that I was seeking was Sarah's secret. But when I realised that Colin did not share it with you, I decided that it would be high time to search for it myself in the caves of Wemyss."

"Colin never spoke of a secret. It's just another one of your lies, you just used me to gain control over the caves and their riches you deceiving lowlife."

"Oh you ignorant female, you have no clue of what I speak, but let me enlighten you," the Lord said with a hateful sneer. "As a very young lad, I learned of King Somerled's sword and that anyone that holds it would rule over Scotland and the kingdom of Elfame. So I sought employment at the castle of Clyde MacDougall, who I knew to be a direct descendant of King Somerled. I soon learned that the secret of the sword's whereabouts was solely passed on to the eldest daughter of Clan chief and realised that I had to accompany Lady Sarah to Kilchurn. I read all her messages to her father, her personal diary. I even tried to squeeze it out of her as she lay dying after giving birth to her son. I told her that I would convince Lord Campbell to kill their son if she did not reveal the secret to me, but she chose to take it and her son to her grave.

After years of searching the caves for the sword I found the enchanted Sapphire of the Goddess Cailleach and tried to lure the secret out of her in exchange for the stone, but she only laughed at me. So I had no choice but to abduct Lady Murigen's mortal husband and to banish her to the island. But still, she did not give up the secret. My last chance to get the sword now is through their daughter Amanda, and trust me I will. It's now only a matter of days before I hold it in my hands."

Julia had heard enough and screamed in his face.

"Don't you dare speak about Amanda, you heartless double-tongued miscreant! Your time to pay for all your cruelty has come at last. Amanda and her companions are at the caves right now to free her father along with all the other captives. She will retrieve your precious Sapphire and return it to the Goddess Cailleach."

Lord Dougal stared at Julia in disbelief. His eyes were narrow, rigid, and cold. The blood drained from his already ashen face as he realised what Julia had said. In his rage, he pulled a dagger from his belt, lurched forward, and threw her on the ground. He was on the cusp of slitting her throat when he was stopped by the shouts of his commander.

"My Lord, a large group of armed men, has assembled on the ramparts lead by all the clan chiefs of Argyll an escape from the castle will be impossible."

"Not for me, follow me," hissed Lord Dougal! He let go of Julia and raced out of the Great Hall towards the submerged tunnels just as William and his grandfather arrived at the castle's ramparts where they were met by Argyll's chiefs and their troops.

"My Lord we have come to swear our alliance to your grandson the rightful heir of King Sumerled. We are prepared to fight at your side against that swine that had terrorised the good people of our lands for far too long."

"Well, well, I say, that is a welcome surprise. We can use every man we can get to end the reign of this murderous villain," Lord MacDougall said. He led the group of men across the lowered drawbridge into Kilchurn Castle, where they were eagerly awaited by Julia and her guards.

"I am so glad that you are here! Lord Dougal and his men must be hiding in the castle somewhere, there is no other way out than over the drawbridge."

"There is Julia, you've forgotten. But he will not be able to get through without the help of the Goddess Coventina," replied William. He rushed with a group of armed men to the submerged passage he and Maighread had used to escape from the castle. Once they arrived, he was stunned to see that the tunnel was dry and that there was no sign of Lord Dougal or his men. He hurried down to the shore of Loch Awe and was horror-struck when he saw that he had managed to escape. Five of the Ashray warrior's that guarded the waters in front of the castle lay slain on the ground.

"William, he is gone," Ariana said, appearing out of the mist. "You have to get a message to Amanda we can't reach her in the dead forest, but Cait Sith can. You must hurry, he is going to kill her and her friends. He has large groups of Red Caps and armies of prisoners with him. I must leave you now and take my fallen brothers home," she spoke before she disappeared in the darkened water of Loch Awe.

William returned to the castle's Great Hall with a heavy heart. *How many more of our friends have to lose their lives by the hands of this ruthless murderer,* he thought as he walked up to the large banquet table, where his grandfather sat with his face buried in his hands.

"What's wrong Grandfather? What happened?"

"It's all my fault, William I should have been more cautious when I told your mother about the sword."

"What sword? What are you talking about?"

"Our ancestor King Somerled knew about the greed and thirst for power that poisons the hearts of even the noblest men. That is why he decreed that only our first born daughters should receive knowledge of the swords secret and its location through their mothers. My beloved daughter Sarah was still a small bairn when her mother died, so the secret was passed on to me, and I revealed it to her shortly before she left Oban. The bastard must have overheard part of our conversation."

"I am lost, you will have to tell me all about this afterwards. Right now, I need your help getting a message to Amanda."

"Very well, me lad, but I don't know where she is."

"Never mind, all you have to do is to get my message to Adelaide. She should already be at the Guildhall to take care of Marisell, and you can be sure that she is accompanied by one or two elves."

"Aye, so what is the message, William?"

"We have to let her know that the so-called Lord knows all about her quest and is on the way to stop and kill her."

"Crivens, will this bastard never rest! James, you must return to the Guild Hall and hand this to Adelaide!" said Lord MacDougall, handing his commander a small roll of parchment.

29 LOCH NESS

Ralston's words were kind and heartfelt, but they couldn't ease Amanda's mind. She needed time alone to come to terms with all that had happened since she had left the inn all these months ago. She yearned for the serenity of the fairy pond. Its warm crystalline waters and rainbow coloured pebbles. It seemed as if a lifetime has passed since she had been happy and free of worry or fear. She gazed at the pearl in the palm of her hand when she suddenly felt something moving behindher.

"Ralston, is that you?" she exclaimed in surprise.

"No Amanda my sweet, it is me. I am so glad to see you unharmed and well." Cait Sith said, as she appeared from the thickets and gracefully lay down in front of Amanda. Her black fur shimmered like silk in the faint moonlight, and her green eyes glowed like emeralds. Amanda was delighted to see her. She always felt safe and at ease in her presence.

"Oh, Cait Sith it is wonderful to see you again. It has been such a long time. But what are you doing in this forsaken place?"

"I bring a message from William, for you."

"Oh how wonderful, is he all right?"

"Aye, he is. But he is very concerned about your safety. Lord Dougal was able to escape from the guild hall. He stabbed Marseilles, ruthlessly murdered five Ashray warriors, and is now coming for you."

"How? He has no clue where I am," Amanda replied.

"He does! Lady Julia, unfortunately, let it slip, and now he is heading to Ben Nevis. You must arrive there before him, to return the Sapphire and break his power," Cait Sith urged.

"There is no way that we can make it there before him. He will make that journey in less than a day," Amanda said with nervous laughter.

"Oh no, he won't, Amanda! He must go to Black Mount first to make up for his losses at Kilchurn and Dalmally. It will need at least two days for the rounding up of more Red Caps and arming his troops. And two more to make it to Ben Nevis. You, on the other hand, have three days to get to the Blue Glacier." Cait Sith said.

"You make it sound so easy, Cait Sith. But tell me how we should make that distance in three days. There is no way that Lord MacDougall's galleons can sail to Wemyss and back in that time. And to make the journey by land is out of the question. Lord Dougal has his murdering squads spread throughout the land and can summon them with his dark magic." Amanda uttered trembling with frustration.

"There is a way Amanda! We are going to catch us some Kelpies and ride to Moray Firth," interjected Ralston who had overheard the conversation.

"Cait Sith, you must haste back to Kilchurn now. Tell Ariana to meet us with a group of warriors at Moray Firth as soon as the sun sets tomorrow. And ask William to join us with his troops at Achterawe by midnight."

"Aye, Ralston will do! Good luck with the kelpies and keep in mind that they very cunning," Cait Sith replied. She spun around and disappeared in the dark of the forest.

"Ralston, what did you mean when you said, we will catch us some Kelpies?" Amanda inquired.

"He was referring to the water horses!" Glen exclaimed with excitement as he appeared right behind Amanda. "I have always wanted to see them, but never dared to dream of riding one – much less living to tell the tale."

"Blimey Glen, where did you come from?" Amanda uttered overjoyed.

"Well, straight from Elfame!" giggled Ursula as she jumped out from behind Glen.

"Ghilli Duh brought us back to help you! You would be lost without us!" Glen added as he embraced her.

"Aye, right! I am so happy that you are back. We have so much to tell you, Glen."

"No need, Ursula filled me in," Glen responded with a broad smile and winked at Ursula.

"I really don't like to break up this happy reunion, but we better hurry down to the beach, and catch ourselves a ride! Follow me!" Ralston interjected and led the friends deeper into the forest.

"What beach you are talking about Ralston? All I can see is a dark, dying forest!" sighed Amanda impatiently.

"Well, mo ghràdh, my ancestors occupied many more caves in Wemyss. And some of them have passages that lead straight to the seashore. Come on!" Ralston said and chuckled silently as he lead the group to a large standing stone covered with strange symbols. He raised his left arm and placed his fingers on five indentations. He closed his eyes and recited a strange sounding incantation when suddenly a large cloud appeared right above them shrouding the sun like a blanket of absolute darkness.

"Take each other's hand and follow me," Ralston whispered, taking Amanda's hand and leading the group further into the darkness. Amanda was mesmerised and followed him into the abyss without hesitation.

The ground under their feet soon changed from the soggy forest floor to soft beach sand. Every step led them deeper into the blackness and silence of the underground passage. After a while, the musty smell of the cave was replaced by the scent of the sea, and a faint, blue light appeared in the distance. It took about another hour before the friends reached the mouth of the cave and walked out on to a beautiful beach. The soft, silvery light of the moon illuminated the night sky and made the wave's crest shimmer like silver. A crisp sea breeze filled their lungs and blew away the memories of the dying forest and the deadly battle.

"I am sorry to rush you again," Ralston said breaking the serenity of the moment. "But we must find the kelpies to get on our way."

"Aye, that's fine with me Ralston! But how will we find them and lure them to us?" Hugh asked looking up and down the beach in search of the magical horses.

"Oh, that is not hard to do Hugh. All we have to do is have a good time, cheer and laugh. Kelpies target mortals that are in a cheerful and slightly reckless mood."

"Brilliant that's not hard, Glen is naturally reckless," Hugh replied with a broad smile tapping his brother on the shoulder.

The friends began to play silly games, running up and down the beach laughing loudly while keeping an eye out for the beautiful jet black horses.

"Here they come! Be ready! Let them come right up before you try to grab their bridles. Once you have taken hold of the bridle, they have to submit and do as you wish," Ralston whispered turning to face the group of Kelpies that came ambling up the seashore.

Amanda and Ursula were taken aback by the horses' beauty and grace. They began to caress them by gently scratching their necks, and combing their silky mane with their fingers. The men followed suit, and soon everyone had gotten hold of a Kelpie's bridle.

"Be careful now! Watch them close!" Ralston warned. As the horses raised their heads and began stomping and pawing the ground.

"Hold on tight! And remain on their side! If they rear up and strike you, you'll be very fortunate to walk away with only a bruise. A strike from a Kelpie will chatter your bones if it lands a kick to your head, you'll be dead!" Ralston shouted holding on to the Kelpie's bridle with both hands.

The horses flared their nostrils and began to snort angrily. Then threw back their heads, raised their front legs high up in the air and started to kick violently.

"Pull their heads down! Don't be shy! Put your whole weight into it! Come on, folks!" Ralston shouted when he saw his friends struggling with the water horses.

Amanda released the tension on the bridle slightly and used the opportunity to swing herself on to the Kelpie's back as it lowered itself to slip out from under her grip. She held on to its mane tightly, squeezed its sides gently with her thighs and began patting its neck calming it down. To her great surprise, it stopped fighting and so did the other four. From now on the horses obeyed and reacted calmly to their riders' commands.

"Well then let's get on the way we have quite a ride in front of us!" Ralston exclaimed and nodded satisfied as he galloped into the breaking waves. The four friends followed and soon found themselves speeding across the sea's surface and over towering waves.

Amanda turned to take a last look at the tree-covered mountains of Wemyss as they disappear in the distance. It was an exhilarating feeling to soar over the water with giddying speed on the back of these magical beings. A cold breeze picked up and blew across her face, tousling her long brown hair and filling her nose with the salty smell of the sea.

The hours were flying by just as quickly as the horses. Soon enough a hint of copper appeared on the horizon, sending its radiant light up into the sky and across the sea. The sun was being born again from the darkness of the night with the promise of a new beginning.

"We have reached Moray Firth! Take a look over there! Can you see the dunes?" Ralston exclaimed pointing to one of the most spectacular sights the friends had ever seen. About five miles ahead of them lay a group of sand dunes that glowed like pure gold in the light of the sun.

"Aye, I see them! They are magnificent! But tell me what do you call these crazy creatures?" Amanda asked, laughing when she found herself surrounded by a large pod of jumping dolphins.

"Aww, they are here too! They are all around us!" Ursula cheered as she bent down to try to touch one that kept jumping out of the water close to her.

"They are Dolphins" And look at the group of Selkies over there. They all came to greet us!" Ralston exclaimed overjoyed.

The Dolphins accompanied and entertained the friends all the way to the inlet of Moray Firth and only turned around as waves began to break close to the shore.

"Thank you my black beauty for carrying me. I hope that we will meet one day again." Amanda whispered in the Kelpies ear. She gently slid off its back and kissed it on the forehead as she let go of its bridle. In a blink of an eye, all five Kelpies turned around and disappeared in breaking waves of the Northern Sea.

"Well then, here we are! What's next? Where are we heading?" asked Hugh looking at Ralston with high expectation.

"I suggest we head towards that smoke! It might lead us to a fisherman's lunch!"

"Aye right Glen, as usual, all you can think of is food!" Replied Amanda and broke out in laughter.

"It may come as a big surprise to you, but I agree with Glen!" Ralston said smiling. "Let's see if we can get some food before we make our way to the River Ness."

After a tricky and pretty strenuous climb across the dunes, the friends reached a vast plain covered with soft beach grass and edged by shading trees. After just a few steps Glen had found a campfire nearby.

"Now that is strange!" mumbled Glen looking around for the fisherman.

"Not as strange as you think my dear brother!" Hugh chuckled while exchanging looks with Ralston.

"Right, there are no fishermen Glen. The fire and the fish broth were made by Selena. She saw us coming and knew that we would need food. She and her family took care of our lunch."

"Selena? Are you telling me that there was a lassie out there? I didn't see a boat. Did you see a boat?" asked Glen looking at his friends with wide eyes.

"Selena is a Selkie! A shapeshifter! She can turn into a beautiful young woman. I am sure you heard of them. They are very shy, and cautious. Too many men have stolen their skins to make them their slaves. Selena's mother was caught by a very brutal boat builder. She endured cruelties for many years before I found her and returned her to the sea," Ralston explained.

"Since she died, her daughter Selena provided me with fresh fish whenever I come to her shore. But enough of that, let's have a quick bite and head to the River Ness," Ralston said, sitting down and helping himself to a bowl of fish broth and some fresh water. The friends finished their meal, hid the cauldron and put out the fire before they walked over to the mouth of the river.

"Well you guys, I hope you feel refreshed and well rested now."

"Sure, but why are you asking Ralston? Sunset is hours away so I think this would be a perfect time for a nap," Glen replied, spreading his blanket under a large weeping willow.

"There is no time for a nap! We have to set up the boat for the journey. Come on! I am sure you had enough rest in Elfame," Ralston replied with a broad smile.

"Alright! What do you want us to do, master? The boat looks fine to me. All that's missing are our provisions and water."

"Oh Glen, you are terrible! What would you like us to do Ralston?" Amanda inquired as she stepped into the boat.

"We have to make it invisible," he answered.

"We what? How are we supposed to do that? We are no magicians!" Amanda exclaimed, looking surprised.

"There is no need for magic, mo ghràdh! All we need are some branches and a reasonable length of rope. Come with me I'll show you." Ralston responded reaching out his hand to help Amanda to step back on land.

"I think we found a perfect disguise for the boat!" Ursula and Hugh shouted as they appeared from the nearby rush pulling a sizeable hollow trunk behind them.

"Take a good luck at this beauty! The trunk will slide over the boat's bow easily." Hugh boosted proudly as he rolled the trunk right up to the boat. "And the web of roots will make excellent protection against arrows."

"Aye, and not to mention the Boobrie!" Glen said in a sarcastic tone of voice doubling over laughing.

"Ah, you think you're funny Glen! Well, you are not!" Amanda hissed and steppedcloser.

"Let's not fight! We need our strength for far more important things. Come on, let's get to it. It won't be long before the sun sets and Ariana will arrive with her brothers," Ralston said stepping between Amanda and Glen.

The friends settled down and created a masterpiece. After their work, the boat was no longer recognisable, and the tangled roots offered an impenetrable shelter.

"Well done! Maybe we are magicians after all! Just look at this. It will be as slow as a snail, but will be invisible," Glen teased, bursting into infectious laughter. Soon they were all laughing so hard that they did not notice the Ashrays arrival.

"I'm sorry to interrupt especially since you all seemed so happy! It's wonderful to hear you laughing!" Ariana whispered with a warm smile.

"My brothers and sisters are ready to accompany and protect you on your way through Loch Ness. The trooping Sluaghs will secure the skies, while the Dryads guard the forest," Ariana announced, pointing to the sky and the wooded shore. "No corrupt mortal, hideous beast, or dark magic will harm you on your journey while we are there," she added.

"Thank you, Ariana! We are ready when you are," Ralston replied ushering the group into the boat.

As soon as the friends had taken shelter under the canopy of gnarled roots, he signalled for the Ashrays to move out. In an instant, the river began to boil around the boat as countless Ashrays started to pull the boat away from the shore.

It took forty Ashrays to pull against the current which rushed past the boat, stony banks, and tall, beautiful bull rushes down to the sea. The cold and crystal clear water was churned into froth around them by hundreds of silver carp, river trout and salmon that tried to reach their spawning grounds.

"Hugh! Look at that! All we have to do is reach into the water to catch us some supper!" Glen exclaimed and was about to leave the roots cover to catch some fish.

"Are you totally bonkers Glen? Are you trying to give us all away for some blimey fish? I swear your love of food will kill you one day," Ursula hissed, grabbing his tunic and pulling him back down.

"What? There is no one anywhere near us. Don't get your knickers in a knot, Ursula," Glen responded, red-faced.

"How can you be so sure about that Glen? Just look at all the movements along the river banks," Ralston whispered, pointing to a group of shadows rushing through the thickets along the river's edge.

"Damn! How did they know that we will come this way? Do we have a traitor in our midst?" Glen asked looking at Ralston with a stunned expression.

"I am afraid something much more dangerous has given us away!" Ralston sighed while keeping a close eye on the river banks.

"What do you mean?" Hugh inquired, looking concerned.

"I was not sure at first, but I thought that I heard the howling of Cu'Sith just before we entered the cave."

"The howling of what?" Glen asked. He looked perfectly terrified.

"Cu'Sith is a dog the size of a young bull with shaggy green fur. I am certain he followed Cait Sith and overheard our conversation. Which means that Lord Dougal is now aware of our plan," Ralston explained.

"Blood bas! That's bad, very bad! I better get my bow ready and tell Ursula to strap on her slingshot," Hugh whispered as he crawled back to the bow of the boat to talk to Ursula.

"Do you think that they'll attack the boat?" Glen asked tensed.

"Not for now, I think we are too fast. But I will feel a lot better once we enter the loch."

"Aye right, which should be just now. But we should inform the Ashrays about our suspicion," Glen suggested. He leaned over the side to share the information with Ariana.

The friends were now at high alert and surveyed their surrounding with eagle eyes. Ralston shot an arrow fetched with white feathers up into the sky to get the Sluaghs attention.

"Lord Ralston, what's your concern?" Lian Cael, the leader of the Sluaghs, asked as he hovered over the boat.

"Lian Cael, we are being followed, and I am worried about the safety of our friends down at Achterawe."

"Say no more, Lord Ralston. I'll send some of my brothers to keep an eye on things," Lian Cael replied in a deep, droning voice. Before he flapped his powerful black wings and shot back up into the nightsky.

The Ashrays picked up speed and reached the loch quickly. Soon the wooded shore receded as they pulled the boat to the centre of the loch.

"Crivens that was scary! Can we relax now, or are we still in danger Ralston?" Amanda asked sounding weary.

"We should be fine for now, at least until we reach closer to Achterawe. You guys can come out and take a breather." Ralston said while helping Amanda to crawl out from under the canopy of roots.

The friends breathed a sigh of relief and calmly gazed at the moon's reflection in the dark blue water of Loch Ness. Everything seemed calm. The wooded shores around the loch remained still, and the sky above was well protected by the trooping Sluaghs. The gentle bopping of the boat felt very soothing so that the friends had to fight to keep their eyes open.

"Wake up, you guys!" Ralston shouted in alarm, ripping them out of their daze just before the boat capsized. Ursula gasped in shock as she hit the freezing water of the loch and had to fight hard to stay afloat. She had the feeling her armour was pulling her down, no matter how much she struggled. Just as the water threatened to close over her head, a hand grabbed her arm, pulling her back up to the surface.

"Damn, don't tell me that you can't swim Ursula!" Hugh exclaimed perfectly horrified.

"I can! But the bloody armour was pulling me down as if it was made of lead!" Ursula answered spitting water.

"It's not your armour, Ursula!" Amanda called out pointing to a dead soldier floating close to her.

"What? How!" Ursula screamed and looked wide-eyed at Amanda.

"I'll tell you later. There is no time now, look at the boats! They are full of Lord Dougal's men. Swim to the shore I'll meet you there later," Amanda said and disappeared in the dark water.

Amanda joined the Ashray warriors as they circled the approaching boats, capsizing them one by one. Many of the armed men were unable to swim and drowned quickly. Others managed to stay afloat and were swimming towards Amanda to grab her, when all of a sudden, the water got ice-cold and began to swirl faster and faster.

The Ashrays recognised the danger in an instant and soared through the water, grabbing Amada and pulling her away. Not a moment later, a gigantic black shadow appeared from the depth of Loch Ness. It breached the water directly next to them and crashed back down on to the group of swimming soldiers.

"Crivens, what was that?" Amanda exclaimed in shock and surprise.

"That was Nessie! She came to your rescue. We would have lost many warriors if it wasn't for her," Ariana replied and sighed with relief.

"Hm, Nessie. I heard of her, but always thought it was just an old wives' tale," Amanda muttered nervously.

"Well, now you know different. She just doesn't trust mortals and therefore stays in the depth of Loch Ness and Moray Firth," Ariana replied, looking at the whirl of water in which Nessie had disappeared.

"Ariana, I have to leave you now and join the others. I hope that I will see you again soon." Amanda whispered and swam to the shore of Achterawe.

Ralston paced up and down the shore, tormented by thoughts of if Amanda had been hurt or worse. His heart had almost stopped moments earlier when Nessie launched herself out of the water, twisted in mid-air, and crashed back into the loch, taking the lord's men with her. He knew that Amanda could breathe underwater and that Nessie would never willingly harm her, but he could not stop the distressing thoughts until he saw her walking out of the loch.

30 THE BLUE GLACIER

Amanda walked out of the water feeling like a wet rag doll limp, cold, and bruised.

I hope the others made it out alright before Nessie breached, she thought as she removed her scabbard and loosened her armour.

"Mo ghràdh, I am so glad that you are alright!" Ralston exclaimed, pulling her into his arms.

"Aye, I am fine! Just a little bruised, but still in one piece, which cannot be said about the Lord's men. They have been smashed to pieces by Nessie," Amanda said and could not suppress a burst of laughter.

"Well, I saw! And so did all the men. Soon everybody will know about her. Let's hope she will remain safe," Ralston responded. "Speaking of remaining safe, William has some important news for us. Let's go and join the others," he said, taking the scabbard from her hands and placing his arm around her for support.

Luckily, it wasn't a long walk to William's camp and the warm glow of the fire. Hugh and Ursula were sitting by the fire warming themselves and chatting with Seamus and James, while Glen was busy cutting a chunk of meat from a boar roasting on a spit nearby.

"I am glad that you haven't lost your appetite, Glen!" Amanda shouted shaking her head in disbelief.

"Och, that will never happen! You know how much he loves to stuff his face!" William chuckled as he walked up to greet her. "We have to talk," he said, sounding very excited.

"I now know what the so-called Lord is after. Let's take a few steps and sit over there. It's not something we could share with everyone." William added in a low voice while leading Amanda and Ralston to a broken down crofter's cottage.

"We should have some privacy here," he continued, making sure no one could overhear them, "Alright. The Dryads had searched the area before we arrived and are watching over us now from the surrounding trees while we get ready," he explained.

"So what do you have to tell us that's so secret that we need to hide in the bushes?" Amanda asked impatiently, stepping from one foot to the other. "I hope it will not take too long I am cold and hungry," she added.

"I am sorry, my bonnie lass. But what I have to tell you could change Scotland's destiny and that of Elfame," William replied in a hushed voice. He proceeded to tell Ralston and Amanda what he had learned from his grandfather.

"So that is what he is after! What do you think we should do first? Return the stone or try to find that sword?" Amanda asked, looking at William and Ralston with great curiosity.

"We must return the stone to break his power before we can even think about the sword and it's where about!" Ralston replied, looking bewildered at the two of them.

"Aye, I agree! Our first and utmost concern should be to free this land from him and his dark creatures!" Amanda responded with chattering teeth.

"Well, we have to get you into some dry cloth quickly so that we can head out while we have the help of the Sluaghs!" Ralston responded. He wrapped his cloak around Amanda and led her back to the camp.

"I like that thought. But where will you find dry cloth for me? I don't think that it would be something the troops would carry along," Amanda whispered while breathing on her hands to warm them.

"No, they don't! But we do!" responded a soft voice from the trees nearby.

"Oh, my goodness, Oren, is that you?" Amanda exclaimed surprised.

"Aye, Laratbogh and I brought you some new

clothing," Oren responded.

"And a helmet to protect you and render you invisible from above," Laratbogh cheered.

"Come on, let's get you changed," Oren exclaimed pulling Amanda behind a large clump of fern.

Amanda was more than happy to get out of her wet clothes and very impressed by the beauty and comfort of her new outfit. She loved the helmet Ghilli Duh had made for her from green dragon hide and embedded with gold. She was quite a sight in her dark green suede truis, tunic and jerkin. Her armour and braces had been cleaned and dried and felt so much more comfortable than before.

"Well, I am ready and hope that you are too!" Amanda said spinning around to show off her new and improved outfit.

"You look stunning, mo chridhe," Ralston whispered. He pulled her into his arms and kissed her.

"Love your helmet, Amanda! You look as if you are wearing a crown," Ursula exclaimed in admiration.

"Alright folks, enough of that! El Cael just told us that about two hundred armed men are heading our way. Let's move out!" William urged, signalling his men to get in the saddle.

"Two hundred armed men! How shall we get pass them? We have no more than a hundred men," Amanda said, a look of despair washing over her face.

"Leave it to us! We'll split them up and led them astray!" Oren chuckled and winked at Amanda before she and Laratbogh disappeared in the woods.

"How? Do you think that they can lure them away, Ralston?"

"Aye, they can! All they need is a little help from the Hinky Punk," Ralston responded laughing.

"The what?" Amanda asked, perplexed.

"The Hinky Punk, Amanda," Ralston replied. "Come along, I'll show you."

"Hugh, we'll ride up that knoll to have a closer look. Keep an eye out for the Wulver. He should show himself at any moment now to guide you through the bog," Ralston shouted over to Hugh who was busy checking the weapons. He took the reins from Amanda's horse and pulled it along.

The horses had a hard time climbing the knoll and staggered a few times before they reached the top. Amanda and Ralston slid off their horses and hid under a large ash tree, from where they could see the entire meadow and nearby swamps.

"Oh dear, look at this! That must be far more than two hundred men. The riders alone come up to about fifty," Amanda whispered, sounding very distraught.

"Never mind, that will change just now. Hang on and keep looking. Do you see the flat area over to your left?"

"Aye, I do Ralston! What about it?"

"Well, that's where the bogs and swamps begin. One has to be very careful not to leave the narrow path, as there is no coming back if you stray," he said, lifting Amanda's chin and kissing her gently.

"I understand that. But that is why the riders have torches for the men to follow," she replied.

"Just keep looking mo ghràdh," he said, wrapping her in his cloak to shelter her from a stiff breeze that came out of nowhere. Moments later, the breeze reached the marshes and blew out the torches. Amanda was stunned and turned to Ralston to ask him what would happen next. But he just smiled, placed his finger on her lips, and pointed down to the meadow. Hundreds of small, blue, flickering lights appeared in the bogs drawing soldiers away from the safe paths.

Amanda gasped when she saw that the men were following these ghostly lights and then disappeared in the bogs.

"There is no need to talk. I know how you feel, Amanda. But remember, they have chosen a path of death and destruction. And that is what they have found. Let's return to the others to give them the good news," Ralston said as he helped her into the saddle.

She did not speak a word until they had caught up with the troops, and even then she left it to Ralston to inform William and the commander. She knew very well that these men wouldn't have hesitated to kill her or her friends. But she still could not manage to bring herself to see the death of so many men as a victory. She had just started to tell Ursula about the Hinky Punks when a blood-curdling scream echoed through the meadow. A moment later, one of Lord Dougal's men dropped from the sky directly in front of her. Her horse was spooked, reared and began to kick violently. Amanda had to wrap her arms around its neck and hold on with all her might to avoid being thrown off.

"Ho, ho, my sweet! Calm down! It's all right, sshh!" Ralston said soothingly as he took the horse's reins to calm it down.

"The Sluaghs just prevented an ambush from Lord Dougal's men!" William announced as he galloped pass Ralston and Amanda.

"Alright, Amanda that means that you Ursula, Glen and Hugh have to ride as fast as you can into the forest!" Ralston said. "The Sluaghs must leave by sunrise so we will be a target for the Boobrie, which I am sure is lurking somewhere nearby," he added. He turned his horse around and followed William, James, and Seamus with flying huffs.

"You heard what he said! Let's get us some cover!" Hugh and Glen shouted, urging the girls to follow them as they dashed towards the forest.

The horses crossed the meadow with long strides. Their hooves barely touched the ground as if they were being carried by invisible wings. The sky above them began to change from the twilight grey to a brilliant gold as the morning broke.

Amanda's eyes were fixed on the sky, expecting to see the menacing shadow of the Boobrie, now that they were without the protection of the Sluaghs.

Just moments later, her worse fear came true as the silence was broken by the cry of that murdering beast. The girls exchanged looks and nodded to one another in silent acknowledgement. Ursula turned around in her saddle and lay down on the back of her horse with the slingshot raised and drawn ready to fire.

Amanda pulled her swords out and stood upright in her stirrups, ready to slash the beast wide open. That's when she heard the call of the golden eagle. Ioroth had come to their defence. The Boobrie was so startled by the arrival of the magnificent king of the sky that he chose to retreat.

A few more strides and we are safe, Amanda thought as the edge of the forest came closer. She sheathed her swords as soon they reached the tree cover, dismounted her horse and breathed a sigh of relief.

"Well, we made it," she said, smiling.

"Aye, we did," Ursula replied as she slid off her horse. "But where are the lads? I can't see them anywhere," she added.

"Right here, mo lennan," whispered Hugh as he stepped out of the thickets.

"You have to leave your horses. They would not be able to make it through the forest," Hugh said taking control of their reins.

"Why would they not make it? You're talking rubbish, Hugh. I won't abandon my horse," protested Amanda looking at Hugh with flashing eyes.

"Who said anything about abandoning? The Pixies will take care of them," Hugh replied pointing to four tiny faces peeking through a blueberry bush.

"Well then, let me introduce you to our four new friends. Alida, Sindri, Nolana, and Pooky," announced Hugh bowing to the group of Pixies.

"Honoured to meet you," Ursula and Amanda

exclaimed smiling.

The Pixies did not say a word but giggled loudly while beaming at the girls with their big brown eyes. A mischievous smile flashed over their faces as they took the reins and lead the horses away.

"Aye, so that's taken care of," sighed Hugh, relieved as he rolled up his sleeves.

"Fine, but what are you up to now?" Ursula inquired.

"Helping you up into the tree, it's high time we get off the ground," answered Hugh. He bent over and formed a step with his hands to lift the girls up to Glen, who sat on a branch above them waiting to give them a hand.

"But why?" Ursula asked, pushing him away.

"Oh come on, don't be so difficult," Amanda, interjected. She stepped into Hugh's hands and disappeared in the tree.

"It will get real ugly here in a moment," Hugh said impatiently. He grabbed her and lifted her up to Glen, who pulled her on to a large branch where Oren and Laratbogh were waiting,

Ursula was furious. She honestly did not like to be manhandled.

"What did you do that for?" she hissed as Hugh swung himself up to a branch next to her.

"Goodness Ursula! He had to do it! No one will be safe down there as soon as Ghilli Duh speaks his enchantment," Oren sighed.

Not a moment, later the forest floor shuddered. Moss covered rocks broke through the ground as if they were pushed up as by invisible hands. The trees began to entangle their branches and pull their roots out of the ground to form tall arches making it impossible to pass.

"Oh, how bloody brilliant! Amanda cried out in sarcasm. "Why did Ghilli Duh do that? Now we'll never make it to the Blue Glacier before Lord Dougal," she exclaimed in frustration.

"Sure you will! The only ones that are slowed by this

spell are Lord Dougal's men," replied Oren and winked at Amanda.

"They have to take the long route around the forest. That will buy you at least half a day," added Laratbogh smiling.

"Amanda, my dear, the only ones that will risk passing through this forest now are the Red Caps as they blindly follow your scent not realising that they will meet their doom," Ghilli Duh said in a voice that made Amanda tremble. For the first time, she felt his immense power and determination to annihilate everyone and everything that dared to threaten her.

"Alright, I understand that," she replied. "But how will we get through?"

"Oren and Laratbogh will guide you through the treetops. You'll reach the foot of Ben Nevis by midday," said Ghilli Duh before he disappeared right in front of her.

The group moved through the treetops effortlessly like a gentle breeze and reached the edge of the forest by midday, just as Ghilli Duh had predicted. The friends bid Oren and Laratbogh goodbye and returned to the ground, where Asanopirh and Sorcha were waiting with their horses. After a brief welcome, the group decided to find some shelter for a short rest and to exchange information. Amanda was relieved when Asanopirh told her that her father was now looked after by Adelaide and that her friends had returned their families.

She leaned back and had some water before she shared the information about the sword with the group. The friends listened intently to Amanda she could tell they needed some time to come to terms with this new development. Except for Asanopirh. He stood a few steps away from the group and stared aimlessly into the distance. "Asanopirh, are you alright?" Amanda inquired, laying her hand on his shoulder.

"I am fine, Amanda. What you said brought back beautiful memories of a time when mortals and the Seelie

Fae lived peacefully side by side," Asanopirh replied, smiling.

"Sorry to interrupt, but William and his men have arrived. It is time to get ready for our final battle. Let's go!" exclaimed Sorcha as she stepped up to Amanda and Asanopirh, handing them the reins of their horses. The friends joined the others and rode in full gallop to the foot of Ben Nevis.

"Let's split up and provide cover for Amanda and her comrades while they climb up to the Blue Glacier," ordered William. He threw Amanda a kiss and joined his men.

"Alright, let us hide the horses. From here on we have to walk," Ralston said dismounting his horse and tying it under a large oak. Hugh and Glen were already on their way when they heard Ursula's scream. Amanda turned around in horror, swung herself back on her horse and rode to where she thought the voice came from.

Ursula's horse had been hit by an arrow and fallen on top of her. She was pinned down by the large animal and could not free herself. Amanda jumped off her horse in full trot and landed on her knees right next to Ursula. The two girls tried to raise the horse's shoulders but did not manage to lift it high enough to free Ursula's foot that was caught in her stirrups.

Amanda stood up looking for help when she saw two of Lord Dougal's men flying towards her with their lances raised ready to impale her and Ursula. She could not pull her swords between the large boulders around them. There was no way out. Amanda and Ursula were certain that their end was near and braced themselves for the defeat. Suddenly at the last possible moment, the saddles of their assailants slipped off their horses, sending them flying. The men hit the ground so hard that their necks snapped on impact. The girls gasped for air, wasting no time as they frantically tried again to free Ursula.

"Shall we give you a hand," asked a soft voice coming

from the dust cloud. Four tiny Pixies appeared.

"Goodness, where did you come from?" Amanda said, looking at them in disbelief.

"We jumped on to the horses of these buffoons as the passed the oak," the four blurted out, giggled and slapping their knees.

"Well and then we cut their saddle straps," screamed Pooky dropping to the ground laughing.

"I don't know how to thank you," sighed Amanda as she helped Ursula to stand. "But we have to go now. You better return to the forest, it is too dangerous for you out here," she said before she and Ursula returned to the oak tree, where they hoped to find Ralston and the lads.

"Crivens where are they," exclaimed Ursula turning around in panic when the discovered their men were not there.

"Calm down, my bonnie lass, they are safe," called Bilobeal from a gap between the roots of the tree. "Come on and mind your head, we had to go underground to shake off this bloody scum," he whispered holding out his hand to help the girls. Once again Amanda found herself in total darkness and had to trust the one that lead her. The girls had to stoop down low to make it through the tunnel and were glad when they finally saw the light. Ralston waited at the end of the tunnel and gave a sigh of relief when he saw Amanda.

"Well, it's high time to make it up to the glacier. Lord Dougal and his armed men are drawing close, some of the Red Caps were able to escape Ghilli Duh," Sabaltalab informed the group as he and his brother Phaervlon carefully hid the tunnel entrance.

The friends tightened their bootstraps and began their ascent. It was a strenuous climb from rock to rock while trying to avoid loose stones. Moments after the friends left the tree cover rain began to fall and soon changed into hail. Thousands of little icy balls hit their faces, making it impossible to check their surroundings. Once in a while, the wind carried the sound from the battle that raged in the meadow below up to them.

But there was another sound, one that was eerie familiar. Amanda recognised it right away as the sound of the Boobrie. Before the friends were able to make him out in the sky, another scream filled the air. It was Glen. The Boobrie had caught him by surprise and grabbed him with his sharp talons.

Moments before the beast was able to disappear in the clouds, Ioroth shot through the sky like a lightning bolt. The eagle circled him once to assess the situation before he turned and attacked the beast. He sunk his talons deep into the Boobrie's eyes, blinding him and sending him into a mad flapping frenzy. The creature had lost his sense of direction and flew straight towards the rock wall when Ioroth returned for another attack. In its attempt to escape Ioroth's attacks, it let go of its prey.

Glen was now falling fast and seemed to be lost when at the last moment Ioroth returned and caught him just before he hit the ground. When Ioroth returned him to his friends, he was as white as snow and trembled uncontrollably. They all had tears in their eyes as they wrapped their arms around him and sighed.

"This was close!" Glen said in a trembling voice.

"Too damn close! But I think that this was the last attack from the Boobrie," Amanda replied, pointing at a black heap of feathers at the foot of Ben Nevis.

"Bloody brilliant! Let's hope that it was the last of our worries," exclaimed Hugh with a faint smile.

"It won't be, Hugh, we are not there yet," Ralston said, pointing to the snow-covered peak of Ben Nevis. "But at least we no longer have to watch the sky," he chuckled and pulled Amanda closer.

The friends unrolled their blankets and wrapped them tight around their shoulders before they approached the snow line. But once they had reached it, they realised it wasn't just snow. It was packed ice, which made it very difficult to even make slow progress. Frozen to the bone and out of breath, the group finally reached the cave entrance atop the Blue Glacier.

"We have arrived, Amanda," whispered Ralston stepping aside to make way for Amanda. She stood and gazed into the blue cave in awe. She felt happy to have made it, but she couldn't deny that she was also reluctant to meet the almighty Goddess Cailleach.

"Go mo ghràdh, Lady Cailleach is waiting," he said encouragingly.

"Give me a moment! I have to let it sink in that I have reached the Blue Glacier before I can return the Sapphire to the Goddess," Amanda said.

"Oh no!" she screamed in terror. "I don't have the stone! Asanopirh never gave it to me."

"Calm down, Amanda. You had it all along. Take off your helmet and have a look," Ralston uttered, looking at her with the softest smile.

Amanda removed the helmet and was mesmerised when she looked into it and saw blue Sapphire.

"I had it all along?" She exclaimed as she removed it. The stone felt amazingly warm to the touch and tingled with energy.

"Oh no you won't, you bloody bastard!" shouted a small voice behind her.

Amanda spun around and saw a Red Cap in mid-air. Pooky had tripped him so that he fell into his own pikestaff. Half blinded by the plum of yellow ashes, Amanda saw how a second Red Cap raised his pikestaff and killed Pooky. She was horror-stricken and filled with burning fury as she drew her sword and slashed the Red Cap. Amanda could no longer keep her pain bottled up and released it with a scream that echoed through the cave like a clap of thunder. She sank to her knees, picked up the tiny lifeless body of the Pixie, and held it close to her heart.

"Leave him to me, my sweet bairn! I will take him to summer land where he will be with his ancestors, happy and free," whispered a voice in her. Amanda looked around but as it seemed no one other than her could hear the voice.

"Follow me!" said the voice, just as a blue light appeared in the distance. Amanda followed it into a large cavern, where a crystal bowl was floating above the blue ice of the Glacier.

"Return the Sapphire to its birthplace and release your light, daughter of my beloved sister Murigen," the voice spoke.

Amanda lowered her eyes and saw that Pooky was gone and that the Sapphire was surrounded by a pulsating light. She stepped up to the bowl, opened her hand, and released the stone. Her heart felt as if it could burst. She drew a deep breath while gazing at the walls of blue ice that surrounded her, then raised her arms as if in a trance. She suddenly found herself engulfed by a bright white light, which melted the glacier and created a magnificent river.

"The water you freed will give life to all that was once dead and lost and releases the sword of the mighty King Somerled," said the voice of the Goddess as the sword appeared from the bowl and floated towards Amanda.

"Take it mo ghràdh, it is a gift from our beloved Goddess Cailleach," uttered Ralston from behind her. "We have to leave now and free your mother," he urged, taking Amanda's hand and leading her to a large ornate gateway.

"But we have to get the others first," replied Amanda, about to return to her friends.

"No need, mo ghràdh! Our Lady Cailleach has returned them, together with William and all his men, to Kilchurn Castle were they were awaited by Adelaide and their families," replied Ralston.

Amanda followed his lead and soon found herself in a beautiful fragrant garden surrounded by butterflies and showered with flower petals. She recognised the garden and the sweet voices of the fairy chorus from the night on the frozen lake when she heard her mother's voice for the very first time.

"Amanda my beloved daughter, you have finally returned to me." It was the voice of her mother that spoke. Amanda turned around and there right in front of her stood her mother, the Goddess Murigen. Her long silver hair framed her beautiful face, and her gentle green eyes reminded Amanda of Cait Sith.

"Let us join your father before I let you both go and rest," Lady Murigen said in a gentle voice ushering Amanda and Ralston to a palace surrounded by the brightest white light Amanda had ever seen.

"Welcome, Amanda," Gregor said in a voice as soft as velvet. He had not only completely recovered from the years in captivity but regained his youth and strength.

"Ioroth just brought a message for you. Read it and then rest. We will see you when you wake. We have all the time in the world to hear each other's stories," the Goddess said before she and Gregor disappeared in the white light. Ralston unrolled the small parchment and read it out to Amanda.

Amanda and Ralston,
We thank you from the bottom of our hearts
for all that you have done for us,
And all the sacrifices you had to make. We would have loved to have you here with as at Kilchurn Castle to celebrate your great victory over Lord Dougal and his dark magic.
But we understand that you need time to get to know your parents and recover.
William and I have agreed to travel
to Touraine to bring Anne, Lucie
and Harris back home, now that William has taken over the Lordship of Glen Orchy, and Argyll.

I send you all my love
Adelaide

Ralston lay down the parchment took Amanda into his arms and carried her to their bedchamber where they finally were able to rest and dream without worry of fear.

ABOUT THE AUTHOR

Ursula Williams was born in Berlin Germany and is the mother of three beautiful children.

She left Germany and a successful but very hectic career in marketing in search for the place she could call home.

She lived and worked for over 27 years on a small island in the Caribbean, travelled the USA, Canada, and the British Isles.

It was Scotland where she finally lost her heart. Its beauty, rich history and fascinating mythology inspired her to write her first novel which undoubtedly will be followed by many more. Ursula now lives and works in Berlin but returns Scotland whenever time permits to visit her family, further her research and to walk through its mystic forests, glens and ancient cities.

42859890R00157

Printed in Poland
by Amazon Fulfillment
Poland Sp. z o.o., Wrocław